HIS NAME IS LEGION

HIS NAME IS LEGION

WAR OF THE ANGELS™ BOOK SEVEN

MICHAEL TODD   MICHAEL ANDERLE   LAURIE STARKEY

His Name Is Legion (this book) is a work of fiction.

All of the characters, organizations, and events portrayed in this novel are either products of the author's imagination or are used fictitiously. Sometimes both.

Copyright © 2019 Michael Todd, Michael Anderle, and Laurie Starkey
Cover copyright © LMBPN Publishing
A Michael Anderle Production

LMBPN Publishing supports the right to free expression and the value of copyright. The purpose of copyright is to encourage writers and artists to produce the creative works that enrich our culture.

The distribution of this book without permission is a theft of the author's intellectual property. If you would like permission to use material from the book (other than for review purposes), please contact support@lmbpn.com. Thank you for your support of the author's rights.

LMBPN Publishing
PMB 196, 2540 South Maryland Pkwy
Las Vegas, NV 89109

First US edition, April 2019
eBook ISBN: 978-1-64202-177-6
Paperback ISBN: 979-8-89354-735-1

HIS NAME IS LEGION TEAM

JIT Readers

Misty Roa
Nicole Emens
James Caplan
Peter Manis
Dorothy Lloyd
Micky Cocker
Larry Omans

If we missed anyone, please let us know!

Weapons Consultant
John Kern
Proprietor
Spurlock's - Henderson NV

Editor
Skyhunter Editing Team

DEDICATION

*To Family, Friends and
Those Who Love
to Read.
May We All Enjoy Grace
to Live the Life We Are
Called.*

1

Although the demons were gone, Rio was still very much in disarray. Troops scoured the city looking for any signs of survivors. The lava had hardened, and although that was a good thing, it made it nearly impossible to get into areas where the housing had collapsed. If there was anyone in there who had found a bubble or a catacomb to hide from the magma, they were basically entombed. That was probably one of the hardest things for the soldiers and mercenaries to deal with, and they did everything in their power to not think about it.

Katie and Pandora kept as good a watch over things as possible, but their time was growing short. There were other places they needed to be, including New York, where there were demons and Damned running amuck through the shadows and alleys. They knew, though, that they would be back as soon as they could, and that they were only two, compared to the millions who needed their help.

Down through Rio de Janeiro, past the streets and coffee shops, past the shopping and touristy locations where the echoes of laughter and excitement still hung like a deep, thick fog, haunting the town, was a small suburban neighborhood. They were nice homes, nicer than the slums, at least, but they were nowhere near the luxury of the rich. Then again, how could they be? The rich sequestered themselves behind bars and walls to keep the poor and moderate out of their presence.

Three streets into the quaint neighborhood and four houses on the right was a blue home with black shutters. The whole neighborhood had basically been destroyed, if not by the tidal wave of lava that washed through, then by the demons destroying their very lives as they hid, weeping, in the corners. The blue house, though, was not completely gone. The roof had collapsed, and it had begun to fall in on itself.

"Hello?" a small voice cried. "Is there anyone out there?"

Isabella, a short eleven-year-old girl with long, silken dark-brown hair and crystal-blue eyes, sighed, squinted at the cracks above her that permitted streaming beams of light through them. Home alone, her brother had grabbed her and taken her down to the basement to hide after they heard the news about the incursion from neighbors who were fleeing. When huge demons had plowed through, it had knocked the three-story house down on them, creating a cave of rubble. Her brother, trying to shield her during the collapse, had fallen victim to several tumbling slabs of concrete that had landed on one of his legs.

The little girl hopped down and grabbed her bookbag off the ground, the only thing she had with her. She reached in and pulled out a Fanta, then popped the can open and crouched, shuffling on her knees toward her brother. She put her hand under his head and lifted it slightly. "Here, drink some of this," she whispered to him. "It's the only thing we have, and it's the last one."

Her brother roused enough to get it down, but at that point, he was barely conscious. Isabella whimpered, putting down the can of soda and wrapping her arms around her shoulders. As a tear fell down her cheek, voices whispered above them. Isabella looked straight up, eyes piercing the rays of light, and watching as someone above dragged their feet, knocking small pebbles and dust into her cave.

"I can lift it myself," one of the voices said pointedly.

The other voice snapped back at her, "It might collapse. We will do it together."

The first voice grumbled defiantly. "Ugh, why? You are being a glory hog again about something that isn't glorious."

A stone hit the floor above Isabella and the second voice snipped in irritation, "Fine, Mom. Whatever. God, such a Nervous Nancy."

The first voice grumped, "Don't call me Nancy."

Katie was standing above the rubble pile, looking around for any clue as to how bad the damage to the humans trapped below was. Pandora stopped in front of a huge slab of concrete, the one that seemed to be the culprit behind the implosion of the building. They each took a side, grunting as they used their angel energy reserve to lift it from the rubble and then leap up, beating their wings as hard as they could.

Isabella put her arm up, squinting as dust fell around her and the sun burst into the space. She was covered in dirt and grime and had smears of black soot across her cheeks and forehead. Small bright-red cuts ran across her filthy skin, but nothing too severe. As her eyes adjusted to the light, she saw the familiar faces of Katie and Pandora. By that point, there wasn't a soul on Earth who didn't know them.

The little girl gasped and hurried over to her brother, dropping to her knees next to him. She pushed on her brother's chest. "Manuel, wake up. They have come to save us. Manuel."

She bit the inside of her lip, looking around for anything that would help her wake him, but there was nothing. Her mother's voice floated through her head, and she remembered the many times over the last few years she had raised her voice to Isabella's brother to get his attention because, despite being her protector, he was also a normal teen.

Turning back to him, she began to yell in Portuguese. "Manuel Oliver Ortega, *acorde. Acorde agora! Eles vieram para nos salvar. Voce proeteu que ficaria comigo!*"

Isabella grunted loudly when her brother only groaned, not opening his eyes. Behind her, Katie landed. "Hi, there. Don't be scared."

Isabella turned to Katie with a sad look on her face. "I am not scared. I am never scared. My brother, he is trapped, and he needs help."

Katie walked over and knelt, putting her hand on Isabella's shoulder. "Don't worry. We will help you both."

Pandora grunted. "If you get over here this century."

Katie winked at Isabella as she stood and walked over. "You want me to lift or grab?"

Pandora glanced down at the guy. "Normally I'm all about grabbing, but this one looks like he might need a gentler touch. I'll lift, you get him out of here. Take him to the hospital, and I'll follow you with the mini-badass back there."

Katie rubbed her hands together and crouched, waiting for the boulder to be lifted. She didn't know how long Pandora would be able to hold it, so she wanted to be ready to get him out of there. Pandora puffed out her cheeks and squatted like a sumo wrestler, wrapping her arms around the slab of concrete. She grunted and lifted; this one was heavier than the last. Katie lunged forward, scooped him up as gently as she could, and took off.

Pandora dropped the slab, waving the dust from in front of her face. She glanced at the little girl, who was just staring at her. Sniffing, Pandora cleared her throat before she turned and got down on one knee, looking over her shoulder. "All right, kid, get on. Let's get you to the hospital. You have a brother to look after."

The girl jumped slightly as Pandora's long wings folded all the way out. Slowly her mouth curled into a smile and she ran, hopping onto Pandora's back and wrapping her legs around her waist. Pandora took off, reaching up with a gasp and adjusting Isabella's arm so it was a little less tight around her neck. "Relax, kid. I'm not a flying squirrel. Don't have to hold on for dear life."

The girl giggled and Pandora smirked, and they headed after Katie.

"The key to it is, you have to brush a lot of the sauce over it and let it sink into the massaged meat," Juntto explained to the group of Brazilian police standing around him. "The meat of a lion can be a fickle thing. Where I come from, we don't have lions like your Earth ones, but we have a creature very similar in stature called a 'larimore.'"

One of the cops, his eyes narrowed and his head tilted, was slightly confused. "I don't think they eat lions on this planet."

Juntto shook his head. "I understand your concern, and initially I thought the same. When I came here, I was shocked there was no lion meat in the grocer. I thought you just didn't eat them, but there is actually USDA certified lion meat that you can purchase in the United States, and there are people everywhere who either eat it or have tried it. Most think it is unpalatable, but that is because they don't know how to cook it."

Another cop wrinkled his nose. "My wife would kill me if I started eating lion."

The other guys chuckled, nodding their heads. Juntto scratched his chin. "Come to think of it, my girlfriend might do the same. Either way, that is the next show scheduled for *Cooking with Juntto*. I'm just glad you guys agreed to bring me some local recipes. International cooking at its best: recipes right from the source."

Sousa, one of the longer-term cops, reached in his pocket and handed Juntto a folded piece of paper. "This is my favorite cheese bread recipe. Bread's made from scratch, too."

Oliveira, a rookie, handed his over. "This is a family recipe for *feijoada*, a stew we love to eat. If you make it on your show, I would appreciate you give the Oliveira family, especially my *Avó*, a shout out. She will be thrilled. She thinks you're very handsome."

Juntto grinned. "That's so sweet. *Avó*...what?"

Oliveira beamed. "*Avó* Marietta Oliveira. Actually, would you mind signing an autograph? I would become her favorite of her twenty-three grandchildren."

"Of course," Juntto replied, the excitement of his small-time fame bubbling over.

Katie and Pandora, after dropping Isabella and her brother at the makeshift hospital in the rich neighborhood, circled the area and spied Juntto below. They landed next to him and lifted their eyebrows as he signed papers, magazines, and even a shoe for the Brazilian police and others.

Three twenty-something girls came up, all of them whispering and giggling. Two of them nudged the third, who nervously walked up to Pandora. "My name is Francisca, and my friends and I were wondering if you would sign some things for us. We are big fans. We started a Pandora fan club when you first started fighting on your own. I'm the only one who speaks English, so they sent me over."

Katie's eyes rolled. "Oh boy, here we go. Ego inflation."

Pandora ignored her, putting her hand to her chest in shock. "You have a Pandora fan club?"

The girl nodded. "We have t-shirts, see?" She pointed to I <3 Pandora on the top right of the shirt and then turned around, revealing a picture of Pandora with her wings spread and a saying on the bottom: If you're going to fight crime, you might as well do it with tits for days. What else am I going to distract them with?

Katie stood with a deadpan look before glancing over behind her. There was a line beginning to form, and she sure as hell hoped they weren't part of Pandora's fan club.

It turned out they were not, at least not most of them. So Katie, Pandora, and Juntto stood in the small section of the town signing autographs and taking selfies with everyone around them. It was actually a really nice way to be able to relax for a bit and be renewed by the idea that people still liked them, and still relied on them. For Pandora, though, it was a chance to grow continuously cockier by the second.

Katie smiled, taking a selfie with two guys. They shook her hand, praising her lovingly as a soldier approached. "Sorry, ma'am, I was sent to let you know that your plane is ready."

Katie nodded. "Thanks. We'll be there in a few."

She looked across the sea of people who had gathered, finding Brock to the side next to a tent, talking to several of his guys. He glanced over and found her staring, his mouth fighting the smirk that wanted to take over his lips.

The throne room was bustling and loud, the servants running all around making sure that everything was on the up and up. There was a long wooden table set up in the center, with Baal, Lucifer, and Mania seated around it. In front of them was a projection replaying the end of the Battle of January River.

Lucifer pointed excitedly. "Wait, wait, this is the best part. Goodbye, head."

He leaned back and chortled in jubilation. Baal forced a smile, his body vibrating as he faked a deep laugh. Mania smirked in amusement as she lifted a strawberry to her lips and darted her eyes hatefully at Baal. He immediately returned his attention to the screen as Lucifer waved his hands, bringing up what looked like live footage of the event.

With a deep sigh, Lucifer leaned forward and grabbed a live shrimp by the tail, tossing it back. "And now they are rescuing all the meatsacks down there, praying way too much for one city and shaking their fists at me. Even those who were followers of my ways have gone silent, due either to melting in the lava or allowing their disgusting human emotions to twist their minds back to *Him*. It really is disappointing. I am not going to lie. I was hoping I would have more followers who were true."

Baal shrugged. "Humans have a propensity to scurry off like rats to Him when they feel real fear. That is something that cannot be changed. Of course, they will return. Once the darkness has entered their souls, they will never truly be free of it."

Lucifer groaned, swiping away the scene in front of them. "I know. But why can't I have true soul followers like I do demons?"

Mania pursed her lips, her eyelids low, leaning forward with her tits bursting from the top of her corset. "Because He offers them a way out of that fear. A comfort that is sickly to think about. Of course, you get a few here and there who escape his glory. Bundy, Gacy…"

Lucifer clapped his claws. "Don't forget Ridgway. He is my favorite tortured soul. Sent me seventy-one beautiful, voluptuous whores from Earth for my collection."

Baal glanced at him. "Your collection?"

Mania giggled. "He has a collection of whore souls he keeps in a small fish tank. He likes to drop fresh virgins in there and watch them attack. It *is* rather amusing."

Lucifer dropped a rat down his throat, wincing as it tried to bite his tongue. "It was very kind of you to arrange for a chef to prepare brunch for us, Baal. A nice surprise after all of the turmoil these battles have put me through."

Baal cleared his throat, keeping a calm demeanor. "Of course, My Lord. Anything to help you enjoy your kingship a bit more."

Lucifer nodded at Mania, who swept from her chair, throwing the back of her cape around in a cascade of shimmering fabric. Her six-inch stiletto boots clacked across the stone floors as she sauntered toward the doors.

"Oh, and don't forget...the thing. The one I like," Lucifer called after her.

She turned back around, tugging on her mini-skirt, her waist tiny in the black lace corset with a twisting black ribbon laced up the back. "Of course, My Lord."

After she disappeared, Lucifer turned toward Baal. "I want to ask you something, Baal. You have shown a, let's say, *affinity* to walking beside the less intelligent demons of hell, but you somehow stay out of the major ambushes. Is there a reason you don't pair with a superior type of demon?"

Baal's broad black-scaled brow creased and his lips

puckered. "I suppose you could say it's because I don't wish to be personally involved in unsanctioned attacks, although I do offer wisdom and advice to any of my fellow lost souls. What type of brother in hell would I be if I did not? Sometimes it gets a bit complicated, but usually, it's the dumb ones who ask for advice. Only after attempting and failing on their own, of course."

Mania came back out with an armful of tools, three equally burdened servants walking quickly behind her. She reached the table and Lucifer swiped his hand, moving all the food to the end. Baal put his hands up as a bowl of marinated sloth toes whizzed by him, spilling some of the juice in his lap. Mania dropped the pile of torture implements in front of them, followed by the three servants.

Lucifer selected a four-pronged device, each prong sharpened to a glistening point. He ran his tongue over his fangs and put the device to his teeth, picking them. "Were you loyal to Beelzebub? Or Moloch before him? Or T'Chezz before *him*? Were you loyal to those who made decisions that ended with them disappearing into the void of nothingness? If so, does that send you down the same path, or do you have some nefarious plan, something that pushes you to get rid of the weak and climb toward the strong?"

Baal showed no sign of fear. He knew the spiked nut clamp Mania was playing with was a form of intimidation, and though part of him *was* intimidated, he could not show his weakness. He had played the game long enough to know better. "No, My Lord. I am only, and have only ever been, loyal to you."

Lucifer scanned him for a moment, still picking his teeth. A small smile pulled at the corner of his lips. "We'll see about that…"

2

Brock tucked his arm tightly around Katie's waist and pulled her close to his body. With his other hand, he smoothed down the wild, wind-swept hairs on the top of her head. His hand moved slowly down her cheek and cupped the side of her face. Their eyes stayed locked as he pulled her toward him, tilting his head to the side. His lips opened, pushing against hers as he deeply penetrated her mouth with his tongue. The kiss was hot and breathy, more passionate than either of them had shown in a public place before.

Katie couldn't help but close her eyes, pressing her body into his, the air catching in her lungs and fluttering with the adrenaline beginning to simmer wildly in her chest. When he pulled his face from hers she kept hers in place, her eyes closed for another couple of moments. Lifting her hand to her lips, she shuddered, wanting more, but knowing that was not the course her day was taking.

After a few moments she cleared her throat and opened

her eyes, her pupils a glistening blue and slowly changing back to normal. "That was intense."

Brock chuckled, releasing his grip on her and putting unwanted inches between them. "I figured it would be good to start lingering when I say goodbye. Get in those last few minutes."

Katie's hand reached up almost without her control, and she rubbed her thumb across his bottom lip. The sound of a soldier walking past made her jump, dropping her hand back to her side. "So, where are you headed, again?"

Brock groaned, shoving his hands into his pockets. "Back to Bahrain. I will be taking several soldiers back with me to assist. We have to start working faster, although I'm not completely sure how that will be possible. We already kill ourselves out there, but more hands may help move the process along. You're going back to New York?"

Katie nodded, looking down at the ground and kicking small lava stones across it with her boot. "Yeah. Me and Pandora and Juntto. I know Angie wants Juntto back. He wants his YouTube career back, and Pandora and I have some business to attend to with the local police. I think we have cleared this area well enough to leave it in the hands of the Brazilian soldiers."

Brock's eyes scanned the area. "Yeah. I think most of the American soldiers and the others from across the globe are going to be heading out in the next couple of days as well. Everyone needs to get back to their forts and continue fighting off the small-time demons that are a huge thorn in our sides. Hopefully, with that big guy gone, things will quiet down for a while."

Katie rolled her eyes. "Yeah, well, we will see. We always seem to get our hopes up, but nothing ever happens the way we want it to."

Brock scoffed. "I know, tell me about it. I think maybe when we are done with the walls and forts, I'll come spend some time in New York if it's possible."

Katie's cheeks burned, but she pushed down her old nervousness when it came to boys. "That would be nice. You know you're always welcome, and there are so many things we didn't get to do during the times that you have been able to come. To be honest with you, I would really like to take you on a date. Like a full-on date."

Brock gawked. "Oh, yeah? Like a real date? Will you buy me a corsage for when we fight the demons in the city?"

Katie chuckled. "First of all, yes on the corsage. A yellow lily would really compliment your eyes."

They both laughed.

"Secondly, I am not talking about a mercenary date," she explained, running her finger down the front of his shirt. "I am talking about an honest-to-God real date with candles and food. Something out of the house, and maybe, just maybe, a kiss at the end of the night. But definitely no fighting demons, no chasing Leviathans, and no exorcising anyone. That is the kind of thing I reserve for date number six."

Brock bit his bottom lip and reached out, pulling her close to him again. "Six? Wow. I was hoping to get to second base before we even left for the date."

Katie shrugged. "You know me. Taking things slow is my motto."

They both smiled broadly and began to lean in for another kiss. Pandora was walking past them and stopped, getting in close to their faces. "You know, you guys have time for a quickie. You would have to make it a *real* quickie. Like no nonsense, pants down, bend over, go to town, but at least you won't have to continue to torture each other like this. Remember, Brock, she's an angel now, not a demon. They don't make handcuffs covered in golden prayers, although they should. Might make them a lot less grumpy."

Katie lifted an eyebrow as she and Brock pulled apart. Her eyes shifted from Pandora to Brock, and she shook her finger in Pandora's direction. "Also, speaking of that date…"

Brock was blinking wildly at Pandora's words. "Mmhmm."

Katie smacked her lips. "One that doesn't involve Pandora, either."

Pandora's huge smile quickly faded to a pout. "Rude. Come on, get your ass together. We have a plane to board so we can get back home and you can go back into Emo, unpleasant Katie."

They both watched her walk off, smacking one of the soldiers on the ass as she passed.

Pandora put her arms up. "And…recovered. You can't hold me down, bitch. You can't hold me down."

The plane seemed like a five-star resort compared to how they had been spending their time for the last few days.

Everything was sparkling clean. There were donuts, milk, and coffee waiting for them after takeoff, and the seats felt like feathers plucked from their own wings. Immediately all three of them, Katie, Pandora, and Juntto, put their feet up and tried their best to relax. For Juntto, it was pretty easy. He had spent centuries witnessing, and often participating in, the mass deaths of entire countries. It was different for Katie, though; the initial look on Isabella's face still figured in the visions in her head.

Her body was relaxed, but as usual, with the world the way it was, and her responsibilities looming in the background, her mind was on overdrive. She was just starting to get used to it. In the past, Pandora had slowed it down for her, but at that moment, she did not feel like dealing with Pandora's constant snarky banter inside her head. At least with her in her own seat, Katie could combat it.

Juntto, however, had just laid back and was enjoying the ride. He had pulled out a notebook and a pen and was jotting ideas down in it. The flight attendant walked up with a Cherry Coke in a glass with ice. Juntto glanced up, his eyes going wide as he reached up and took it from her. "I got bored a couple of weeks ago and found myself in a bowling alley. They had Cherry Coke, so I tried it with crinkle fries dipped in mustard and a huge pretzel. It is pretty much my favorite thing now."

The attendant smiled kindly, her face clear and smooth, but the creases beside her eyes showed her age. "Don't you just love the simple things? I mean, who doesn't adore a lavishly prepared meal, but those little quirks? Those are the things that make you let go of things for a little while."

Juntto put down his feet and sat up. "Yes. *Yes.*

That's exactly it. And this dimension has so many things like that. They seem strange at first, but in the end, they aren't. I didn't even bowl while I was there. They don't make bowling balls big enough to be comfortable for me as a frost giant, and I hadn't shifted. No matter who I shift into, though, it's like throwing a paper ball down a hallway. So light. Anyway, I went back and started planning for the next cooking show."

The attendant pointed at him. "That's right, *Cooking with Juntto*. I heard you made some amazing cookies on there."

Juntto crossed his arms with a pleased smile. "You have to make sure when you go online to follow me on Insta and smash that Subscribe button. I need more followers, for sure."

The attendant thought for a moment. "Have you been promoting on social media? I swear, you can sell anything on there if you hype it enough. Like the Fyre Festival. I won't lie, though, seeing all those pissed-off little rich kids with cheese and bread for lunch on a deserted island made me a little giddy on the inside."

Juntto laughed. "I heard about that. How ridiculous can you be? I don't understand it, not in the least. But then again, I make food for a living. I don't put together festivals, or in Ja Rule's case, put together a broken-down FEMA site."

Pandora smirked, turning her head from Juntto to Katie, who was staring out the window. She knew that look on her face, and she knew who she was thinking about. She unbuckled her seatbelt and dove right into

Katie. With a groan, Katie's arms lifted and then dropped back to the armrests.

I've said this a thousand times: you need to tell me before you jump into my body, Pandora.

Pandora sniffed. *Well, you were over here daydreaming about Brock, so I figured you wouldn't mind if I just strolled in to try to shift your thoughts.*

Katie got comfortable again. *Why do I need to shift my thoughts?*

Because it's getting serious with the guy, Pandora replied.

Katie pursed her lips, watching the small patch of ice on the outside of the window begin to spread across the glass. *I guess it is, but what am I supposed to do? I care about him. I want to spend more time with him, and putting it out of my mind is really not an option.*

Pandora faked a gagging sound, but Katie didn't respond. With a sigh, Pandora switched her tone to a somewhat more serious one. *You have a crazy-busy life. I just don't want to see you get hurt because you want it one way, but that is not the reality of this world.*

Katie reached up, tracing the ice with her finger. *Who knows? Maybe dealing with Beelzebub on a very public stage will teach the fucking demons to stay in their lane. I mean, how many huge asshole overlords do we have to kill before they stop coming after us? Not to mention that our response times and angel powers just keep getting better. Seriously, maybe this will free up some of our time.*

Pandora scoffed. *Not too fucking likely. But what do we do now? I mean, usually we don't even have time between shit shows to have our milk and cookies, but this one seems pretty quiet.*

Katie shrugged. *I don't know, exactly. No one has called. I know the station and the NYC cops could use our help, but that's tiny stuff. I think at this point, I am going to rely on my angelic powers to lead me where I need to go.*

And if demons come back like they did before?

Katie shut the sliding cover on her window and grabbed her glass of wine. *I'll be ready. And if they do come back, they better hope to God that I am not armed.*

Normally the wind in the desert would blow the sand up one side of the base and down the other. There was a constant stream of dry grains pelting the eyes, noses, and throats of everyone there. On that evening, though, the sand stayed put. It was wet enough from the drifting and fluttering snowstorm that had passed across the desert that there was no way it was going to shift and whirl like usual. It might have been really close to March at that point, but someone had forgotten to tell the weather gods that.

Stephanie pushed open the doors to the barracks and walked out, her breath steaming up and over her head like she was smoking a cigar. She put her clipboard between her knees, and with shaking hands and chattering teeth, she zipped up her winter coat and pulled the collar up on each side. Straightening up and shoving one hand in her pocket, she gazed at the small fluttering flakes that drifted toward her. One landed on her nose and she smiled, seeing the shimmering ice crisp melt quickly.

The flapping of a piece of tarp caught her attention, and she made her way over to her garden. She had been told that the winters in the desert were unpredictable, sometimes not sputtering out until May. She didn't believe them, however, and even though she'd lived in Vegas for a long time, paying attention to the desert weather patterns had never made its way onto her daily list of things to do. She was more of a test-the-weather-when-you-walk-out-the-front-door kind of gal.

She knelt and tucked the piece of tarp back into the winter cover. She wanted to make sure that the plants survived if such a thing actually happened. Plus, the sheets were designed to keep the frost out in the early spring.

A soldier walked up and stood straight at attention. Stephanie glanced up, putting her hand on her knee and standing as she grunted through her words. "Nice evening, huh?"

The soldier's eyes shifted to her, and he smiled. "It's a bit nippy for my taste."

Stephanie chuckled, waving her finger. "At ease. I called you over because I want you to snatch up four of your best guys to do something out here. It's supposed to drop down in the teens tonight. I need you guys to double-check anything that could be affected by a freeze. I'm talking water lines, septic, the well—just about anything that could be a catastrophic event for the base. We don't need to be worrying about that stuff if we happen to find ourselves in the middle of an incursion. Let's not shut the base down because we were too focused to remember the basics of taking care of things."

The soldier nodded, his hands behind his back. "Yes, ma'am."

Stephanie pulled the hood over her head and squinted,

the snow hitting her face. "Good. I'll be on in Comms if you need me."

When the soldier left, she scanned down her to-do list, finding the next thing to be checking in on was Timothy and all of the systems that were up and running, and any complications he might be anticipating. Heading into the main building, she could feel the bitter cold windburn on her cheeks simmering in the warmth of the hallways. She walked to Timothy's computer dungeon and slid her keycard through, opening the door.

"Well, howdy, sister lady," Timothy said, moving his chair over and clicking one of the buttons. "You look like you just walked out of a snow-covered hellscape."

Stephanie chuckled, unzipping her coat. "Yeah, definitely not a blizzard, but weird for here. I just wanted to come in and check on the incursion data."

Timothy swung around in his rolling chair and typed wildly on the keyboard. "If I had known it was going to be a windy, snowy hell, I would have pulled out my vintage fur jacket and pranced across the base catching snow in my fur."

The screen changed, but it was relatively quiet. Stephanie walked up and looked at it. "Looks like you could be prancing anywhere you wanted, with as quiet as this shit is."

Timothy put his hands out. "This isn't abnormal, not right after a big incursion—especially with the girls killing yet another major demon. Just enjoy the winter wonderland for now, and we'll keep an eye on it. Before we know it, it will be so hot in this bowl of hell, we will *wish* it would be cold."

Stephanie smirked. "So you would take sunny beach against hell frozen over? Check. I grew up between SoCal and Las Vegas, so hot was the norm for me."

Timothy crossed his arms. "Mmm, girl, I grew up in Montana. They have snow that snows there. I came out here and lost fifty pounds just by taking the snow gear off. Though I do have to admit, there are times that I miss it. Then I remember the whole hat thing, the knit cap, and realize that world was not for the fashion-forward."

Stephanie laughed as she sat down in a chair. "When it's cold, I don't give two shits. I just want to be warm, hobo-style or not."

Timothy smirked and glanced up at the cooking show on the television. He opened his mouth to inquire about Sean, but before he could say a word, the door opened and Calvin walked through. Timothy hid his sigh, not wanting to talk with someone else in the room. He figured that Sean and his security clearance could be discussed later. It wasn't like he was going anywhere, and he couldn't really screw up anything where he was right now. He was pretty much not allowed near anything important.

It was a slap in the face to Sean, but it was what it was.

3

The time just seemed to keep passing. Katie and Pandora spent weeks in New York doing small jobs, but nothing crazy or life-threatening, at least to Katie. On the one hand, she really enjoyed the downtime; on the other, she feared she was getting out of practice. Pandora was feeling it too, and as preparation to their trip back to the base, Katie had to help her pack her bag. She kept forgetting her underwear, although Katie had a hard time believing it wasn't intentional.

"You need to put them all together, fold them tightly, and remember to put them the fuck on," Katie said, pushing the pile of Pandora's clothes down.

Pandora shrugged. "Who needs underwear? And seriously, what is with these clothes you are packing?"

Katie sighed exhaustedly. "You need to take clothes with you for the base. Not just your super-tight fighter gear, but all kinds. We aren't going there to work this time. You know this."

Pandora groaned. "Please tell me I'm only lugging this shit through the portal."

Katie shut the lid and pushed down, struggling to fasten the clasps. "We are going on a plane as a family, and if you can carry a boulder, a person, and your ego, you can make it from the car to the plane carrying your suitcase."

Pandora shook her finger at Katie as she walked to the door. "I'll have you know, my ego is actually light as a feather."

Out in the hallway, Katie grabbed her bags. "Great, so you have more strength to carry the suitcase. Come on, the plane and the others are waiting for us." She shook her head and started toward the door, still talking. "You can jump to it for a damn donut, but this is like pulling teeth."

Pandora dragged her case to the elevator, and they headed down to the car that was waiting to take them to the airport. When they arrived, pulling into the private hangar bay, Angie and Juntto were waiting for them. Angie was jumping up and down and rubbing her arms, trying to stay warm as steam rose off Juntto. He was watching something on his phone and laughing.

Katie raised her eyebrow at Angie, who shrugged and followed her up to the steps to the aircraft. "He recorded a new show last night, and he finds himself incredibly funny. There was some incident with a piece of beef and an animation of sorts. I don't know. I stopped trying to figure it out."

Katie giggled, putting her arm around Angie as they reached the door of the plane. "Don't worry about it. We are going to the base to celebrate our dear friends and their baby. Sofia's baby shower should be really interesting, with everyone there."

Angie rolled her eyes. "Great. I get to watch grown men sit around a pink and blue room and talk about babies. Exciting. Thrilling. What I've been waiting for all my life."

They all boarded and took their seats. Pandora sniveled, looking at her finger. "Broke a nail on that damn suitcase."

Katie buckled her seatbelt. "I love how everyone is in such a fantastic mood right now. Come on, guys, get excited! How often do we board a plane without having some sort of bloodthirsty demon attack going on?"

Angie smiled. "You're right. Changing mood...*done*. So tell me, what have you guys been up to for the past few weeks? I feel like we see each other for breakfast, and that's about it."

Pandora smiled at the healed nail and looked at Angie as the plane went hurtling down the runway. "Katie and I have had the pleasure of working with New York's finest the last few weeks. And no, it is not as bad as it sounds. They love donuts, they find me funny, and the case is really interesting, even to me. That, and I have managed to yank off a couple of the guys in the evidence room."

Katie scowled. "That was too much information, just like we talked about."

Pandora looked at her with wide eyes and mouthed the words, "I'm sorry" to her. Katie chuckled and looked at Angie. "It actually *is* pretty interesting. There is a case, or several together, involving mass hallucinations. People in apartments have been seeing things. Weird shit, really."

Angie looked at her with fear on her face. "Oh, my God. That sounds terrible."

Katie raised her eyebrows and tilted her head from side to side. "It doesn't seem to be too bad. At first, I thought it sounded like we had another Kabbus the Leviathan on our hands, but the reports don't line up with that. No one is reporting nightmares, or anything else overly horrifying. I don't know. It's an ongoing case right now, and we get the fun of tagging along."

Angie snorted. "Better you than me. I have a gaming tournament coming up, and I'm actually starting to make money doing the Twitch stuff. Nothing more than a coffee fund for the month, but still."

Katie nodded. "Hey, that's good. Coffee is expensive in New York. That can't be too bad a check. And you get to do something fun for you and entertaining for others. I'm glad it didn't interfere with your work with us. I wouldn't want to lose you."

Angie flapped her hands. "Please. I love my job. It's more like a lifestyle than a career. It's great. This is just something fun on the side. Like Juntto here."

Juntto looked up excitedly. "I have twelve subscribers now on my YouTube channel, so I would say that things are going great for me. One day it's twelve, the next day it could be a million. You never know."

Pandora giggled. "A million morons finding entertainment in animated beef patties."

Juntto opened his mouth angrily but then put his arms up in excitement. "You watched!"

The plane's door opened, and Calvin hurried up the steps and waited at the entrance. He could hear Sofia grunting as she got up from her seat with the help of the attendant and shuffled toward the doorway. As she appeared, the light cascaded over her warm tan skin, her eyes were glistening brightly, and her smile was slightly crooked. She hurried forward with a slight waddle with one hand on her lower back and the other on her stomach. She was VERY pregnant at that point.

Her eyes flashed and she giggled, shaking her head. "Come here and kiss me to remind me how much I love you. Your kid here has been trying to convince me otherwise with a good shove in the pelvic bone every few minutes."

Calvin put out his bottom lip and pulled her close, kissing her deeply. As he pressed his body against her stomach, he felt the baby kick. Calvin chuckled and moved back, getting down on one knee and pressing his hand to her belly. "Don't worry, buddy. From the moment you came into the picture, I became, and will forever be, the second most important person to your mom. And I'm not even mad."

Sofia chuckled as she rubbed the back of his head. He stood back up and offered her his arm. "You ready to get off this plane?"

She rolled her eyes. "Three bathroom trips ago, which was like ten minutes. And I'm freaking starving."

Calvin helped her down the steps slowly and carefully. "What are you in the mood for?"

Sofia thought carefully about it. "Definitely some

vanilla ice cream, ooh, and those little sweet pickles that you get. Not the bread and butter, the mini sweet pickles."

Calvin chuckled. "Very cliché of you."

Sofia got to the bottom of the steps, winded. "Wait until you hear what I eat the rest of the time. I want to orgasm and die every time I eat a meal. It's terrible."

Calvin threw his head back and laughed. "You forget that I live with a whole bunch of young guys. The shit they shovel in their mouths sometimes baffles me. Did you finish that paper you wanted to get done before you came?"

Sofia took her small carry-on from the plane's staff, smiling. "Yeah, I did. This semester has thankfully been very easy. Still, I am looking forward to taking a few months off once the baby is born. I am burned out, to say the least."

Eddie and Turner were training some troops just to the right of them. Eddie looked over and waved excitedly at Sofia. Turner glanced over his shoulder and then whistled, yelling at the troops, "Everyone, drop to one knee and freeze! Now bow to Mrs. Calvin and the future Killer in her belly!"

All the troops did as they were told. Sofia giggled and returned their bows awkwardly as she passed them. Calvin gave them two thumbs-ups. Eddie laughed as the guys got back up and continued their exercises. "Baby shower weekend!"

Turner raised an eyebrow. "Uh, why did you say that like I would say 'stripper weekend?'"

Eddie shrugged. "Family time, man. We were both invited."

Turner stopped and turned toward him, putting his hands on his hips. "Wait, you're actually *going* to the shower?"

Eddie furrowed his brow. "Uh, yeah. I was invited, and my demon Coco was once inside of Sofia."

Turner blinked at him. "Why does that have anything to do with her baby shower?"

Eddie scratched his head. "The way I see it, that makes me and Sofia practically cousins, you know? And Coco was the first being to have met the baby. Actually, the only one so far, so he should be there for moral support and all."

Turner rubbed his face. "You *do* realize you're talking about your demon, right?"

Eddie nodded with a grin on his face. "Yeah, sure. You know how it is. It's an intimate experience, and I don't mean that in a creepy demon lover way. Just, a soul in your soul. It makes you attached in a way."

Turner put out his hands. "Dude, it's a *baby shower*. Seriously? Like pink and blue puffy things and diapers, and women with all kinds of emotions and crazy thoughts going on in their heads. It's a total chick thing. Dudes don't usually go to them."

Eddie looked around him. "But we're all a family, and let's face it—there aren't that many women here. Sofia's party would be like three or four people."

"But the games!" Turner laughed. "You are going to have to play like pin the diaper on the baby or something."

Eddie winced. "Remind me...if I ever knock anyone up, don't let you babysit."

Turner pointed at him. "That's a deal I can make. I just think you are going to want to claw your eyes out by the end of it. I've seen the pictures of baby showers. Weird cult shit goes on in those."

Eddie snickered as he picked up some of his gear. "Right, but there is also one really amazing thing."

Turner's eyes shifted. "What? And I hope you're not getting creepy."

Eddie smacked his lips. "They have those little cakes."

Turner stared at him for a moment. "Petit fours."

Eddie shook his head, putting his fingers out in measurement. "No, what? Those little cakes. The delicious ones."

Turner let out a slow annoyed breath. "I know what you're talking about. The little cakes, they're called 'petit fours.' That is what you are going to the baby shower for? A fancy little cake?"

Eddie lifted his stuff onto his shoulder and gave him a toothy grin. "Hey, they're going to have really good food and booze, even if Sofia can't drink. So yeah, I'm going. If it means I have to play dumb games, then bring it on. I'll wear a diaper and hit a pinata."

Turner covered his mouth, trying not to burst into laughter. "I feel like the two of us have a really unhealthy view of what actually happens at a baby shower."

The evening service bells of Westminster Abbey could be heard echoing across London and through the cracked window of one of the most prominent members of the British Intelligence Committee, Powell. Though the bells were loud, the sounds coming out of the place were a bit more interesting.

"Whoop," Powell squealed, adding a light giggle behind it. "That's right. Daddy was a bad boy today."

One of the women behind him put her shiny, high-heeled latex boot on his back and pushed him down, then reared back and flung her arm forward, cracking a fringed leather whip across his ass. He hissed and began laughing. "This was just what I needed after a full day with those stuffed shirt blokes on the Committee. Come on, then, don't be greedy. Give it to me some more. I thought you were supposed to be dominating me?"

The woman knelt, grabbed his cheeks in her hand, and squeezed. "Then shut the fuck up."

She threw his face down and whipped him again, his eyes popping hard this time and a smile tugging on his lips. Walking over, she grabbed him by the shoulder and flipped him on his back. He put his hands up, his laughter weasely and high-pitched. She stepped down, her foot just centimeters from the leather bikini bottom covering his balls. She dangled the whip over his chest, tickling his skin before reaching down and tugging hard on the rings through both of his nipples.

He rolled his eyes back and groaned, tilting his head. His phone began to ring but he ignored it at first, hoping whoever it was would call back later. It just kept ringing, though. His eyes opened and he growled, his lip quivering. "Fuck. Goddamn it!"

He tried to get up, but the woman raised an eyebrow, wagging her finger. Powell shook his head and tried to grab the phone. "Stop. Wait. What's that bloody safe word? Uh…grapes! No, that's not it. Oh! Tangerine!"

The woman pouted and stepped back as he picked himself up clumsily and stumbled over to the phone, putting it to his ear. "There's a limo waiting out front. Dismiss your weird freakishly tall woman with the boots and get your ass dressed. It's not safe to talk on this line. Be downstairs in fifteen minutes."

The phone clicked off, and he shrugged at the woman. "Sorry, love, duty calls. I'll call yeh next week. We'll set something up. I owe you, after all."

She clomped over to him, reaching down and roughly cupping his balls. He grunted and smirked as she ran her lips across his cheek. "Damn right, you do."

Powell got dressed and wiped the red smear of lipstick off his cheeks and chin, then grabbed his wallet and shoved it in his back pocket before heading down to the limo waiting for him out front. The driver nodded, opening the door and keeping an eye out around him. They drove across town to an older building with no lights on the outside, and one car parked out front. Powell got out of the limo and headed inside and down the hall. Walking through the last door, he sneered. It was a tech room just like Timothy's, but it looked more like an old run-down factory version that hadn't been cleaned for pretty much ever.

Inside were tables upon tables of technological gadgets. Guts of computers thrown in heaps, falling to the floors in piles. Near the back, a single light hovered over a slightly neater desk with several computers hooked up to large state-of-the-art screens. The man nervously switching from keyboard to keyboard looked up, his shimmering sweat highlighted by the bright bulb swinging gently over him.

Powell put his hand up to block the reflection. "Xian, I was rather unfortunately summoned here. Please tell me it was worth getting up and walking away from a very good time in my condo."

Xian pushed his black-rimmed glasses up and nodded, not caring what he was talking about and, quite frankly, really not wanting to know. "The World Council put a lot on us. This system is so complex. It's almost ridiculous how much I have to do to just keep up."

Powell grimaced at a rat running along the wall. "Yes, well, it's not exactly the most pleasant of jobs. And the system is that Timothy fellow's work. We all knew he was a genius hacker, but we are tracking down the Leviathans for the Council. This is incredibly important, not to mention that it is good for both our careers."

Xian pulled up an image on the screen and nodded at it. Powell walked over closer and squinted at the screen. "What are we looking at?"

Xian typed a few more things in. "I think it is a Leviathan. It's huge, and seems to lumber in the oceans like an underwater land mass."

Powell dropped his head and groaned, rubbing the bridge of his nose. Suddenly he turned, grabbed Xian by the collar, and lifted his feet from the ground, slamming him against the wall. "You bald idiot, that's Baylahn. You have been wasting my precious time and resources hunting down a Leviathan that's being tracked in all of our intel offices."

Powell was pissed. "You were supposed to correct for the ones we know about. Juntto and Baylahn are already here."

Xian nodded nervously and Powell dropped him to his feet, pushing him toward his desk. "Find something! Do not stop looking! Fucking useless! Everyone is fucking useless."

4

The plane touched down on the runway to the base, coming to a gentle stop at the hangar. Katie looked out the window, seeing, besides the base, only miles of sand stretching as far as the eye could see. Never in her life had she ever thought the sight of sand and dryness would be so warm and inviting, but there she was, delighted at being back home without some crazy emergency messing up her plans.

Pandora, on the other hand, snickered at the scenery, slung her carryon over her shoulder, and started flipping her hair around. "I love the family, don't get me wrong, but this place is so drab and sad-looking."

Katie grabbed her bags as well and laughed. "It's a military base. What do *you* think it should look like?"

Pandora shrugged and grumbled as she walked to the door. "Less like Alcatraz and more like Beverly Hills."

The door opened and Pandora pulled her sunglasses down, raising her arms. Katie ducked so as to not get popped in the face and looked down, smiling at Stephanie and Calvin, who were waiting to greet them. They went down to the bottom of the steps and set their bags down. Katie walked over to Stephanie and gave her a big warm hug. She knew that she was struggling without Korbin, and really felt for her.

Pandora, on the other hand, grabbed Calvin and yanked him into her. She hugged him far too tightly, so much so that he was struggling to get oxygen. Calvin's eyes bugged, and he jumped as she slapped her hands down on his ass and cupped both of his cheeks very tightly. Closing her eyes, she sighed, grinning from ear to ear. Calvin couldn't move, and his hands were straight out, not touching her.

"Good to see you again, Daddy," she cooed.

Calvin's lip twitched, and he felt her release enough for him to actually breathe. "You know, when anyone else calls me 'daddy,' it's cute and sweet and full of the idea of my child. When you say it, it just sounds weird, and slightly creepy in a 'you keep locks of my hair in your drawer' kind of way."

Pandora giggled. "I like momentos. Just be glad it's hair. I've been known to take much more precious samples. But that's all behind me now that I've got my wings back."

Stephanie and Katie looked at Calvin, who was still struggling to get free. Stephanie laughed hard but Katie shook her head, rolling her eyes as she walked over. She gripped Pandora's hand and began to pry it away slowly, one finger at a time, off Calvin's ass. Pandora struggled for a moment, then finally let go, putting her hands up and backing away. "Fine, fine. You just don't like the fact that I am a proud white woman with a connection to this Nubian prince."

Straight-faced, Calvin shook his head. "No. See, no, you can't... Don't say shit like that."

Stephanie giggled, waving at them. "Come on, you guys. I'll walk you to your quarters. We've done a few upgrades, and Pandora, we went through and completely redid the bedroom that is yours now. Tried to make a bit more like home, so when you come here, you don't feel out of place."

Katie and Stephanie held hands as they walked down the hall. Pandora reached for Calvin's, but he slapped it away. They stopped and let Katie throw her bags in her room before heading down to Pandora's. Katie was excited to see what they had done, especially since it was the only way to keep her out of her hair, at least while she was sleeping.

When they walked into the room, Katie almost gasped in surprise. It was beautiful, with long black velvet drapes and a deep turquoise on the walls. The furniture was a deep chestnut color, and the bed was a queen size, with pillows and fluffy blankets all over it. Pandora walked around, rubbing her chin and nodding.

Stephanie just smirked, knowing Pandora all too well. Pandora scoped it out for several minutes and then turned to Stephanie. "It definitely has potential. You did a good job. Now, of course, I will need to invest in a bigger bed. Gotta have room to really roll around with my lovers. And of course, one of those swing thingies."

Stephanie tilted her head in confusion. "A hammock?"

Pandora pursed her lips, thinking. "Can you bone in a hammock? I always felt like I would go spinning around and then get stuck like that."

Stephanie shrugged. "I mean, *technically* you could bone

in one. I would tell you to be careful not to get cocooned, but…"

Katie rubbed her face and groaned. "She means a sex swing, the ones specifically made to bolt to the ceiling and strap in for the ride." She turned to Pandora. "We're not buying you a sex swing."

Pandora narrowed her eyes at Katie. "I don't need you to buy me one. I can purchase it on my own."

Katie lifted an eyebrow, hands on her hips. "Oh, yeah?"

Pandora nodded defiantly. "Yes."

"With what money?" Katie asked.

Pandora giggled, flipping her hand and walking over to her bed. "Why, with half of whatever you get for saving the world. If I'm living out here and not in you, I need my own cash, baby."

Katie scrunched her nose. "Yeah, well, we'll have to talk about that one later."

Stephanie put her palms together. "Oh, yeah. Speaking about talking. I need to put my head together with you and Angie about supplies. We are running low, and figured this would be the perfect time to go over everything and revamp the budget. But it can wait until later. I know you guys are exhausted."

Katie jerked a thumb at Pandora, who was prancing around her room. "I don't think I've stopped being exhausted."

Korbin ran his hands over the stone wall, newly constructed and very nicely done. Several of the Damned hurried beside him with pads of paper, jotting down notes as he talked. He stopped and looked up and over the wall, rubbing his chin and scoping out every inch of the place.

He pointed at the scaffolding to the right. "All of those sections need to be cleared. That is where the platform for the gun turret will go. They should be here soon to put up. Until then, I don't want to give anyone the idea that we are vulnerable."

The Damned soldiers nodded, making the note. They already had about five pages worth. It was a very mixed group of Damned out there, not like the other places. Most of the men wore *thobes,* and a few wore turbans on their heads and sported short curly beards, while others were clean shaven, donning the military helmets in case of falling debris. Korbin wasn't picky about what they wore as long as they were on top of their game. The military forces in Bahrain weren't either, especially with religious exemptions.

Korbin turned, putting his hands on the railing of the walkway. He peered down below, where the other workers were bustling in and out of the armory buildings and technology hubs. A man dressed in a long black trench, wide-brimmed hat, and combat boots stepped out of the shadows and glanced up, nodding to him and patting the front of his jacket. Korbin nodded back and turned to the Damned. "Take a break, then start working on what we talked about so far. I have some things to take care of. We can pick this up later."

The guys walked off, talking to each other about the plans. Korbin glanced around and then headed down, following a distance from the guy and turning into one of the not fully completed buildings. The guy stood with his back to Korbin as he entered the room. "Did you bring the goods?"

The guy turned around, dirt on his cheek and a toothless grin. His voice was low and raspy, and he reached his long crooked fingers out. "Did you bring the money? This was incredibly hard to find, and I put a lot of work into it. It's a good one, too."

From all indications, they were about to complete a major drug deal. Korbin pulled an envelope from his breast coat pocket and handed it to the guy. The creeper smirked and thumbed the envelope, then opened his jacket, carefully pulling a small plant from his pocket, the base wrapped in a wet cloth and plastic bag.

Korbin grinned. "A plant for my wife's garden. She loves the exotic ones."

He bowed his head as Korbin took the small plant from his hands. "The Jasmine Sambac, better known as the Grand Duke Supreme. Enjoy."

Korbin smiled as he held the small plant up. Nodding, and without another look, he headed out of the building and through the fort to his car. He jumped inside and drove back to the house they were staying in. Korbin didn't want the plant to be exposed to the elements, and knew he had to take good care of it until he could get it to his wife.

As he entered, Brock looked up. He was making himself a sandwich. "Hey, you finally got one."

Korbin smirked. "I did, and she is beautiful. Worth every penny."

Brock chuckled. "You guys are strange, but I like it.

Everyone is going to be at the base. Probably already there."

Korbin nodded, setting the plant carefully on the counter. "It's baby shower weekend, isn't it?"

Brock took a bite of his sandwich and nodded. "Mmhmm. Should be a lot of fun. Don't you want to be there?"

Korbin sneered. "Nah. Besides, I sent a gift."

"I feel like this is bullshit duty. We are being put on fucking *teddy bear* duty," one soldier said to another as they climbed into the empty plane.

The other soldier shrugged, walking up to an eight-foot teddy bear with limbs taller than the soldier. "Hey, at least we get to chill at the party afterward. Calvin is one tough motherfucker, and the least we can do is make the party a good one for him."

The two soldiers grabbed the bear under the arms and awkwardly wended their way down the steps and across the base. They struggled through doorways, grunting and tripping the entire way, to the common room. The thing was freaking huge, and they could barely keep it off the ground.

Timothy moved to the side as the guys squeezed it through the common room door. The whole place was decorated from top to bottom in beautiful shades of yellow and green. There were amazing artist creations of floral blooms, vines made out of papier-mâché, and candles flickering all over the room. The tables were the same, covered with soft linens and piled with specially-made food. Curled into rose shapes, a wall of streamers provided a focal point, celebrating the unknown sex of the baby.

Calvin patted him on the back. "Looks good, brother. Thank you for doing this."

Timothy took a small bow. "It, as always, was my pleasure. Can't let this girl have her baby shower in the slums, now, can we? Had I had more time, I would have turned the whole place into an enchanted forest, but I did what I could."

Calvin chuckled. "You did more than enough, so relax, have a drink or five, and enjoy the party. Everyone is here. Even Tweedle Dee and Tweedle Dum over there."

Timothy glanced at Eddie and Turner, who were playing with tiny plastic babies in one of the bins brought in for the festivities. He looked back at Calvin. "Right, the riff-raff. Sean isn't here. Not sure if he is coming."

Calvin could tell it bothered Timothy. "He'll come around. He's being really hard on himself."

Timothy snapped out of it. "You know what I'll never get over?"

Calvin raised an eyebrow. "Tweed going out of fashion? The misuse of alligator hide for ugly boots?"

Timothy smacked his lips. "Oooh, boy, don't get me started on those ugly-ass cowboy accessories. Damn shutting down the world, killing all the animals so we can feel fancy before we die off. But no, that is not what I was talking about. I was not, and still have not, been told whether this is a puppy dog tail or something sweet in that belly. I could have played up the sex of the baby *big* time in these decorations. Personally, I think your wife is a sadist, finding pleasure in torturing me."

Pandora walked across the room, grabbing a Danish from the table and breaking off a piece. She walked up to Sofia, who was sitting quietly near a wall, looking out happily at the decor. "So, you gonna tell me that name yet?"

Sofia smiled, her eyes shifting to Pandora. "You have asked me a million times, and just like all the other times, I will have to decline. It is a complete and total secret."

Pandora sneered. "I *hate* secrets. But worry not, I have faith in my abilities. I will get the truth out of you one way or another."

Across the room, Juntto and Angie stood talking and looking around at all the decorations. Juntto shook his finger. "Humans are strange in the ways they celebrate. In my dimension, when a female started having the child, we would hold a moonlight ceremony where we would slaughter a *sheeba*, a cow-like creature, collect the blood, and all watch as the child was born. Then the doctor would dip the baby in the blood and show it to the moon. It was a ritual."

Angie wrinkled her nose. "Oh, God. That's terrifying. What if the baby wasn't born at night?"

Juntto shook his head, reaching over and tugging the bear's ear. "The women held the babies in until the moon rose. It was customary."

Angie shook her head. "Sometimes I think about taking back the whole 'coming to your dimension in the future' thing."

Juntto laughed at the bear next to him and snapped his fingers. Angie stood back and crossed her arms as he morphed into a giant blue version of the bear, the only difference being, his body didn't sprout hair. Timothy stopped next to Angie and glanced at Juntto, jumping. "Good Mary, Joseph, and baby Jesus, what in the Holy God is that thing? Is that Juntto? He looks like a huge version of Sheev Palpatine without the black robe. It's absolutely terrifying."

Stephanie stepped up to the front of the room and clapped her hands. "All right, everyone. Thanks for coming to celebrate the new arrival. We are going to get started on our first game! On the table, you will find decorated eggs and wooden spoons. Go ahead and collect yours and line up. Your goal is to get down the line and back again as fast as you can without dropping the baby!"

Eddie and Turner were all about it, putting down their glasses and grabbing their eggs. Turner reached into his pocket, snickering, pulled out a doll's army jacket, and put it on his egg. Eddie pulled out a small piece of fabric and tied it around his egg like Rambo.

The guys got really into the subsequent game, drinking far too much alcohol, and rooting for the frozen plastic babies in their cups, wanting to be the first to scream, "My water broke!"

Their competitiveness was amusing to everyone, but Calvin didn't want the shower to turn into a rager. He walked over to the guys and peeked into Eddie's cup. Eddie pointed at the frozen baby ice cube in his glass. "She's coming, man. The foot is out. The foot is *out*."

Calvin patted him on the shoulder and moved between the two guys. He reached up and firmly grasped the backs of their necks. "All right, Ricky Bobby and Cal Naughton, I need you two to quiet it down over here."

Turner chuckled, nodding at the ice cube baby. "Sweet baby Jesus."

Calvin shook his head. "Chill out before I put *you* on ice."

Pandora strolled through the party, winking at a couple of the soldiers. She walked up to Sofia and smiled at her belly. "Look at you."

Sofia puffed air out of her cheeks. "I know. I'm *huge*."

Pandora ran her hand over the belly. "Your belly is a little high. I think that means conception occurred during doggie-style."

Stephanie's eyes widened. "Pandora!"

Pandora shrugged, keeping an innocent look on her face. "What? It's logical. Right, Calvin?"

He walked back over after taming the terrible twins and just shook his head. "I don't even know what you asked, and because of that, I decline to respond."

Pandora waved her hands at Calvin. "Calvin's such a prude. Sofia? Back me up?"

Sofia pursed her lips and did her best to look innocent. Suddenly Eddie yelled, putting his hand up with a small plastic baby in his palm. "*My water broke*! I'm so proud. Just so proud."

Sofia giggled and Calvin groaned as Eddie held the small plastic baby in the air like Mufasa holding Simba. He began turning in a circle as Turner sang *The Circle of Life*.

Once they had calmed down, Sofia called for everyone's attention. "If I could just have you for one minute. I want to make an announcement."

Pandora walked over to Katie excitedly. "The name! It's going to be the name."

Katie slowly turned her head toward Pandora. "I really don't know why you're so excited. Do you think she'll name the baby after you? 'Pan' if it's a boy, 'Dora' if it's a girl?"

Pandora kept a smile on her face, her lip flickering slightly. "You're making fun of me, but you suck at it."

Sofia put her hands together. "I know all of you really want to know if we are having a boy or a girl."

Everyone cheered. Sofia patted her palms downward to quiet them. "But I will not be revealing the gender or the name of the baby until it's born. So you can stop hounding me."

Pandora sneered. "Killjoy."

5

Stephanie stared down at the paper in front of her, reading through the most recent intel on the Leviathans and demonic issues cited by the World Council. She had been reading them three times a week, yet she still found more intel in Timothy's work than she got from the big guys. It was more proof that they had been on the right track the whole time—maintaining friendly relations with the governments of the world but not putting their faith in them fully.

She took her glasses off and leaned back, rubbing the bridge of her nose. A knock sounded on the door, and Angie stuck her head around the corner. "Knock, knock. I come bearing coffee."

Angie held up the cups and Stephanie let out a deep breath, waving her in. "You are the real angel here, lady. The real one. You even heard my prayers."

Angie handed her a mug and sat down in the chair on the other side of her desk. "Got a lot going on?"

Stephanie shrugged. "No, not this second. I was just reading the World Council's briefing, and it says pretty much nothing, as usual. I read them anyway, just in case. How about you? You glad to be here?"

Angie laughed. "I am always happy to be part of the family and get to see everyone. It's nice that we can be here and not have to fight off demons, knock on wood."

They simultaneously tapped on the desk three times, then Stephanie leaned back, holding her mug in both hands. "Yeah, I do too. I miss Korbin like crazy, but I have to say, I really do love running the base. I think most of that is because we have such good people. Plus, I'm not fighting someone every day."

Angie nodded. "I hear you. I love this position, or lifestyle as I consider it, but I also enjoy learning about myself. I've got my Twitch channel for video games, and that really fulfills that lingering feeling that I am not doing enough constructive stuff to feel good about myself."

Stephanie swallowed a sip, shaking her head. "Yes, girl. I think the one thing about this and every other business I've owned is being a cattle herder. Wrangling people when something needs to get done. I'm sure you know how that is. I mean, you are the official herder of the group with Katie."

Angie snorted. "Except now I feel like she is a piece of cake. Try wrangling the big blue frost giant for a couple of days, and you will feel a lot better about the rest of it."

Stephanie rolled her eyes. "No, thank you. Mine are a bunch of grown people who often decide to retreat into their inner babies. That's always fun, especially when you need those babies to get their shit together and get on the ball."

Angie sighed, looking up at the picture of Stephanie and Korbin on the wall. "The things we do for the people we love."

Stephanie put her coffee down and scooted forward. "Amen to that. I'll just add, the things we do for all of humanity."

The stack of papers on Stephanie's desk was ever-growing, but luckily she was able to find her list three pages down. "So, it was good timing that you came, since we need some of the larger-type shipments."

Angie reached out and took the paper from her. "Yeah, and Katie, of course, said to just get whatever you need. We know you aren't frivolous."

Stephanie smirked. "Sometimes I wish I was, but I can't let myself do that."

Angie chuckled. "I think you live wild enough to just pass that one by. As far as what you need, I can order all of it for you. I think I still have the ordering information you gave me a year or so ago, but if it's changed, just let me know."

Stephanie pursed her lips, thinking about it. "I am pretty sure that for the stuff we need on here, none of the companies has changed. If there is something on a list that we haven't ordered, I wrote in the distributor information."

Angie skimmed down the page. "Excellent. You *are* on top of it."

Stephanie laughed. "We need these things to keep going, so I have to be on top of it. For example, we need additional materials to make more of the special metal, plus all normal stuff that we need to run the base. Right now, with how we have been rolling, these will possibly become a regular order—something I call you and you check off an order sheet for."

"Hopefully, eventually you can just make whatever calls you need yourself, so you don't have to go through me. I don't mind since it gives me something to do, but it's kind of an unneeded step. I don't think Katie has taken the time to think that through," Angie replied.

Stephanie shrugged. "Whatever is best. I don't really put much thought into it these days, with so much going on. But yeah, I made a list, then pared it down to the most important things."

Angie glanced at the list again, stopping about five lines down. She glanced up at Stephanie. "Kimchi?"

Stephanie giggled. "Yeah. Sean has been cooking, and now half the base wants Korean twice a week."

Angie smirked. "Sounds like he has a job in his future. Okay, okay. It all sounds good. The only thing I was specifically told I could not get was a sex swing for Pandora."

The room was silent for a moment, then Stephanie laughed. "That girl is hopeless. If she really wants one, there is no doubt in my mind that she will rig one. We'll be walking down the hall hearing the drill going, and there will be chains and straps and all kinds of shit all over her room."

Angie put the list in her book, still shaking with laughter, then they each took a deep breath and settled into their chairs. Angie tapped her pen on her notebook for a moment. "So, there is still the matter of the security breach."

Stephanie pressed her lips together, hating to even think about it. She felt bad for Sean from the bottom of her heart, but it was what it was. "We've got a division of duty there. Calvin's taken over the defense of the base. I think he is talking to Katie about that right now. He has my proxy."

Katie and Pandora walked into the dining hall, finding Calvin sitting at the big table with a box of donuts and coffee. Pandora stretched her arms wide and yawned. "Lookie here! My lover from another life has set me up with a box of donuts." She turned directly to Calvin, speaking loudly. "No, Calvin, you cannot bribe my vag with a box of donuts."

Calvin shook his head and looked up at Katie. "Hey, there."

Katie laughed. "Hey. So, we're here to get to the nitty-gritty and talk about Sean's breach of security."

Calvin clasped his hands, trying to ignore Pandora shoving an entire donut in her mouth. "Yep. It's a tricky situation. Obviously, none of us truly believe he helped her steal those documents and software. He would have been arrested by now if that were the case. At the same time, he *did* fuck up. It's been hard on all of us. He is part of Brock's team, and they all highly respect him. He is a true warrior, and has proven himself time and again by putting his life on the line."

Katie glanced down at her hands and coughed, finding the story all too normal. "But he put his trust in the wrong person and let them take valuable information. And regardless if he knew it or not, he was still responsible for it. Any word on Carmen?"

Calvin took a deep breath through his nose and shook his head. "No. She's still missing, and Timothy hasn't been able to find anything about the robbery on the dark web, so we are assuming that whoever her contact or buyer was, they did everything through face-to-face contact. That's rare, but if it is deep, then we know they know what they're doing. There isn't a system to detect someone having a conversation without completely taking away all human rights and listening to *every* conversation, which is impossible at this point anyway."

Katie shook her hand. "That's not the only choice, though. We can figure out things much more complicated. To be honest, there is a good chance she is either Damned or dead by now. Anyone who would be looking for the information Timothy had would have to be in a pretty high position, either legally or illegally. That is just semantics. The point is, they were strong enough to burrow into our base and collect secret information that only a handful of people had the ability to find. But there she was, taking it right in front of Sean without him knowing, and on the first try."

Pandora swallowed her donut and wiped her lips. "Honestly, I think we could discuss this until the cows come home, but we need to get to the source. We need to bring Sean in here and use our powers on him to find out what the hell happened."

Katie tapped her fingers on the desk. "You're right. Let's bring him in."

Calvin pulled his cell out and called down to the administrative offices. "Yeah, can you send Sean up to the main dining hall? Thanks."

Calvin changed chairs, coming over and sitting next to Katie. Pandora cracked her neck and her knuckles, taking the conversation very seriously. She liked interrogating; it let her be a bitch without having to apologize, at least most of the time. Sean wheeled into the room, pausing briefly as his eyes fell on Katie and Pandora.

Katie smiled sweetly and Pandora leaned back, resting her ass on the edge of the table with her arms crossed. Katie stood up and walked over, shaking his hand. "Hey, good to see you."

Sean nodded. "You too. I heard you guys were here."

Katie put out her arm. "Why don't you come to the table? Then we can talk."

Sean wheeled over, glancing uncomfortably at Pandora, who was glaring at him. Katie followed, beginning to pace next to him. She kept her voice calm and kind, not only to play the good cop but because she genuinely cared about him. "I've read the report on what happened. I just want to go through some things, maybe jog your memory. So, you and Carmen were friends?"

"Yeah," Sean replied. "We hadn't been friends that long, though. She had just gotten here. She seemed funny, sweet, and kind. I didn't give it two thoughts."

Pandora narrowed her eyes. "But she was grounds, and you were tech. How did you cross paths enough to actually become friends?"

Sean opened his mouth and then shut it, not having really thought about that. "I guess I met her at something with a bunch of people. But now that I think about it, she did seem overly interested in getting to know me. I just assumed she had a crush."

Pandora shook her head, turning into the bad cop. "Really? After all of the training that you've had, you didn't get an instant red flag? Look, here's the deal. We don't have the rest of eternity to sit here and talk to you about it." She slammed her hand on the desk, making him jump. "Tell us everything, or we'll start pulling fingernails! And trust me, I have some experience with that."

Katie shook her head, putting her hand up. She sat back down across from him. "This is going to go nowhere if we start yelling at each other. Sean, we have known each other for a long time now. We have fought beside each other and done all kinds of things. We *want* to trust you. If we didn't, you wouldn't be sitting here in front of us."

Pandora shifted, stepping into Katie's body. *Just want to verify this. Are you sure we can actually trust Sean? We've seen some good players in this game before.*

Katie had thought she was sure until Pandora questioned her. *I think so.*

Pandora clicked her tongue. *I'm going to come out of you full angel. We have some unique abilities that I think will help us here. I want you to follow along with me.*

You got it. Just don't physically hurt him.

Pandora jumped back out of Katie, and they both immediately spread their angelic wings.

Calvin shifted in his chair, feeling his demon Nate Dogg shift inside him. The demon freaked. *What the holy hell? I knew I would be getting into some shit with this, but you never mentioned I might be facing two angels. Calvin, this is not cool, man. Not fucking cool.*

Ever since Calvin had caught and thoroughly chewed Nate out for messing with his emotions and reaction times back when Sofia's house was attacked and afterward at the base, the demon had been quiet. Now, though, he was too scared to be careful about how he was affecting Calvin.

Calvin's heart started racing, and he stood up from his chair. "I'm just going to step outside. If you guys need anything, let me know."

Katie and Pandora continued to question Sean. One of the most important aspects of their angel abilities was that they could detect how other people felt. They focused on his responses, finally seeing, thanks to Pandora's hard-on for crime shows, that there had been no ill will or deceit in Sean's actions.

Katie folded her wings back up and walked over, hugging him tightly. "I'm sorry you had to go through this. I can tell you have no malice in your heart, and I forgive you for what happened."

Powell hopped out of the limo and brushed the crumbs from dinner out of the folds of his suit. This time he was entering the complex looking like he normally did: dressed to a tee, calm, and slightly intimidating. He entered through the same door and walked back past the sea of cadaverous ruins—once-great machines now reduced to rubble.

Ahead, standing under the light was Xian, but he was no longer bald. He was wearing a wig. Powell pressed his lips together, trying not to laugh. He actually looked pretty good in it, and had Powell not known Xian, he would have assumed that was his real hair.

Xian waved at Powell without looking up. Powell meandered over and stood next to Xian. He took a deep breath, pushing the giggles down. "Is there something different about you? I feel like there is."

Xian shook his head. "Nope. Just been working through this stuff."

Powell persisted. "You sure?"

He continued to shift the conversation away from the tuft of hair on the top of his head. "The technicians are out on break, but they are all chomping at the bit, and to be frank, I am too. We found something new."

Powell dropped his act and walked over to look at the screen Xian had pulled up. "You found one?"

Xian pointed to the screen. "I think so. It has the same signature as all the other Leviathans, only this one we found in Iraq. There is something common between the Leviathans that is not seen in humans— various uncommon traits."

Powell looked at him with a furrowed brow. "Yeah, that was way too complicated."

Xian didn't repeat himself, running his hands gently over his wig and stepping back. "So, what is next? What do we do from here?"

Powell composed himself, knowing he was now in charge of the decision. "We have to decide if this warrants pulling the trigger."

Xian shifted his gaze down to a file. He picked it up and read through it. "So, we have a team that is awaiting orders."

Powell nodded. "Yeah, a platoon led by a Damned lieutenant who is extremely capable. He is the only other person who knows we are looking for this thing. They are pretty much floating until we make the call."

Xian stood still for a moment and then jumped, punching Powell's shoulder lightly in excitement. "We found a fucking Leviathan. Even the guy who created this shit couldn't find any more."

Powell rubbed his hands together excitedly, a smile moving over his lips. He was a strange guy, and got even stranger when excitement ran through him. He reached up and started pinching his nipples through his button-down shirt. "So, we kill it?"

Xian bit his bottom lip and slapped his hands together. "Yes. We can't let another Kabbus free. We are going to be hailed as heroes here."

Powell's eyes went big. "If it's another Juntto, the World Council could use big guns in the demon fight. You would be able to see it from space."

Xian's mouth formed an o. "And if it's something like Kabbus, we could be unleashing a new hell on Earth. That would be the opposite of good."

Powell squeezed his nipples hard and shook his head. "It's a risk either way, but even more so if we wait for this motherfucker to wake up on his own. That is when we would have to try to be on top of it. That's a problem, though. It's always been the problem. If we can destroy these sonsofbitches before they even open a crusty monster eye, then we wouldn't have to watch all these people die. No, that's not going to happen. Let's kill it. Call the number in the file."

Powell walked closer to the screen, really pinching down hard on his nipples. "Send a team in."

6

It was night, and the hills and valleys south of Al Fatsi, Iraq were barely lit, besides the random farmhouse with lanterns in the yard. The sound of the helicopters overhead was barely audible as they swiftly moved into place, dropping closer to the ground and allowing the trained team of twelve to rappel out. As soon as the soldiers hit the ground, they scattered, staying low and aiming their weapons around them. They had done jobs like that a million times, but their target was a bit different on this go-around.

The last to rappel down was their commander, Lieutenant Vinders. When he hit the ground, he took a knee, opening his map and positioning his mic in front of his lips. The helicopters took off, leaving nothing but a small breeze in their wake.

The Lieutenant spoke in a quiet whisper into the comm, directing his soldiers where they needed to go. The team worked together seamlessly, moving straight into their positions. The area wasn't unnecessarily dangerous for them, but Americans in Iraq always created some sort of stir. They weren't there for political or idealistic reasons, though; they were there to find a Leviathan, the one thing that threatened everyone in the world despite their religious preference or political ideas.

As the lieutenant turned, bringing up the rear, his eyes glowed red. He was Damned and had been for a long time, finding solace in the system and an ability to excel when it came to rank and missions. The team walked carefully through the hills using night vision goggles, keeping watch for anyone who might open fire out of fear of their presence in the open hills of Al Fatsi.

It didn't take them long to arrive at the destination, a tomb with a boulder in front of it. One of the soldiers joked over the comm, "Is this when we find out that Jesus wasn't a god, but actually an alien sent here to pit us against each other? I mean, I'm cool with that, but I need some time to prepare my mother."

The lieutenant called for the explosives. "Don't worry, Jones, I'll let your mother know when I see her later tonight."

The whole team chuckled but kept their focus. They attached the explosives and fell back, taking cover wherever they could, then blew the boulder, crushing most of it into dust. Half the team moved fast, rushing into the cave-like tomb. As they entered, they shined their flashlights around, finding carvings on the wall and a stone altar.

Jones pulled off his night vision goggles and shone his light on the altar. "What the ever-loving fuck is that?"

Another guy got closer. "Uh, looks like some sort of mummy. A short one."

Jones nodded uneasily and clicked his comm. "LT, it's a mummy. Over."

Vinders shifted his eyes to the side and cleared his throat. "Uh, come again? Over."

Jones pursed his lips and blinked. "Mummy. M-U-M-M-Y. Not shitting you; this isn't a joke. Shriveled little guy. Do we light it up?"

Vinders was confused, but he wasn't taking any chances. "Affirmative."

Jones pointed at the mummy, and everyone gathered around, arms ready. "On my mark…"

Suddenly, a small pebble dropped from the edge of the pedestal and Jones stepped closer, looking up at the ceiling. When he looked back down, the mummy snapped into a sitting position, and everybody freaked out.

Vinders looked down at his watch, trying to get the other half of the team on comm. He didn't hear any gunfire, and he had given the order. "Jones. Jones, come in, please. Over."

Nothing.

He bit on the inside of his cheek as his team stayed steady, ready for anything to attack from any direction. They scanned the area behind them as a line of team members pointed their weapons toward the opening of the tomb. One of the guys, Tracker, looked up at the lieutenant. "So, should we go in there after them?"

The guy next to him, Alvarez, shook his head. "No fucking way. You heard what he said; there was a mummy in there. So, if the thing didn't spring back to life and feast on their bones, then all of them will be cursed for eternity. I know my mummies."

Tracker raised an eyebrow and looked at the lieutenant. "Are they shitting me? A *mummy?*"

Vinders shrugged. "Apparently. He knows he can't fuck with me like that on a mission."

Tracker laughed. "No shit. Like in the movies?"

Vinders gave him a deadpan look. "No, *not* like the movies. There is very little reality in movies, especially ones like that. And Brendan Fraser is not going to be running from the tomb."

Tracker glanced at the face of the tomb, gritting his teeth. He looked back at Vinders. "But it's supernatural shit? You know, beings as it's the spot where the Leviathan is, and all."

Another guy scratched his head. "Huh. Well, fuck. Yeah, I guess it *is* supernatural."

Tracker nodded dramatically, putting his hand out to the guy and looking at the lieutenant. "See? It *is* like the movies."

Vinders sighed and shook his head. "This is why I don't take you guys anywhere. You are all conspiracy theorists. Who knows, they might have gotten the thing wrong. It might have moved. This could be some archaeological site we just happened upon."

Tracker grinned. "It's a supernatural Leviathan mummy, and it's going to go all kickass on us any second now."

Vinders ignored him, starting to get worried about the guys inside. He clicked his mic on again. "Strike team, I want you to bring whatever you have out here. We're just going to burn the damn thing."

Vinders gazed at Tracker and Alvarez, the rest of the team listening. "Seems legit, right? Whatever it is, fire will probably kill it. Fire kills everything."

Tracker chuckled. "If you can't shoot it, burn it. The motto of the military. The *real* military, that is."

The lieutenant shook his head, trying to convince himself that he was making the right choice. The only problem was, the rest of the team wasn't answering. He couldn't take them down, too. He clicked his mic again and spoke into it. "Come back, Strike Team. Strike Team, do you copy?"

He waited a bit longer, checking his comm to make sure it was functional. "Tracker, call the strike team, just in case my comm is fucked up."

Tracker pressed his button. "Strike Team, do you copy? Over."

They waited a few moments before the lieutenant pulled his pack off his back and his gun around in front of him. Tracker and Alvarez watched him for a moment. "What you doing, LT? Should we be preparing?"

Vinders shrugged. "Why the hell not? Fuck it. Let's go inside and figure out what is going on. That's our job."

The guys had started to stand when they heard a low rumble from inside the tomb. They all froze, including Vinders, who was getting his gun up and aimed. "Everyone hold. Let's see who's coming out of there. Might be the team."

Tracker sulked, bringing his gun to the ready. "Or, what is that? This shit is getting really creepy, LT. Really creepy, really fast."

They all squinted at the opening to the tomb as the sound grew closer, and suddenly a leg emerged. The strike team was coming out, but there was definitely something wrong with them. Not only were they stumbling forward with little or no rhythm or understanding of where they were, but they were not carrying their packs or guns. It was an incredibly confusing development.

The lieutenant called to the main guy. "Hopper, report. What happened in there? We've been calling you on the comm."

Hopper didn't even flinch. He just kept stumbling forward. As the rest of the team emerged, Vinders' team backed away from the entry with their guns at the ready. They couldn't see themselves killing their teammates, but were they really in there anymore, or had something taken them over?

The group was mumbling low and slow, and the team outside listened hard. The team that had gone in was chanting, almost. "We. Are. Legion."

Tracker stood up and shook his head. "Their eyes—they're purple. And they are like the living fucking dead, with less rotting skin."

Vinders was Damned, which made him the strongest member of the group. He'd known almost immediately that something wasn't right, even before the guys went into the cave, which wasn't well hidden. He raised his gun again, hollering out orders. "Strike team, cease and desist.

Again, Strike Team, stop where you are, and we will get you medical attention. You have been exposed to some sort of chemical agent, and we need you to stand still."

None of them paid a bit of attention to him, continuing to zombie forward without any awareness of the world around them. Vinders growled, lowering his gun and then raising it again. "Strike Team, stop! I *will* engage!"

The lieutenant looked for Tracker, but he was no longer sitting next to him on the ground. He found him with the rest of the team, their weapons on the ground and their feet shuffling like the inside team's. After a few more moments, all of the troops stopped. Those walking toward the tomb turned, showing their glowing purple eyes.

Vinders backed up, tripping over a stone and hitting the ground. His finger pressed the trigger of the gun, spraying special metal bullets all over. The group began to advance, their eyes fixated on the lieutenant, looking for revenge of some sort, or maybe just to bring him into the fold. Luckily his demon had been strong enough up to that point to keep whatever was happening at bay.

Suddenly there was a hand on his arm, and he saw Tracker beside him, gripping his arm tightly as his eyes burned a deep purple. On the other side, Alvarez walked up, followed by the rest of the team, grabbing him. Vinders screamed as the team pinned him to the ground, his legs spread and his arms stretched out.

"Oh, God," he begged. 'Let me go!'

But it was too late; the mummy had already come through the door to the tomb and was shuffling toward him, tilting his head. He climbed over the soldiers holding down Vinders' feet and looked down into the leader's eyes. The lieutenant went quiet when he saw the swirling wildness in the mummy's eyes. They looked like a Caribbean sea, crystal-clear but hiding secrets beneath. Just looking at him made the lieutenant want to give in to the deep power they held. He could feel it and was fighting it with everything he had.

The mummy leaned farther forward and gripped the lieutenant's collar. Without moving a muscle, mostly because it no longer had a true form, it whispered close to his cheek, "We are Legion."

Vinders sneered but dropped the expression. His eyes went wide for just a moment before he began to shake from head to toe. His eyes burned bright red, but the glow began to flicker. Like water running down glass, a purple haze shifted in his pupils until his eyes glowed like the mummy's. Slowly the mummy let him go, and he sat up, staring at the others. He put his hands on the ground and got to his feet, not concerned with his weapon or his things. The troops began to move out, following the mummy. Vinders, his shoulders slumped, arms crossed, and head tilted to the side, turned around and stared at the people walking past him.

He coughed, then began to whisper with the others, "We are Legion."

Powell banged the phone down on the table and then put it back to his ear. "Hello? Vinders? I thought we had a deal. You need to answer."

Xian worked tirelessly trying to use the satellite phone to reach Vinders' personal cell and then those of his troops. They rang and rang, but no one answered. Powell finally put the receiver down and set his hands on his hips. "What the fuck could they be doing that they can't talk while they walk?"

Xian groaned, sweating so badly that his hairpiece had tilted to one side and become matted. He looked up at Powell and shook his head. "I don't know what else to do. None of the team is answering the comm or the phones. I'm not even getting their signal on satellite. It's like they fucking disappeared into nowhere."

Powell growled, clenching his hands and pacing in the small space among the ruins of technology. "What *can* we do? We can't go there, and no other team has been briefed on this situation."

Xian grabbed the folder. "Not specifically, but there is a backup group. They understand it's a top secret/need to know kind of thing, so technically, you could deploy them."

Powell shook his head, putting out his hand. "Not yet. There has to be something more to this. Do I just leave them, cut ties, and act like none of this ever happened? Do I send in the other team and risk losing them as well? What the ever-loving fuck happened out there?"

Xian stood and then plopped down in the chair again, clasping his fists together out in front of him. "I don't know what happened. There is no reading on it, and the last thing we heard was them talking to each other, then a couple of seconds later, there was radio silence. There was no warning, and we have an explanation for it. We have to assume that *something* is out there, quite possibly the Leviathan, and they are either unconscious or dead."

Powell was getting more anxious as the moments passed. He couldn't help but feel it all the way up his chest. He gripped his nipples, tweaking them hard. Xian sneered, smacking at Powell's hands. "Stop that!"

Powell rolled his nipple in his fingers. "I can't help it, it's a weird nervous tick."

Letting out a deep breath, he pulled his hands away and turned toward the monitors. "I am the one who opened this can of worms. I sent them in, so I am going to have to deal with it."

The chopper started, roaring up to speed. A team of six tough military boys walked out of the hangar toward it carrying guns, ammo, and supplies. It was Strike Force Gamma, the backup team for the Leviathan. Although they had been on call for an important mission, they had only just been briefed on all of its details.

Lieutenant Croner was leading the team and had directed his troops to take everything they could fit into the chopper. They handed the gear down the line, throwing it inside. The lieutenant handed the first soldier, Lennon, a bag, and Lennon shook his head. "A Leviathan! Man, this is fucking amazing."

"Damn right it is, boy," the lieutenant barked in his deep, commanding voice. "We're gonna go out there and save the fucking world from some dipshit alien monster."

The guys all cheered. Lennon passed that bag and

turned back for the next, excitement gleaming in his eyes. "My little boy, when he is born—he's gonna have a hero as his daddy."

The lieutenant spat to the side, a string of tobacco-infused drool hanging from his lip. He wiped it off with his shoulder and nodded. "Yes, he is. When is the baby due?"

Lennon grinned. "Just two months, LT. Just two months."

Lennon passed a box of ammo to his teammate, Crowley. Crowley took it and turned back to Mishler. "That's right, I bought the ring. All I got to do now is, when we get back, get down on one knee and ask her to marry me. I swear she is the most beautiful woman I have ever met. Just the sweetest little thing."

Mishler grinned. "I know exactly how you feel, although I'm not buying a ring just yet. It's only been four months, but I knew when I saw Amy that she was the girl for me. Hell, she looks more like an angel than any of the ones on Earth right now. Just can't believe my luck. Don't want to jinx it, not for anything."

Mishler turned and handed the ammo box to Geiger, who nodded and handed it to Phillips. Geiger took a deep breath and shook his head. "So that's when I did it. I just signed the papers, and I have my own house. Me. The kid that grew up in the slums, his family barely having enough food to eat, owning a house that was just passed down from generation to generation. I can feel it, I am breaking that cycle, man. I am finally breaking that cycle."

Phillips tossed the box into the helicopter and wiped the back of his head. "Man, that's some sweet shit. I am not anywhere near house-buying, but life has been sweet.

Stationed out here, easy most days, out having a blast at night, doing what I please. After my marriage ended, I thought I was done for, but life really came back to me, you know?"

The guys talked and laughed, getting ready to load in. They were pumped and didn't have a care in the world.

7

Pandora wrapped her arms around Sofia and hugged her tightly. She lingered for a moment, whispering in her ear, "I might not have kids, but you stick around for centuries, and you learn quite a bit. As soon as you are one minute overdue, you just jump right on that man and ride him home. That labor will roll right up on you. The elixir of life, bringing life, and bringing the pain."

Sofia giggled. "Thanks, I'll remember that."

Katie walked up. "You'll remember what?" She looked at Pandora and then at Sofia, rolling her eyes. "Are you giving out advice again? Seriously, leave this woman alone. She does not need to know how to deliver her baby in a sixteenth-century carriage."

Pandora blinked at Katie. "There you go again, trying to be funny, but it just plummets and explodes on itself."

Katie shoved Pandora out of the way. "Have a good and *restful* rest of your pregnancy, and let us know as soon as anything happens. You understand?"

Sofia nodded, kissing Katie on the cheek. "You guys are just headed back to New York, right?"

"Yeah, with Angie and Juntto," she replied. "Gotta get back. Working on an interesting case with the cops, and hopefully, we will crack it soon."

Sofia chuckled. "If it's like anything else you guys do, you'll have it figured out by the time you get back to New York."

Pandora came up next to Katie, and they gave each other a side glance before staring inquiringly at Sofia. She ran her hand over her belly and shifted her eyes up, feeling their stare. They gave her matching toothy grins. Sofia sighed and shook her head. "Get out of here. I am *not* telling you the baby name. You have to wait like everyone else."

Pandora's bottom lip came out, and Katie snapped her fingers. "Dammit. We were *so* close."

Angie walked up and looked at them all for a second before letting out a small grunt. "They're trying to get you to tell them the name by being fucking weird, aren't they?"

Sofia scrunched her nose and held two fingers up a fraction of an inch apart.

Angie shook her head and turned Sofia toward her. "Don't do too much. Let Calvin wait on you hand and foot. It's the least he can do when you are going to be pushing his spawn from your lady bits. And I added some extra things to the supply list just for you and the baby."

Sofia smiled excitedly. "Aw, thank you! And thank *you*, Katie."

"Of course," Angie replied, pulling a piece of paper out. "I would let it be a surprise, but I don't want you to buy the stuff and have two. So, we got you diapers, duh. And I mean like a pallet of damn diapers. The kid can poop his or her heart out. We also got you a crib for the base, some décor for the room, and a really techie baby monitor. Oh, and some Daddy books for Calvin so he can make himself useful."

Just then Katie's phone rang, and she stepped away from the girls to take it. Accepting the call, she put it to her ear. "This is Katie."

"Katie, it's Detective Schultz," he replied. "Sorry if I caught you at a bad time."

Katie squinted into the sun. "No, not at all. What's going on? Has there been a break in the case?"

The detective groaned. "Kind of, but not really. I tell you what, something really strange is going on around here. Shit, there is something strange going on all over New York right now. We sure could use your help. I waited as long as I could to call you. There has never been anything like this before."

Katie glanced back at Pandora. "Are we talking like *Ghostbusters*, StayPuft Vigo kind of strange, or are we talking regular demons kind of strange?"

Schultz coughed loudly, letting Katie know he was out smoking. "It's a little bit of both. No slime buildings just yet, but I am not ruling anything out anymore."

Katie picked up her bag and flung it over her shoulder. "I was actually just about to get on the plane back to New York City. Like, it is literally in front of me right now, and Pandora, Angie, Juntto, and I were headed back as fast as we could get there. Of course, saying our goodbyes always takes three times as long than we think. In any case, we are packed up and ready to come home. I will call you when I get there.'

Detective Schultz was silent for a minute. "I need you to come as quick as you possibly can. This stuff isn't *going* to happen, it is happening as we speak and I really need some help from you and Pandora to know what the fuck is up. I've been here for three days straight."

Katie shook her head. "All right, so tell me what kind of hell this is. Sleet and lightning?"

"No. Actually, there is another mass hallucination, and this time, it is at your apartment complex."

Katie stopped in her tracks, glancing at Pandora to let her know this was not just a routine call from their friendly detective. Pandora came over, looking concerned. Katie repeated what Schultz had said so Pandora could hear. "So, there are a bunch of hallucinating people making their way to the condo. Got it."

Pandora immediately became pissed. "Oh, hell no. One of those bitches puts one grubby hallucinating finger on my stuff, and we are going to fight to the death."

Katie shook her head. "Schultz, we'll be there ASAP."

She pressed End and tossed her bag to Juntto. "You guys mind taking our luggage back? We are going to portal back because there is something pretty huge going on."

Juntto shook his head. "Nope, and if you need me just call."

Katie blew the rest of them a kiss and turned, opening up a portal.

The guys looked out the windows of the chopper as it sped along close to the ground, trying to find the other team. They were attempting to be discreet, but the Iraqi government had given them permission to be there, so they were only in minor danger as they soared up and over the hills that led to the tomb. There were storm clouds in the distance, and the mood had gone from playful and talkative to ominous very quickly.

The pilot of the craft came over their headphones. "We've got a big group of what looks like soldiers over to your right. They are in a gaggle, but I feel like there is something wrong with the situation. I'm going to circle around and see if we can't catch their comm. I'll go quiet until you are done, LT."

Everyone looked out their windows, staring at the group of soldiers below. They tried to signal, knowing how frustrating it was to be down in the pit with soldiers flying over safe and sound. Unfortunately, they couldn't get any of them to even look up at the passing chopper.

Geiger narrowed his eyes, peering at them more closely. "Where are their weapons and packs? They are just walking along with no gear like they don't even hear us."

The lieutenant shook his head, something in the pit of his stomach not feeling quite right. He looked out the front at the hill ahead. "Land over there. We'll take a closer look at what's going on."

"Roger that," the pilot said, whipping the chopper around and heading over to the spot.

As they landed, the lieutenant opened his door and looked out in the distance. He stepped out, pulling his binoculars from the belt around his waist. He looked through the lenses and jumped slightly, lifting his head up and lowering it again. Through the binoculars, he could see the lieutenant, as well as the rest of the guys. Their faces sagged, and their arms were lower on one side than the other. They dragged their feet, and their eyes were a sparkling wild purple in color.

He turned and hopped back in the chopper, grabbing his satellite phone. "Everyone sit still for a minute. I gotta call in for an order on this one. Those boys are not in their right mind. Something got to them bad."

He dialed Powell, who answered on the first ring. "LT, did you find them? Are you taking care of the Leviathan?"

The lieutenant looked out the window again at the affected men, who were getting closer. "We have a situation. We have found the team, but they seem to be possessed in some way. Bright purple eyes, and acting like motherfucking zombies. They don't have any weapons or packs, and we can't get their attention."

Powell let out a long, deep breath and stayed quiet for several seconds. "Dammit. I shouldn't have sent them in there like that. They were supposed to make it out. Look, we've got to clean house. We are dealing with a threat level that is off the charts here."

The lieutenant's mouth fell open. "Sir, are you suggesting—"

"Trust me, it pains me to say this, but you need to terminate them. Try to make it humane, but we can't take any chances. This war is brutal, LT, but I need to know I can count on you to execute orders from the heads of state," Powell said, standing and pacing in his office.

The lieutenant frowned and nodded. "Yes, you can trust

me. We've got this. I'll report back in thirty minutes with an update on the Leviathan."

They hung up and the lieutenant reached over, switching the blade toggle so the helicopter would turn off, then got out and called for his men. The other team was steadily approaching, so he needed to make them understand. "Listen, I have orders that I know are brutal. It's a very good way for us to judge how you handle the really serious shit. The team is gone. They are already gone, and they pose a significant threat to all of mankind, so...we are to take them down. If there is anyone who cannot perform this task, I understand, and you will not be penalized."

All of the guys looked at each other and took position with their guns. The lieutenant couldn't have been prouder of them than at that moment. He needed to be brave too, so he turned around and rolled his neck, staring at the lieutenant of the other team—someone he had played cards with six months or so before.

He pulled his gun around and up to his shoulder, sighted it, and cringed as the x moved over their faces. When everyone was ready, he cleared his throat. "Open fire!"

Not a single bullet was fired. Every single one of them sat there, their fingers on the triggers, but their minds unable to wrap around what was happening. The lieutenant looked up, realizing that the other team was coming toward them fast. "If you're going to do it, now is the time."

The troops looked at each other and put their guns down in unison. They stood and rolled up their sleeves, ready to take the men by force. They just couldn't kill their brothers. Unfortunately, the others didn't have that thought, or any thoughts at all. They had wasted so much time that the Legion was upon them. As they attempted to grab the soldiers, they looked into their sparkling eyes. They all slowed, and the first team began pulling the second to the ground and pinning them down.

The chopper pilot stared fearfully out the window, watching the entire team be taken down. Suddenly his eyes bulged, and he pushed the buttons and started the chopper again. The first team moved to the sides, parting as a purple mist flowed between them. Shuffling from the back was the mummy. He moved from soldier to soldier, whispering to each and watching as their bodies stopped struggling and their eyes shimmered to the new color. As they assimilated, they rose to their feet, the life force drained from their sparkling purple eyes.

The Legion had grown.

Katie and Pandora stepped through the portal, which closed quickly behind them. Of late, they had usually just walked straight through, not even noticing the different worlds, but on that one, there was no way they couldn't at least take a quick glance around. It was a peaceful world, quiet and beautiful. There were no huge cities jutting from the landscape or loud planes flying overhead. All around them, things shimmered and sparkled in their star's light.

There were diamond trees, crystal rivers, and flower buds that looked like they had been created from flawless rubies, emeralds, and sapphires.

"Wow," Katie whispered. "This is like a woman's dream

come true. One of those flowers would make you rich for life."

Pandora crossed her arms, pouting. Katie frowned. "What? Why are you upset?'

Pandora shrugged, twisting her top half around. "Because it makes me think about my favorite dimension. The city was perfect, the sky was perfect, there was no smog or trash, and everyone there was butt-ass naked and fine as hell."

Katie rolled her eyes. "Yeah, I remember. But why are you upset? I thought you could get there anytime you want."

Pandora sighed. "I can, but I'll never go back. I went there and met an amazing man. He wanted to take me home and pleasure me, and then it all went to hell. He said the most egregious thing I have ever heard."

Katie looked at her with concern. "What? Oh, my God. Did he say it to you?"

Pandora wiped a tear from her eye and leaned in to whisper, "He didn't know what a donut was."

Katie just blinked at Pandora as she threw her arm up to her forehead and cried. "I can't bear to ever go back there. It hurts too much. Just too much. But I figure maybe the old adage is true. If you love something, let it go."

Katie wanted to pick on her and tell her how dramatic she was being, but oddly, she actually looked terribly upset, so Katie decided to leave her alone. "You remember that dimension we went to that was like, just white? Everything was white, and there were no discernable shapes? That one was absolutely terrible. I don't ever want to go back there. But the one where everything was chocolate? That one was pretty sweet, pun totally intended."

Pandora put her arm down and sniffled. "I didn't like the white one either. That was fucking freaky. And the chocolate one *was* amazing. Personally, there was one that had, like, nothing but hot firefighters in it. That's the vacation I would like to take. Whoop, sexy men!"

Katie pointed at Pandora. "Oh, man. Remember when we walked into Juntto's dimension? All the massive frost giants. It was wild."

Pandora shivered. "I never want to go back to that one. We would get squashed or eaten in a heartbeat."

Katie wrinkled her nose. "Yeah, that wouldn't have turned out well. But there is a good side to it. We are learning how to choose which dimensions we travel to, at least when we concentrate and are on the same wavelength."

Pandora waved her hand, opening another portal. "Just don't think about the naked freaks."

They stepped through the second portal into New York. Pandora was still grumpy. They were about a block away from the condo building, so they picked the pace up to a jog. When they got there, Detective Schultz and Detective Travers were standing out front with lost looks on their faces.

Katie poked Schultz in the shoulder. "Uh, Earth to Schultz. You in there?"

He shook his head and looked at Katie, elbowing

Travers. "Sorry. We are here. We just got entranced by the scene out there. I don't know what to do."

Katie wasn't really sure what they were talking about. "What is it?"

Travers pointed behind her. Slowly she turned around to find a completely different scene than she was used to. There were no protestors present that day, but even odder, everyone was out in the streets. Not the normal New York City foot traffic, but they were out there, scared and wandering around. The cars were stopped, and everyone just kind of stayed there comforting each other. Some of them would periodically point up at the condos, but Katie looked up and didn't see a thing.

Katie turned right and left, looked up and down. "What are they looking at, and why are they wandering around in the street?"

Travers shrugged. "The only explanation I have is that the city has gone mad. Just absolutely insane."

Schultz nodded. "Yep. We are being controlled by witches or something."

Pandora rolled her eyes. "Come on, witches aren't real. Do you believe everything you see on television?"

Schultz and Travers looked at her. "You *do* realize that you are an angel or ex-demon or whatever, right?"

Pandora snickered. "Oh, yeah."

Katie put her hands on her hips. "The condo is under attack, but by what, I have no idea."

Pandora pointed as the last sliver of the sun dipped behind the buildings. "And there's no better time to figure that shit out than in the fucking dark."

8

Katie and Pandora both took deep breaths and reached up, clapping their hands. A flash of light blew down from the sky and outward, radiating through the streets. Their armor snapped into place, Pandora grunting, "I think I gained some weight."

Katie chuckled. "Come on, Porky Pig, let's take care of this and then run you with a donut dangling in front of your nose."

Pandora looked at her sword. "Now, *that* is a way to get a girl running, for sure."

Katie gripped her sword as she crept toward the door and opened it. She slid to the side, and Pandora went in first. She charged forward, her sword up, yelling her Pandora battle cry: "Sllllluuuut Girlll!"

When she got to the center of the lobby, she stopped, turning with her sword still raised. Katie lifted an eyebrow as she sauntered in behind her, glancing around in case Pandora missed anything in her hasty entrance. "That was anti-climactic."

Pandora looked over her shoulder. "I know, right? Sheesh, throw me a bone here, whatever you are causing this chaos."

She dropped her sword to her side and tilted her head straight back, staring at the giant chandelier. "Well, the lights are working."

Katie walked over to the elevator and pressed the button. It dinged, and doors slid open. "The elevators are working."

Pandora walked back over to the front desk and went behind it. "None of the security alarms are going off. What in almighty hell is going on here?"

Katie shrugged. "Maybe whatever it was ducked out."

Just then something rattled. Katie raised her sword and Pandora crouched, narrowing her eyes at the janitors' closet to Katie's right. There was more rattling. Pandora hurried over next to her, and they held their swords at eye level as Pandora slowly reached for the door handle. As the tips of her fingers touched the metal, the door flew open. Pandora screamed, raising her sword and jumping back. Katie screamed as well, raising her sword to the left over her shoulder. And the inhabitant of the closet screamed, holding a dustpan in front of his face and crouching.

"You sick sonofabitch, why are you doing this to our condo!" Pandora yelled, stepping forward to strike.

Katie lowered her sword and put her hand out. "Whoa, whoa, whoa, Zorro. Calm down. I don't think Harry the Bellhop is the reason we have some strange shit going on."

Pandora, breathing heavily, focused, pushing the dustpan to the side. Sure enough, it was Harry, his glasses halfway down his nose and fear on his face. Pandora let out a deep breath and sheathed her sword. She grabbed Harry by the back of the neck and pulled him toward the door. "Didn't you know that there is something going on in here? Wait the fuck outside."

She tossed him out and closed the door, locking it behind her. Katie stood there pressing her lips together, trying not to laugh. Pandora pointed behind her. "Did you see that? Harry almost got his ass angel-murdered."

Katie laughed, her eyes shifting to the glass behind Pandora. In the reflection, she could see a silvery object jerkily floating up. Pandora looked over her shoulder and narrowed her eyes. "Do you see that, or am I just on an adrenaline high right now?"

Katie shook her head and whirled around, seeing another rise up from the floor and gingerly make its way upward and through the floor. "What is that?"

Pandora's lip twitched, and she slapped her shield on her back. "That is a ghost."

Katie turned to her. "A ghost?"

Pandora sniffed and nodded as another floated up and disappeared into the ceiling. "Yeah. I wonder where they are going."

Katie and Pandora turned and pushed through into the emergency stairwell, making their way up one flight. When they exited onto the first floor, they stopped in their tracks. "Holy shit, that's a lot of dead souls."

Pandora was baffled by it. "That's really wild. They are, like, congregating, and then…"

Katie lifted her chin, looking up at the ceiling. "Continuing up, up, up. Man, I mean, I knew there were ghosts, I saw them with Damian forever ago during an exorcism, but this is wild. I've never seen so many in one place before."

Pandora jumped slightly as one floated past her before vanishing into the ceiling. Katie blinked at her and Pandora put her hands up, flat palms facing the ceiling. "What? Being the queen of the damned means I can't be freaked out by anything? They are tortured and sometimes very dangerous, and they usually look like they did when they died. So, girl who died in her sleep? Sad and pretty. Woman who is forty and died in a vicious car wreck is what nightmares are made of."

Katie puckered her lips, walking forward and then turning back around and putting her arms out. "I guess they really want to see the penthouse."

Pandora snorted. "Or your place."

They chuckled and then stopped, staring at each other in silence. Katie abruptly turned and took off for the elevator. "Oh, shit."

Sure enough, by the time they got to Katie's condo and went in, the place was full of ghosts. Katie and Pandora walked around with wide eyes, staring at all of them. There were leisurely ghosts hanging out in the kitchen, drinking ghost coffee and smoking ghost cigarettes. There were some lounging in the living room and pawing with their dead hands through Katie's books. And then the special one—the one sitting on the toilet with the door open, twiddling his thumbs and glancing around.

Katie winced and shut the bathroom door. Pandora looked around, nodding. "Okay. Okay, I see. So, I guess we're going to need a bigger place."

Soft whimpering caught Katie's attention, and she

walked back to her bedroom to find a sweet and beautiful blonde sitting on the edge of her bed, looking out the window. Every few moments she shed a tear, and then caught herself. Katie stood in front of her, watching.

The girl slowly looked up and floated back in fear. Katie shook her head. "No, no, please. I'm not going to hurt you."

The girl tilted her head and floated closer, gazing at her curiously. Katie smiled. "Why are you here?"

The ghost sniffled and floated over to the glass wall. "I was looking for a safe place. I tried to live in my old apartment downtown, but I just scared everyone. I didn't mean to. I am not trying to haunt people, I swear. But of course, since I scared them, they then scared me, and it was a vicious cycle. So I came here. We've all heard of the angels of Central Park."

Katie smirked, now knowing what the ghosts of the world referred to Katie and Pandora as. Another ghost floated in, wearing clothes that looked to be from the early 1800s. He grabbed his hat and lifted it, nodding to the girl ghost. She curtsied and looked at Katie. She glanced around and then made a quick bow. "How about you? Why are you here?"

The gentleman stopped, one hand in the pocket on his vest. "My home was knocked down, so I had to find a safe place to come. Preferably quiet and not too crazy, so of course I came to the angels of Central Park."

Katie nodded and walked into the living room. She looked to her right as she entered, finding the ghost of a woman holding a ghost baby. Katie knelt and gave her a kind smile. "And why are you here?"

As the woman looked down and back up, Katie noticed

the bloody scar across her ghost throat. She glanced down at the baby, finding the same. "My husband did this to us, and we ran. I had been staying at the shelter, but I was asked to leave by a priest and I had nowhere to go, so we came to the angels of Central Park. We were told that this was a safe place."

Ghost after ghost, everyone had the same answer. They were wayward, cast out, or scared in some way, and had been told by someone that this home was a safe place for them. And while Katie fully welcomed them, she knew she couldn't live with hundreds of ghosts coming in and out through the floor.

Pandora walked up next to her and rolled her shoulders. "At least it's for a good reason, although it really upset the balance for the human beings. This is why they were all off-kilter: so much energy flowing to one place."

Katie rubbed her arms. "We need to help them."

Pandora smiled. "Then let's get our angel power on."

Pandora offered her arm, and Katie wrapped hers around it. They both closed their eyes, breathing in through the nose and out through the mouth in harmony. The energy began to build inside of them, and they could hear the whispers of all the lost souls fluttering through the air. When the energy had built, they kept their arms up and relaxed before releasing it, focusing hard on what they wanted to accomplish. The light flew wildly through the apartment, twisting and turning the corners. Katie's and Pandora's bodies shook slightly, and then the light dissipated.

When they opened their eyes, they were stunned. All of the ghosts were gone, even the one taking a dump.

Everything was quiet and peaceful, and the massive amount of energy they had detected when they came into the condo had dissipated. Someone began to clap behind them.

Pandora and Katie jumped and clung to each other. Slowly they turned around, and Pandora gritted her teeth as her eyes fell on Gabriel in his beautiful robes. "You are such an *ass*!"

Gabriel ignored the comment. "I wanted to come down and commend you on helping the ghosts. Also, just a friendly reminder—a repeat of advice. A friend of your friend can be an enemy."

Pandora threw her hand up, grumpily. "Fuck you, okay? Fuck you."

Gabriel tilted his head to the side with a smirk. "Your strength is your weakness."

"What the fuck does that even mean? We are back into riddle mode because you are bored and want something to do?" She lunged forward to grab him, but he moved too quickly for her, something she had never noticed about him. "You got super-speed now? Trying to show off for the ladies?"

Gabriel smirked, his cheeks high and his lids low. "No, you're just getting slow in your old age."

Pandora gasped, putting her hand to her chest. "Twatwaffle!"

Pandora grabbed the remote off a small table next to an armchair and lobbed it at him. Before it reached his spot, he was gone. The remote hit the wall and landed hard on the ground. Katie gave her a blank look and Pandora stomped her foot. "Why does that douchebag get to torture me, but when I get flustered, you look at me like I'm wrong?"

Katie shook her head. "Oh, no, I totally think you should stand up for yourself. I was looking at you that way because I bought that remote two weeks ago after you lobbed it at what you thought was a mouse, which ended up being a ball of lint from the dryer."

Pandora glanced around. "Ah. Yeah. Sorry about that. Uh, I'll pay you back?"

Katie jerked her chin up. "Mmhmm. Sure. I'll just take it out of the sex swing fund."

Pandora roared, "You monster!"

General Brushwood paced in front of his desk with his hands behind his back. It was his normal morning assistants' meeting, and he had a lot of work to give out. "You know I hate overloading you girls. And gentleman. But we are still on high alert and we are getting wild intel on something boiling under the surface, so my thoughts have to be elsewhere."

He pulled out the sheet of paper that had the assignments. "Mary, Amanda, and Star, the three of you will pull everything from 2016, and especially anything that sounds legit about one of our current elected officials that had not been scoured previously."

Everyone nodded, taking their folders. "Sharyn and Margie, you will be manning the public calls and concerns line. We get a lot of those now, and we try to reply as much as possible."

He kept moving down the list, assigning each person at least one project to begin working on. "If you manage to finish these, Brianna divide the rest among you."

As the assistants got up to leave, the door opened and Jehovivich stuck her head in. The general smiled. "Come in, come in. What a pleasant surprise!"

After the staff filed out, she came inside and saluted. "I didn't mean to come without calling, but a lot of things have been happening. I've been digging through the current affairs, and I think I found something very interesting."

The general showed her over to one of the chairs, then walked behind the desk and took his seat. "You know I like interesting, though in this climate I tend to reserve interesting for good literature or a lecture. You know, something more grounded. But you have come all of this way, so it must be important."

She shook her head. "In reality, I don't know if they are important. But from the sound of them, they aren't something I just want to pass over and never say a word. You know I have your back, and always will. Anyway, within the current intel there has recently been some chatter about strike teams being mobilized. Apparently, there is some sort of operation in Iraq, sent from the UK. The thing is, I looked into it on the national servers, and there aren't any public, or even top secret, missions happening."

The general frowned. "Really? Not even from British military?"

Jehovivich shook her head. "Nope. Not even there. I have a friend over there, and they had nothing. But I did find out one last thing. Apparently, the operation has a code name. It is 'Operation Treasure Hunt.'"

Brushwood narrowed his eyes. "'Treasure Hunt?'"

Jehovivich shrugged. "That's the chatter."

The general rubbed his hand over his stubbly face. "Do you think it has anything to do with the rising conflict in Iraq?"

"I thought that at first, but there are no notes on the conflict, and from what it looks like, they landed in a pretty remote location. The conflict is in Baghdad, mostly," she replied, crossing her legs and sitting back. "Then I thought about the militias; perhaps they were trying to cut the head off of the snake. Many of the militias are centered in the more rural areas, but I would say that ninety percent of them moved after our last mission to rescue POWs."

The general shook his head and tapped his fingers on his lips. "What are they doing?"

Jehovivich shrugged. "I have to say, the chatter didn't feel like it was coming from a military entity. It was a lot less professional-sounding than that."

He pursed his lips and narrowed his eyes. "You don't think… I would hope that… Oh, God."

Jehovivich looked at him confused. "What?"

The general picked up the phone and paused. "There might be people on the Council who are trying to use Timothy's technology to search for something."

He called Katie's base, having the admin transfer him to Timothy.

"General, where have you been all my life?"

Brushwood chuckled. "Saving the world, son, with you

on my team. And while you are on my team, I need you to hack something for me."

Timothy giggled. "I love it. It's been forever. Tell me the details, and let's do this."

"It's a specific location," the general explained. "If I had to guess, they're working out of a London safe house."

Timothy paused. "And this is secret government black-ops-type stuff? Should I be doing this? Just so I know what to fully trash from my drive's memory and what to deny under penalty of treason."

The general smirked. "I am not concerned with that at this point."

Timothy hissed. "Uh oh, sounds like you have reached your bullshit threshold."

"And then some," the general grumbled. "If I'm right, they are conducting missions without any oversight or approval using your stolen tech, so you have my blessing. I'm sending you a secure message with the specific location to look."

Timothy received the message and put the general on speaker as he went into hacker mode. He moved his fingers quickly, pulling up screen after screen and inputting data without conscious thought. He had more than enough experience at hacking government sites and locations, and safe houses weren't usually the most secure of the facilities.

Within ten minutes, he was successful. "And I'm in. Give me just a second to look through the dataaaa—oh my God! It *is* my program. Those dirty motherfuckers are looking for a Leviathan, and what's worse, they think they found one. They've already sent two teams to deal with it.

Are they insane? Have they not learned anything from recent history?"

Brushwood groaned. "I suppose not. I just hope those teams took the beast out and got home safely for all our sakes."

Legion walked through the valley, his form growing. The fabric wrapping his body waved around him without even the smallest hint of a breeze. Following him were several groups of people, including soldiers, a few farmers, and a shepherd. You could hear their whispers echoing through the valley and over the hills, tiny little voices ricocheting through the countryside.

"We. Are. Legion."

9

Juntto and Angie stepped into their apartment, dropping their bags just inside the door. Angie walked over to the couch and sat down, letting out a deep breath, then put her head back and closed her eyes. As usual, she picked up her legs to put them on her coffee table, but instead of hitting it, they fell back to the floor with a thud. She opened one eye and looked up, finding nothing but open space in front of her.

She picked up her head and sat up, looking around. Along the wall under her shelves was her coffee table, sitting just as she had left it, only about seven feet off the mark. Juntto walked out of the bedroom with a hairbrush and a spatula in his hands. "Why were these two things tucked into bed like they were getting ready for a good night's sleep?"

Angie pursed her lips, unsure of what to say. "Yeah, I don't know. The coffee table is under the shelves."

They both started looking around the house, finding things in the strangest places. There were potatoes in the freezer, glassware on the bookshelf, and a box of tampons in the fruit dish.

Juntto and Angie went next door to talk to Katie and Pandora. They were rearranging things as well. "Uh, there is a whole bunch of weird shit going on in our apartment—like tampons-in-the-fruit-bowl kind of weird."

Katie looked up from moving her trashcan off the couch. "Yeah, uh, there was some strange stuff going on in here while we were gone. When we got here, this entire place was full of ghosts."

Pandora walked out of the bathroom with gloves, a face mask, and an apron on. "Not to mention that they might have used your bathroom to take a ghost-dump."

Angie's nose wrinkled, and she covered her mouth. "Oh, my God, that ruins my entire life right there. There were ghosts shitting in my bathroom? That is absolutely the most horrible horror story you could make up. I don't even know what to say."

Katie giggled as Juntto pulled a banana out of a light fixture. "We don't even have bananas."

Angie took the piece of fruit. "*We* did, and now I know where they are. But let's get back to this ghost-dump. I am seriously pledging right now that I am going to go out and buy a new toilet seat for the bathroom. Maybe even seven gallons of bleach, which I will use to hose the entire place down."

Pandora took her gloves off and tossed them in the trash, then pulled her surgical mask down and wiped the sweat from her forehead on the back of her arm. "So, wait. I just need to get this right in my head. Juntto's big blue butt is okay, but an airy ghost bum freaks you out?"

Angie shivered and put her hand up, shaking her head feverishly. "I accept a lot. Demons. Monsters. Leviathans. And it's great. Hey, I take it in stride. But a ghost using my commode? I have limits."

Katie smiled as she walked around collecting random trinkets from all over the house. Juntto shrugged. "Hey, at least they were nice enough to tuck our hairbrush and spatula into bed."

Pandora looked at him, confused, and he shook his head. "Look, this whole ghost thing is new to me. Souls in my dimension have good enough sense to stay dead once they have passed over. There was no visiting your loved ones, or ever seeing them. They died, they are dead."

He walked over and sat down in the chair, lurching forward with a grimace and pulling a fork from behind the seat cushion. Katie took it from him, and he leaned back again. "I can understand people who died in accidents, but even *they* stayed dead in my land. Most of them were killed, so they *would* be ashamed to come back to life. There is nothing more embarrassing than not watching out and getting a Frost Fork in the belly."

Katie grimaced. "What is a Frost Fork?"

Juntto waved his hand. "It's like an Earth pitchfork, except it creates extreme cold. You stab someone with it, and their entire insides freeze. Pretty sucky."

Angie sat on the arm of his chair. "But what about those who died valiantly? I mean, everyone dies, even frost giants. Just takes longer. So, everyone who dies is disregarded?"

Juntto shook his head. "No, no. We respected their conquests, but nobody wants to return to the site of the defeat. At least, that is your mentality in my dimension. Now, I have to admit, my personal thoughts have changed by leaps and bounds since I joined you guys. I don't know how I feel about it, really. I know that if I died now, my soul would still miss the people important to me, so I might come back as a ghost. But the ones here on this planet? They are usually lost souls. The rest roll right up to heaven. There aren't many who would pass that by for a life on Earth, or so I am assuming. Haven't actually been there."

Angie stroked her hand down the side of his head, tucking some hair behind his ear. "You are a very different frost giant. You are kinder, more caring, and—"

He interrupted, squeezing her hand. "Empathy. Compassion. Had you told me three years ago that I would feel compassion for human beings, or anyone, really, I would have probably laughed in your face and then stabbed you to show just how uncompassionate I was. I really was a completely different man back then. I'm glad I am not that giant anymore. Looking back, it was a lonely and angry world."

The safehouse was bustling again, all of the techs stationed around the room, their bookbags lined up next to their desks and their focus on what was going on at the sites. Powell and Xian were not happy with each other. They spent a lot of time together, so it was bound to happen that one day they went their own ways. They were still trying to hold on to the project, but the stress was really getting to both of them.

They had one job, and they had yet to accomplish it. It all came to a head with the accounting of the event right there on the screen in front of them. They were completely mortified, and immediately had a tech hack in and delete the footage.

Xian grabbed a piece of paper out of Powell's hand, whispering in an angry tone, "You think you are so smart, yet you are for some reason, perplexed that I would have a similar feeling. You are too much for my mind to handle."

Powell scoffed, glancing around to make sure no one was watching them as he whisper-yelled back, "You, sir, can't handle me because you are just not as smart as me."

Xian burst into laughter and shook his head. "You are about as smart as a fucking goat. I am the one who set all this up."

Powell tilted his head back, holding his stomach, and cackled. "Please! Without me, you would never have found anything."

Xian put his hands out, still whisper-shouting. "Found what? We are in this fucking mess, and now we don't know what to do about any of it."

Powell hissed, gesturing wildly. "What would you like to do? Run to the World Council and tell the truth about how badly we fucked everything up? Hope they have a soft spot in their hearts because we came clean? That isn't a real thing, and people are only honest about things like that because they know they're going to get caught and want to earn bonus points before they get taken down. We won't survive this. It was off the books, and we royally screwed it up. There will be no mercy, and they will want to make sure we don't talk to anyone about it."

Xian thrust his arm to the side. "Okay, so you are a pussy, afraid of the World Council. Fine. But in case you have forgotten, we have a Leviathan out there who's completely free to roam around the world and take people hostage with whatever sick power it has. We morally can't sit here and just continue to let that stupid alien sonofabitch do whatever the fuck it is doing. It is obvious that this cannot be spun to look good when we are the sole reason people are dying."

Powell clenched his teeth and balled up his fists. "You are so damn impossible. You think I *want* to just let that thing roam around? But how do we stop it when we can't tell them what happened?"

Xian shrugged as he packed things away. "Maybe, just maybe, we can't. Maybe there isn't another answer. Maybe owning up to the failure and facing a possible death sentence is the only way we can make this right."

Powell shook his head. "Are you fucking *nuts*? I am not putting myself on the damn guillotine."

His emotions out of control, he crossed his arms over his chest and pinched his nipples to release some of his tension. He hissed through his teeth, the release cooling his muscles and lessening the tension in his shoulders.

Xian grabbed a piece of paper and balled it up, chucking it really hard at him from close range. "Stop it. That isn't something you can just walk around doing, you fucking freak."

Powell pulled his arms back and very noticeably tweaked his nipples through his shirt, shaking his chest.

"What's wrong, Xian? You afraid of your own manlihood?"

Xian scoffed. "Yeah, like you'll get your freak on it, and suddenly it will dry up and run off. Fucking pervert."

Powell's mouth dropped open. He didn't like being called a freak in the least. "Me? You are calling *me* a freak?"

He swiped his hand hard across the top of Xian's head, knocking his hairpiece off and across the room. It slid across the floor, stopping at the feet of one of the techs. She shifted her eyes before kicking it back. Powell started laughing so hard he could barely breathe. Xian walked over and snatched it off the floor, shoving it into his bag.

Powell leaned forward, slapping his hand on the table and cackling in a high-pitched tone. Xian watched him for a moment, completely disgusted. "You know what? Fuck you, Powell. This was a favor for the Chinese government, but I can't be expected to work with amateurs. Fuck this whole project. Guess what? It's your country, and it's your safehouse. I am going to gather my fucking shit and get the hell out of here. I don't need the money that badly—as if we'll even get paid after you fucked shit up so bad."

Powell wiped tears from his eyes and waved his hand. "Dude, seriously? Wait. Hey, don't go. I was just joking! I mean, when you put that on this morning, did you expect people not to notice that you went from Mr. Clean to Frodo Baggins overnight? It doesn't look bad, but come on, man! Embrace the baldness."

Xian stood with his bag on his shoulder, just staring at him. Powell stopped laughing and motioned behind the desks. "Come on, dude. You know I didn't mean it. Please don't leave."

Xian took one hand out of his pocket and jammed his middle finger into the air before walking away.

Katie beat her wings hard to keep pace with Pandora, who was flying next to her. They were both dressed in everyday clothes so they could go to the bank. Katie was wearing a pair of ripped jeans, heeled black boots, a black sweater, and a peacoat. Pandora had been talked out of a tight bodycon dress and into a pair of wide-leg palazzo pants, and Katie had agreed to the light-blue turtleneck sweater that was cut off halfway down her belly. Over the ensemble, she wore a puffy black jacket with a fur hood.

"So, have you seen *Ghost*? Demi Moore, pottery, the whole nine?" Katie asked.

Pandora shook her head. "We talked about this before, and I hadn't seen it. Personally, I like the ridiculous movies like *Casper*. Most of the other movies are about poltergeists, not ghosts. Two completely different things."

Katie giggled. "That's true. We'll have to look up some ghost movies tonight. There have to be some good ones. Oh! Like *The Sixth Sense*."

Pandora just stared at her with a curved mouth and lifted eyebrows. "Haven't seen that either."

Katie and Pandora began their descent to the street below. Katie wagged her finger. "We are definitely going to watch that one. You have to see it once in your life."

The two landed on the sidewalk outside the bank, and without skipping a beat, Katie opened the door and the two strode in. Several people looked over, recognizing them, and the bank's VP came running over to help. "Why don't I take you into my office so we can do this discreetly."

Katie nodded. "We would appreciate that."

They went to the banker's office and he sat across from them, putting his palms together and pressing his fingertips to his lips. "So, tell me. What are you looking to do today?"

Pandora flipped her hair back. "I want to start with a bank account. After that, we'll see."

He nodded, springing forward and grabbing a pamphlet about the different options. Pandora glanced at Katie, who leaned over and tapped the Silver checking account. "That would be good for her."

The banker smiled, taking the pamphlet back and opening a drawer, then pulling out a folder of paperwork. "Excellent. This won't take too long. I just need two forms of government-approved ID."

Katie pursed her lips. "Actually, that's part of the problem. I'm assuming you know her story?"

The VP nodded. "Oh, yes. Started out as a demon, Damned you, started working with you, both achieving great things, and now she is branching out as an angel."

Pandora smiled broadly at hearing her accomplishments. "Yep. So, you see, I'll be fine, right?"

He kept the huge smile on his face, but he shook his head. "Oh, no. I can't give you an account without at least one form of ID. I'm sure that, as much as you have helped this country financially, someone will agree to take care of the problem."

They sat there at the desk talking to each other, Katie sulking more than Pandora. She couldn't help but feel she was the reason this had gone to shit. "Angie should be doing this. She's much better at this sort of thing."

Pandora poked her in the arm. "Um, I could be wrong, but don't you run a giant-ass corporation? Besides, they are right; I am technically *not* an established person here. It's like I don't exist."

Katie sighed. "One, you do exist; trust me, I have to hear you each day. Number two, yes, I own a huge corporation, but I am only successful because I know enough to hire smart people to work the scene for me and take care of payments and stuff like that."

"She wouldn't probably have been successful either," Pandora sighed.

Katie shook her head. "We're going to fix this, and I am going straight up the ladder. Right to the top. I'll call Brushwood and ask him to get you all straightened out."

Pandora nodded, glancing at the banker every few moments. "Or I could just live inside you all of the time. It worked before, so why wouldn't it work now? I mean, *I* was comfortable, and you didn't seem to mind the ability to eat as much Jessie Rae's or Italian or Mexican food as you wanted while I was making you fit with huge tits. Of course, everything changes, I suppose."

Katie reached over and touched her arm. "Things do change, and beyond how I feel about you being inside me all the time is how you should have the opportunity to have your own life. You don't have to be in me all the time. I think it's important that you allow yourself to have time for yourself. I know it might seem frightening or uncomfortable, but I want you to be your own person. Well, you already *are* your own person, but to rely on yourself and look to me only out of necessity, not because you think you can't do something without me. Come on, you love the freedom. Besides, it will help if you are a legal person."

Katie pulled her phone out. "Here, I'll call the general right now. Maybe he can expedite something, and we can wait here to set it up."

Katie leaned back in her chair, waiting for Brushwood to answer the phone. Pandora slowly looked at the bank employee sitting there. Not only was he engrossed in the conversation, but also, he was obviously weirded out. Pandora was tired of apologizing for that. She whistled to get his attention and blinked at him. He cleared his throat and nodded, whispering, "I'll go work on some stuff out here. When you need me, just yell."

10

The general didn't answer the phone, and Katie knew better than to think the IDs would come the same day anyway, so they told the banker they would be back when they had the proper identification. Stepping outside, they took off straight up to get away from the people who had started to gather for them outside. Somebody in the bank had leaked their location, but that was normal for them. At that moment, though, neither of them wanted to deal with it.

They flew up to the roof of the bank and landed. Katie folded her wings and walked to the ledge, stretching her arms over her head. Pandora came up next to her, shaking hers over the whole thing. "Banks never used to be that way. As long as you paid the bank owner, they would let you open any account you wanted. Everyone had access."

Katie scoffed. "Welcome to capitalism, where they make the good stuff available only to those they deem financially important enough."

Pandora crossed her arms. "That is actually bothering

me a lot. I am a real person. I might have started as a demon, but now I am on Earth. I can have children, I can fall in love, I can hold down a job, and I'm sure I could pass a college course, too."

Katie put her hand on Pandora's shoulder. "Trust me, I completely agree with you. In fact, even when you were in me pretty much always, I still never thought of you as an alien to this world. You had to acclimate and make your choice, and you did that just like a human. You paid the penalty for not making the right choice, and you pretty much have experienced the full range of human emotions and issues along the way. You don't have to convince me. I already know all that."

Pandora sighed. "But you aren't the one who needs to get me this stuff."

Katie nodded, looking out over the city. "You're right. *You* are, but like every other person on Earth, we have to take that leap to do better. For right now, as soon as I get in touch with the general, I'm going to see if he can't get you some sort of ID, even if it's special-citizen status."

Her phone began to vibrate at that moment. The number was unknown, so she knew it was someone important. She stepped back off the ledge to the roof and answered, "Hello?"

"Katie, it's General Brushwood. Sorry I missed your call. What can I do for you?"

Katie glanced at Pandora. "We were out today, and because Pandora is on her own now, she wanted to set up a bank account so she could be given some money and handle it herself. Problem is, she doesn't have any ID, mostly because she was not born here. As you can imagine, it's probably exhausting for her to be someone who is not technically considered to exist by the very country and world she serves."

The general listened intently, giving small verbal cues that he was still with her there. "I understand all of that, and having an ID and everything that goes with it is something that, in my book, she totally deserves. I know I can do something for her, but unfortunately, I am going to have to take care of it later. I know that's terrible, but I have a bit of an issue going on right now."

Katie scrunched her brow. "Uh-oh. Anything I need to be aware of or help with?"

He paused. "Not right this second, no. But if what I am thinking is true, there is a very good chance that I will call on you, so please don't go far, and keep your phone on you. I will say that it has to do with a possible new Leviathan, and if it is awake, it didn't get that way on its own."

Katie shook her head. "What? What the fuck!"

Brushwood chuckled sadly. "That was my reaction exactly, not going to lie. This blindsided me. Anyway, I have a couple of phone calls to make. I will keep you updated, and as soon as I can get to it, I will get Pandora something. But if this goes down, I will need both of you."

Katie glanced at Pandora. "Of course. Pandora and I will make sure we stay by my phone. Be careful, General."

They hung up, and she looked at Pandora. "He'll work on it soon. Right now, he is on some sort of trail that means we could be called up to Leviathan stomp again."

Pandora rolled her eyes. "Oh, so I'm enough of a person to kick ass, but I can't open a checking account without a little picture of myself and a huge entity acknowledging my presence? I don't know, dude—that sounds a lot like hell and Lucifer."

The tech sat at the computer typing quickly, watching the load on the system fluctuate as she allocated different sectors to different jobs that needed to be completed. It was a really old system, but she liked to create and expand technological programs. It was the only way up.

The phone rang and she reached over without looking, putting it to her ear. "Hello?"

"This is General Brushwood." He cleared his throat. "I need to speak to whoever there is using a stolen program to trace specific entities without prior authorization."

The tech stopped, looking up with wide eyes. "Uh, I think you'd better speak to Powell. He has been in charge since the beginning of the project."

The general coughed. "All right, put him on."

The tech told him, "Actually, he isn't here right now."

"WHERE THE HELL IS HE?"

Powell grunted as he swung from the beam. Leather straps bound his ankles, and his head hovered just feet above the ground. He could see the shiny leather thigh high boots of his dominatrix as she stepped up in front of him. She ran the riding crop over his thigh softly before snapping it hard against his leg. He groaned and laughed at the same time.

She walked around him, dragging the crop across his skin. As she pulled back, he prepared himself again for the stinging pleasure he would receive. However, before she could follow through, his phone began to ring. He lifted his head, watching as she walked across the room and picked up his phone. "Secure call?"

Powell's eyes opened wide. "Oh, shit. I need to take that. I usually don't, you know that, but this is important."

She pursed her lips and walked over to him. "Fine, but extra punishment for you afterward."

He smiled as she handed it to him. He was still hanging upside down. The blood was collecting in his head, and he was struggling slightly to get his thoughts together. He wasn't sure specifically who it was, but any time a secure call came through, he knew that it was work in some form or fashion.

He pressed the Answer button. "Hold on, securing the line."

He pulled the phone up in front of him and blinked wildly as he pressed the button to secure and waited for the system to fully cycle through and give him a green light. "This is Powell."

"This is General Brushwood, World Council, among other things," he stated gruffly.

Powell winced. "Yes, General, I am very familiar with you, although I am a little surprised to be getting a call from you. What can I do for you today?"

The general was breathing heavily. "I think you know the reason I am calling. And if you don't, think really long and hard about the last unauthorized mission you sent out. That will answer it nicely for you. I don't have time given the state of affairs in this country to wade through your bullshit, so I am giving you the chance to tell me everything that happened from beginning to end, no details left out. Then, and only then, will I consider not reporting you to the federal government for acts of treason."

Powell gasped. "I... Treason? That is absurd."

The general didn't waver. "Then you better start talking and make me understand."

Powell put his hand over the phone and looked at the dominatrix. "I need you to lower me and leave."

She tilted her head back and laughed loudly. "Are you mad? *You* don't tell *me* what to do, you fool."

Powell held his temper and put the phone back to his ear. "General, I think that..."

Brushwood cut him off. "That was your one free chance. The next words that start coming out of your mouth better be the truth, and nothing but the truth from beginning to end. If you think you are incapable, I can send some MPs to pick you up in your dungeon right now, but they won't be nice enough to let you change before you are brought to our offices. I'm pretty sure you don't want to go to the brig in leather chaps and nothing else, do you?"

Powell glanced at his domme. "No, sir. Okay, so you want the truth."

Before Powell could hesitate again, the domme whipped him hard across the back. He bowed, the straps twisting as he slowly turned in a circle. "Right. So we were hired to use the program that was stolen from Katie the angel's technology guy. One other guy and I worked on it until we figured out the system and found a sleeping

Leviathan in Iraq. We sent our guys in to destroy the beast."

The general grumbled. "But that was not what happened, was it?"

Powell sighed. "No, it wasn't. The team disappeared, and we assumed at that point it was the Leviathan. So we sent a second team."

"And?"

Powell's nostrils flared. "And they haven't gotten back to us. We lost contact about ten minutes after the helicopter landed. They are all MIA right now. We have not sent anyone else in. My coworker and I were given the okay to make all decisions and keep everyone we could out of it, so we did, and then were at an impasse on where to go at this point."

The general laughed. "No shit. You are at an impasse, all right. Do you tell your people how badly you fucked up and risk the very good chance that whoever these men are will dispose of you, or do you tell the big guys so you can help the troops you sent out as rat bait? They will put you in prison, or possibly worse. Seems like a no-win situation for you."

Powell sighed. "Yes, General, it is."

"And where are you at this point?"

Powell glanced at the domme as she circled him. "I'm carefully considering the situation."

She reared back and whipped him again. He shoved his fist in his mouth to muffle the groan.

Brushwood was silent for a moment. "Give me the location of the Leviathan. I am sending my own men in to hopefully minimize the hell you just set loose on this planet. And don't try to leave the country, I've already flagged you. I'll deal with you when I'm done making sure the people of this country are safe."

Korbin's room was dark as hell, the blinds down, the curtains pulled and the door to the rest of the house shut. He had put in a hell of a day's work the day before and was enjoying sleeping until the sun began to rise. There was no way he would be able to handle that job if it weren't for the amazing sleep he was getting here. He was working fifteen-hour days with no days off to try to get the fort up and running.

His phone rang, echoing through his bedroom. Korbin groaned and rolled over, slapping the table to locate his phone. He pulled it up in front of his eyes and squinted, waking immediately when he saw the general's number on the screen. He clicked on the bedside lamp and put the phone to his ear. "General. Is everything okay?"

Brushwood sighed. "I'm so sorry for waking you up, Korbin. I know you are working hard, and I wouldn't call unless it was important."

Korbin rubbed his eyes. "Of course. It's part of the job, and it's a usual thing for me these days. Is Katie all right?"

"Oh, yeah. Yeah. I actually haven't even talked to her about the issue yet. I called you first. There has been a breach, and someone went in search of a Leviathan with no authority. I have over a dozen soldiers MIA right now, as well as a possible Leviathan on the loose."

Korbin's heart fluttered. That was not a good thing. "Shit. What can I do to help?"

The general cleared his throat. "I was hoping you could send a team of Damned to check out Al Fatsi, Iraq. It is a little bit outside of it, and I will send the exact coordinates. I believe that is where the first team went missing. Hopefully, there are clues as to where the rest of them went."

Korbin threw the covers off and stood up, then flipped the lights on and grabbed his glasses, pulling his roster of Damned out. "Yes, of course. Anything that I can do. We are in Bahrain, so that is only a few hours away. And with the military choppers they have here, it's probably even less time."

"Excellent," the general replied. "I knew I could count on you. I'll send over the coordinates so you can go straight there. We don't know anything about what you will be facing. Nothing. So, make sure you go as prepared as possible."

Korbin ran his fingers over a small trinket on his dresser given to him by Katie. "I can call Katie and Pandora too. Since this is probably a Leviathan, they are going to want to know. I think we've all learned not to take these things lightly. And if it *is* a Leviathan, we are going to most likely need them to fight it."

The general had another call to make. "Of course. Do what you think is best. And thank you. Keep me updated."

As soon as Korbin hung up, there was a knock at his bedroom door. "Come on in, Brock."

Brock opened the door, rubbing his eyes. "I swear I wasn't eavesdropping, but the walls are really thin. There's an issue?"

Korbin nodded. "There may be another Leviathan, and there are currently about a dozen soldiers MIA. He is asking for a team of Damned to go scope the situation out. And of course, Pandora and Katie if it is necessary."

Brock nodded. "Have you picked who will be going in?"

Korbin looked down at his list. "I was just looking, but I think I want to go in for sure. These Damned are not experienced enough to face a Leviathan on their own. I feel like I would just be sending them to their deaths."

Brock leaned against the dresser, crossing his arms over his bare chest. "Let me head up the team, or co-lead with you. I think this warrants more than one experienced Damned."

Korbin wrinkled his face. "This is dangerous, and we'll probably have Katie and Pandora with us there too."

Brock shook his head. "Okay, just hear me out. Let's recon the area and figure out what the hell is going on out there before you bring in Katie and Pandora. We can check out the area where the soldiers landed, find any evidence that may suggest a Leviathan, and get all the details Katie and Pandora will need to successfully launch a full-scale attack on this thing. Plus, if we can, we'll save the soldiers who have been lost."

Korbin pursed his lips. "That might not be too bad of an idea."

Brock shrugged. "After all, we set up these forts and these Damned teams just so that Katie doesn't have to be everywhere at once. If this turns out to be something less devastating than a Leviathan, we would have pulled her for no reason. We already have limited resources in this country—no, this world, really—to fight all of these things. We don't need to expend them all in one spot."

Korbin looked him up and down. "And you're sure that this isn't just an attempt to keep Katie safe? I understand, if that's what it is, but still, that is a really dangerous precedent to set."

Brock waved a hand. "Not in the least. I am simply trying to minimize the manpower until we know what the hell is going on. We need to share the burden in all of this, and not sit back and make Katie take care of everything. Even in regular situations, you have a check team that observes the area before the strike team goes in. Well, you should, at least. It's obvious these guys did not, but from what it sounds like, this mission was not authorized."

Korbin chuckled. "No, it was not, and it possibly stemmed from the stolen data at the base."

Korbin sighed, and Brock chewed his lip. "So, do you think I'm right? Share the burden, do the reconnaissance first?"

Korbin's jaw clenched and unclenched, but he finally nodded his head. "All right. Go get your gear."

11

Sean pressed rewind on the video and watched the section again, holding the already de-feathered and butchered raw cockerel meat in his hand. The kitchen was quiet, everyone having already eaten and gone back to their rooms. Sean needed to do something with his time. He was going crazy in his room alone, so he'd rolled up to the kitchen and decided to watch one of Juntto's cooking videos and make cockerel and stinging nettle soup, a very close Viking rendition of a frost giant recipe he'd posted. It was kind of difficult, considering Sean had never worked with those specific ingredients before and Juntto had a habit of talking so much on his videos.

He rewound the section on cutting up the chicken one last time, noting each step. As he reached over to grab the knife, Timothy walked through the swinging kitchen door. "Hey there, Chef Boyardee."

Sean chuckled. "Hey."

Timothy wrinkled his nose and looked at the ingredients. "What in God's name are you trying to poison us all with now?"

Sean nodded at the video. "It's a Viking soup that Juntto made on his video. It looked good when he was done, and it will feed a lot of guys, so I am trying to get it done for tomorrow."

Timothy nodded, leaning against the wall. "I actually came to find you to tell you the good news. Well, kind of good news. They found the stolen software, and the general is taking steps to recover it."

Sean looked up at him with a big smile on his face. "Man, that is really good to hear. Seriously, if you can get that info back, that will at least put some closure to the whole thing—at least on the tech side of things. I don't think it will affect my punishment in the least. Still, I want to know our stuff is back safe and sound since it was my fault."

Timothy shook his head. "It was *not* your fault. You know that. Carmen conned you, and while I wasn't her biggest fan, I did not see *that* coming."

Sean scoffed. "Tell that to the rest of the base. Aside from Eddie and Turner, the whole base seems to be avoiding me like the fucking plague. They all think I had something to do with it, like I let her in specifically to steal the data. After all I've done… Never mind. Doesn't matter. What is done is done. And I just have to move on from here, I guess."

Timothy shook his head, putting his hand on Sean's arm. "Don't do that. Don't close up. You know I believe you, and you know that I wish this would all go away. I'm here. Talk to me."

Sean glanced up at him, then continued cutting up the cockerel. "I don't know, I guess I really didn't think about how I felt until I had no one there to distract me. No job I liked, no friends around all the time to keep me going. And when I finally got to that point, I realized how being demonless made me feel alone inside of my mind. And then Carmen the software thief came along, and for some reason, she made me feel less alone. I don't want you to think you weren't an amazing friend, it's just that there was something about her. I really thought she understood me. How I thought about things. Maybe she did, and she just didn't care because she had a job to do. But the loss of my demon was hard for me, since with him, there was constantly an ally in my head. His reasons weren't necessarily the same as mine, but we had the same goals."

Timothy nodded supportively, listening to him talk about his demon for the first time ever. He always shut that conversation off as fast as he possibly could. "I mean, I don't know how that feels. Yeah, I was Damned, but my demon and I had a completely different relationship; it was like having a homophobe in my head all the time. But I *do* understand that transition from constantly having someone there to absolute silence. It can definitely be lonely. Even for me, the guy who wanted his demon gone so badly he would have done just about anything to make that happen. At first, the silence was almost deafening sometimes."

Sean looked at him with a half-smile, the first close to genuine smile he had produced since before the incident. "Thanks, Timothy. I really appreciate you coming up here and talking to me. And I appreciate how loyal to our friendship you've been. I feel like you're the only one who never had a doubt. I mean, the guys never acted that way, but I could tell that they had at some point at least thought about it. It meant a lot to me to have someone there; made me feel less alone."

Timothy pumped his fist. "Yesss! Gay bestie for the motherfucking, sparkling, fantastic, super-sparkly win."

Sean burst into laughter, shaking his head. "I really hope we get to work together again."

Timothy wiggled his eyebrows. "Girl, me too. Let me tell you, that damn dungeon is sad and pathetic all by myself. Dark and lonely. And the cooking shows just make me feel like a spinster now, not to mention that I do not cook, so I get hungry and never make the recipes."

Sean nodded, chuckling. "So, you want me back for the squeaking of my wheelchair and my cooking. I get it."

Timothy shrugged. "A girl's gotta eat. I am all about the waif look, but I don't really like the third-world-country starving-to-death look. It's not attractive with the whole tailbone-sticking-out thing."

Timothy stayed and cooked through the evening with Sean.

The chopper pilot came over the comm. "All right, boys, we are coming up on the spot where the first and second teams were dropped. We came out here as a dry run with the second pilot. He saw the whole thing, but he clammed up. We haven't gotten him to say anything about what happened."

Korbin, Brock, and three other Damned were pressed against the window, as the helicopter began to descend toward the ground. They were visiting the original location, figuring they would start there and follow any clues they could find. They also hoped there would be some good clues about whatever they found.

The helicopter landed and the five men piled out, taking their guns and some ammo with them. The chopper immediately lifted back off, going high enough to survey the area and keep a lookout for them. When the wind had died down and they didn't need to block their faces from dirt and debris, the five of them scanned the area. There was an eerie feeling over the whole place, from the way the almost-hidden cave-like tomb was indented into the hill to the boot tracks from what they assumed to be the soldiers.

Korbin walked up next to Brock and looked at him seriously. "I'm going to keep the three new guys back a little, and you and I will push closer to the opening. If it looks safe, we'll call them in."

Brock nodded and waited for Korbin to give the orders. When he joined him again, they started down to the cave, which was in a small valley. Korbin put his arm out and stopped Brock, nodding to the right. There were two abandoned helicopters sitting there.

Brock was confused. "I thought the second pilot got away."

Korbin nodded. "He did, but the first team had two helicopters because it was bigger. Looks like we know for sure they didn't get out."

They made their way carefully down the hill toward the flatter valley area. As they approached, they slowed, seeing something scattered around in the tall grass. Korbin squinted as they got closer, the two of them stopping in their tracks when they realized what they were looking at. There weren't just two abandoned helicopters sitting eerily by. The valley was full of guns and personal gear.

Brock leaned down and picked up a rifle. "These are military issue. It looks like they just dropped them here. Why would they do something like that?"

Korbin shook his head. "I don't know. Maybe there was some sort of incursion or a larger number on the enemy side than we thought. Or maybe they dropped everything for some way creepier reason."

Korbin called the three guys down to the tomb after securing it, and Brock began taking spotlights out of his bag and setting them up to point directly into the cave. Brock took the lead, slowly making his way in one step at a time. When he entered, he felt a bone-chilling surge go through him.

The place was a single room with ancient markings on the wall, an altar, and more guns and equipment that had just been dropped. Korbin bent down and examined a boot print under the spotlights. "Military-issue combat boots. These definitely belong to one of the teams."

Brock tilted his head, stepping back and looking at the markings on the floor. He noticed that there were also knee prints. "They took a knee in here."

Korbin's brow was permanently furrowed. He walked over and studied the drawings on the walls. The three other Damned stood in the doorway, slightly shocked by the place. "Can anyone read this?"

Brock shook his head, followed by the other three guys. Korbin took out his phone and scrolled through, finding Timothy's number. "No problem. If anyone can find out the random details of non-famous events, it would be Timothy." He tried to place the call, but predictably, there was no signal in the cave.

They checked out the altar and the rest of the cave before heading back out. Korbin called Timothy as soon as they emerged and sent him photos of the inscriptions, then they all walked along slowly in a line, looking for anything that would tell them which way the guys went. One of the new Damned, Ayrton, waved everyone over. "Look how the grass is smashed. It's not just a single line, it's a bunch of lines. This makes it look like there was some sort of mass exodus or migration of at least, I would say, a dozen people."

Korbin looked in the direction the prints headed. "They are all moving in the same direction too. We should follow it and see where it leads us. Get your guns out and keep them at the ready."

The five of them walked carefully along the valley, following the trail of smashed grass and drag marks. Through the hills of Iraq, an area more than a little familiar to Brock, the team trudged, unsure if they would find anything.

However, as they moved over another hilltop, they found an array of weapons spread all over the ground. There were helicopter skid indentions in the grass, but no helicopter this time.

Brock picked up a shepherd's crook and poked his boot

at a military-issue M-16. "Uh, I think this might be the second spot. Looks like there are more than just military missing unless shepherds just leave their sheep in the middle of the hills."

Korbin nodded. "I have a feeling they may not be far ahead of us. Keep your eyes open."

The chopper pilot did a continuous loop around the guys below, making sure to go out far enough to spot anyone they might be getting close to without them realizing it. Up to that point, all he could see were random helicopter graves and weapons and packs left abandoned on the ground. When he ascended a few hundred feet to see over the next hill, a fair number of people came into view. They were trudging along, some in military gear, others not.

The pilot grabbed the comm. "Korbin, this is the chopper pilot, Lieutenant Andrews. Yeah, I have a group of people in my field of vision, straight ahead of you and moving in the same direction. Some of them look injured, and others seem ill. Over."

A couple of seconds went by before Korbin replied, "Uh, copy that, sir?. Do you see any creature that looks to be from another dimension? Over."

The pilot hovered near the group, looking at all of the people walking along. "That would be a negative. There is no monster down there. I am going to go in, land, and see if I can't put together a plan to get them out of there. If you can, head in that direction, which is straight ahead six or seven more hills. Over."

"Copy that, pilot. We're on our way. Be careful, since we don't know what happened to these people. Over," Korbin replied.

The pilot did another pass and pulled ahead of them, landing carefully on a plateau. Switching off the chopper, he paid attention to his safety protocol and removed his headset, since he couldn't use it out there anyway. He looked in the back, making sure he still had blankets and water. He had no idea what kind of shape these people would be in.

When he turned back, the group was surrounding the chopper. He narrowed his eyes, staring at them. They had blank, almost dead expressions on their faces, and their eyes glowed a bright and brilliant purple. The pilot waved at them at first, but then they began to shake the chopper and claw at the glass.

He was reaching for the toggle to turn the chopper back on when a big military guy leapt up, throwing himself against the glass front of the helicopter. The windshield started to crack, and the pilot panicked. He reached down next to his seat and pulled out his pistol, making sure it had a full magazine. By the time he snapped it back in place, the chopper was rocking wildly. Out of nowhere, there was a loud squealing noise, like tearing metal, and before he could react, they had ripped the door of the chopper off.

With shaking hands, he aimed, shooting and killing three of them. They fell to the ground, their eyes going back to normal almost immediately. The others took a few steps back, their bodies still lethargic. From the back he could hear grumbling, and the sea of people around him involuntarily fell or spun out of the way. The pilot gripped onto the edge of the seat, his eyes growing wide as Vinders lumbered forward. His eyes shimmered from purple to red and back again. The pilot moved to aim at Vinders' chest, but the lieutenant grabbed the gun, ripping it out of the pilot's hand.

Vinders was possessed by both the Leviathan and a demon, so his strength was unmatched as he punched the pilot in the face over and over. The pilot tried to cover himself, but Vinders was far too strong, so he just took it until he was barely conscious. Vinders reached in and ripped him from the cockpit, dragging his body along with him as he approached Legion.

Vinders dropped to one knee and presented the pilot as a gift. Legion moved closer to him, breathing in his pain and anguish. Without any movement of lips or mouth, a whisper emerged from the mummy. "We Are Legion."

The pilot's skin began to heal quickly, and his eyes shot open, shimmering purple.

Korbin and Brock hadn't wanted the pilot to land since it was risky, but Korbin had kept his mouth shut, considering the pilot was not only a career military guy but also a multi-tour veteran who had many medals for his combat actions. When the radio went silent a few minutes later, Korbin had a feeling that something wasn't right. He stopped the troops and had them move to the top of the hill, looking around for anyone or anything.

Brock continued to try to reach the pilot, but there was still nothing but silence. Korbin came up. "Any luck?"

Brock shook his head. "Damn it, no. Fuck. He was right there, but he got sidetracked. I don't know. Whatever this is, it seems to be collecting people."

One of the Damned yelled down, "Hey, there's a car coming down the dirt road on the other side of this hill."

Korbin waved to the soldier and nodded to Brock. "Let's go get this fucker."

They hurried up the hill and over the crest, then down to the side of the road. The rusty yellow pickup truck kicked dust and rocks all over the place before slowing down and coming to a stop in front of Korbin. The window rolled down, revealing a middle-aged man with second-hand clothes and worry lines on his forehead. He flashed a friendly smile. "Hey, do you speak English?"

Korbin nodded. "Yes. What can we do for you?"

The guy looked around the hills. "I am looking for my cousin. He is a shepherd. I haven't been able to find him."

None of the other guys said a word; they had seen indications a shepherd had been nearby, but given the security level of this mission, there shouldn't be anyone out.

"We haven't seen anyone like that," Korbin said. "We are military and mercenaries, here on a mission assigned by US general named Brushwood. Would you mind giving us a ride to the last known location of our pilot? He said he saw a group of people, then he landed, and nothing else came over the comm."

The guy didn't even have to think about it. "Uh, you up front with me to show me where to go. The rest of you can get in the truck bed."

Korbin climbed into the passenger seat, and the guy put out his hand. "Archer, Archer Niles. I am British, but my cousin is from here. Do you think you are going to be able to find your pilot?"

Korbin sighed, looking out the window. "I hope so. I really hope so."

12

Katie knocked on Angie's and Juntto's door. Pandora was behind her, holding two donuts in one hand and eating a third. "Why did you have to bring food with you?"

Pandora shrugged. "I don't get the donut time now that I used to. I have to improvise, okay? Just be glad I don't need dick as bad as donuts right now."

Katie turned back around, then burst into laughter. "I'm sorry, I just pictured you carrying around an armload of dicks instead of donuts."

Pandora lifted both eyebrows. "I mean, it's not out of the question."

Angie opened the door. "Hey, guys. Sorry, I was changing. Come on in."

They walked in and followed Angie to the kitchen, where Juntto was filming his show. Katie bit the inside of her cheek and nodded at Juntto, letting him know they had to talk to him. He took a break, turning off the camera.

Katie walked up, looking at his mess. "Sorry to interrupt you, but we have some news."

Juntto waved it off. "I am getting pretty good with editing. It's fine."

Pandora was down to one donut but had already had six. She looked in the pot on the stove and flinched, the smell hitting her straight in the nose. She took the last donut and tossed it in the trash, holding her stomach. "That's the only thing to ever tear me from my donuts. What are you making, stewed babies?"

Juntto shook his head. "It's a lamb and garlic dish, with some other stuff thrown in because that's what we frost giants do. So, what's going on?"

Katie stuck her hands in the back pockets of her jeans. "Looks like a new Leviathan may have been found."

Juntto's face went perfectly still. "Is it Legion or the Unnamed One?"

Katie shrugged. "We don't know right now. We can't catch up with it. Which is worse?"

Juntto sat back on his stool. "We don't know much about the Unnamed One, but Legion is infamous. He seeks to add the strongest possible beings to his collective, and he's not friendly."

Katie nodded. "Well, then, let's all hope this is just a false alarm."

The truck bounced over the terrain with Korbin holding the oh-shit handle in the front and the guys clinging to the sides for dear life in the back. They made a left turn and raced over a patch of level ground. Korbin leaned forward and put his hand out. "Slow down. Don't get too close."

Up ahead were a large group of people and the helicopter, which now had no door. Korbin opened the door and nodded to Brock. "Let's get around them. See if we can't get some answers."

Brock gave him a thumbs-up and walked back to the truck bed to update the others. Korbin stuck his head in the truck. "Stay here for now. If things go well, we'll call you over."

The guy swallowed hard. "And if they don't?"

Korbin pulled his pistol out. "Then you hightail it out of here and call the Army. Tell them you were sent by Katie's Killers and you need to get hold of General Brushwood. He is the best person to talk to."

The guy nodded. "Good luck, then. I'll be right here."

Korbin shut the door, and the five of them walked slowly toward the group, spreading out far enough to move around them. No one was looking at them. They were just standing there, slightly hunched, their heads hanging low and their bodies swaying. Brock stayed next to Korbin with his gun out and his sword on his back.

Korbin cleared his throat. "Excuse me. Do you know where I can find two British military teams?"

He scanned the crowd, but no one so much as twitched. They acted like they couldn't hear him. He sniffed, glancing at Brock and then back at the group. "It looks like you could use some help. My name is Korbin, and these are my guys. We are here to help you. Can someone tell me what happened?"

They waited, but there was still no response. All five of

them were starting to get antsy. Suddenly the center of the group began to shift, the people moving to the side one by one and creating a walkway of sorts through them. From the center, a creature, something reminiscent of a mummy with its shroud flowing like tentacles around, stepped out. Its eyes glowed bright purple, and Korbin immediately knew it was not there to make friends.

Korbin pulled out his gun. "Oh, shit."

He pointed his weapon at Legion and began to fire, and the other Damned, including Brock, followed suit. Then things started to get ugly. Legion's soldiers, the missing military plus others, suddenly began to move. Legion put his arms up, opening what resembled a mouth and let out a deep and raspy scream. His soldiers popped into action, moving as fast as they could toward whichever of the Damned was closest to them.

The three Damned in the back didn't stand a chance. Seven or eight purple-eyed soldiers came down on them. They threw the Damned on the ground and pinned them. The Damned fought hard, but these creatures were wildly strong. Legion didn't seem to walk; it was more like he floated inches above the ground, moving at a speed that Korbin had never seen any creature on Earth achieve. You could barely make out his body when he moved, just the fluttering white ribbons of fabric that whipped around him.

One by one he stopped at the three Damned soldiers, whispering something close to their ears. He moved to the last and all three went still as he floated in front of them, waiting. Korbin and Brock had backed up and were pointing their weapons at the soldiers. Suddenly the three

Damned began to shake violently, their eyes rolling back in their heads and spittle flying. This continued for about thirty seconds before their bodies went limp.

Brock gritted his teeth, thinking they were dead, but a moment later, their eyes flashed open, turning from red to purple and back again. "Fuck. He is infecting them somehow."

Legion's army then turned to Brock and Korbin and started moving toward them. Brock hated shooting the soldiers, but he was running out of options. Korbin and Brock took a couple of the soldiers down with bullets in the chest and they fell to the ground, their eyes flickering from purple back to their normal hues.

Korbin grabbed Brock's shoulder. "We need to fight, but if it gets too much, we retreat and call for backup, you understand?"

Brock nodded. "Got it."

Korbin looked him straight in the eyes and gave him a nod. For Brock the next few moments were almost like slow motion. His eyes flicked behind Korbin as he turned, slamming a new mag in his gun. Brock saw the flashes of white, but they didn't register until too late. As Korbin turned back around, Legion moved up to face him, reaching out and grabbing his throat. Korbin's eyes went wide and his mouth fell open, struggling for air.

Legion whispered to him, too low for Brock to hear, and then let go. All he could see was Korbin from the back. He stood there for several moments before lifting his chin and taking a deep breath. When he turned around, his eyes shifted to meet Brock's, filled with swirling purple. Brock stepped back, tripping and dropping his pistol.

Reaching back, he slowly drew his sword, putting his hand out. "Don't make me do this, Korbin."

The bubbling and blistering pits of hell simmered in their sulfuric glory deep within the inner circle. Baal rushed around his mansion, ordering servants right and left, trying to get everything straight. Early that day he was awoken by the servants telling him he'd had a messenger from Lucifer. Wrapped in a robe, he hurried out of his bedroom to greet the messenger and take his request for Baal to join him in the throne room. He had no idea what for, but he wasn't about to screw it up.

Lucifer, for as long as he had been the almighty ruler of hell, had been keen to receive splendorous gifts and glorious tithings from his many slaves. Baal was not exempt to those expectations just because he sat on the council since he was still a slave—which is always wise to remember. He just had a bit more room to breathe. He ordered his chefs to prepare all sorts of delicacies to bring with him since he wanted to impress Lucifer. Despite what people said, he was not actually hard to please when it came to those sorts of things.

"Let's go, let's go," Baal roared, holding the door. His staff and chefs accompanied him to the throne room.

There was no way he would pull that off by himself, and he wanted to give Lucifer his utmost attention while there, so putting out all of the food and drink himself was not in the cards for him. It wasn't a big deal, though, since he had more than enough staff to fulfill his needs. It was getting them there on time that was worrying him. He knew how Lucifer felt about lateness.

Everything worked okay, though, and he arrived ten minutes early, enough time to be shown in while the chefs and servants set the luscious feast up on the long stone table that had been placed in the center of the room. It was almost as if Lucifer had known what he would do.

"Ah, Baal, I see you have brought the delicious cuisines of your personal chefs with you," Lucifer said, walking off the dais and waiting as the demon servants removed his robes, leaving him without a stitch of clothing.

He sat down, and Baal did the same. Lucifer sipped from his cup and stared at Baal for a moment. "This was good timing for your food. I have some news from Earth. Somehow those idiots managed to wake up a Leviathan. And not just any Leviathan, at that. Legion is on the loose."

Lucifer waved his hand, bringing up a view of the battle in the hills of Iraq. Baal watched with caution, knowing how powerful Legion could be. He had no soul. He could die, but when he did, he would not linger on any plane. And while he was alive, he didn't care about anything but himself. As they watched the fight, Mania scanned the food that Baal brought. With a sneer, she sat back down and ordered the servants to bring her the fruit she wanted. She wasn't into demon food; she made that perfectly clear.

Baal watched as Legion and his growing army added three more, all Damned, to the ranks, then turned one of Katie's top Damned. "That is Korbin, as in Korbin's Killers. The one who discovered Katie just moments after Lilith entered her body."

Lucifer nodded. "Yes. And that is impressive."

The fight cut out, and Baal put his paws together. "Do you wish me to help Legion?"

Lucifer sucked out the contents of the belly of an African toad and shook his head. "No. Other demons interfered on Earth, but it was never my command or my wish, nor would it have made any sort of impression on me had they succeeded."

Baal tilted his head to the side. "But I thought..."

Lucifer shrugged. "I have to have some entertainment. Why not watching the bumbling idiots around me waste their lives on this nonsense?" He pushed the plate away and slammed his fist on the table. "They were all fuck-ups, and some of them were even traitorous fuck-ups. I don't care about making hell on Earth. As a matter of fucking fact, I don't care about taking over that idiotic ball of rock. I rule here. HERE!"

Lucifer growled, pointing his talon at Baal and taking a deep breath, then letting it slowly out. Mania raised her head from her fruit plate. "Deep breaths, darling. Remember what the yogi taught you. You will only be successful if you learn to control your emotions. Put forth only what you want to."

Lucifer nodded as he took another breath and opened his eyes. He stared at Baal and grabbed a clawful of monkey brains. "What I want is my wife back at my side. That is *all* I want. I have been saying that since the beginning, but somehow my council believes they know better than I do what I want and need. Well, with your assistance, we got rid of the ones who couldn't figure that out, and now what I want is Lilith. Legion is stronger than everyone but me and Him, but we both know that Lilith will not sit back and let him turn her precious humans into slaves. If Legion assimilates Lilith, we will retrieve her and bring her here."

Baal shifted his eyes around. "Here? To hell?"

Lucifer nodded. "Yes, and she will heel at my request. She will do as *I* please, and she will proudly sit on that fucking throne I had made for her. There will be no more games, Baal. The time for that is over. Now I will focus on what is really important."

Brock slid across the ground on his knees, slicing his knife into one of the soldiers charging him in the two-second pause in his fight with Korbin. The soldier collapsed to the ground, screaming in agony. Brock hated it; he couldn't stand the sound. He picked his pistol up out of the dirt and put the last bullet into the soldier's head to spare him the pain.

He jumped back up and ran after Korbin, slashing his sword at him, only to be blocked and then pushed down. Korbin was deadly with his twin swords, making no movement without thought. Brock was barely able to hold him off with his broadsword, but he was almost out of ammo, and the rest was in the helicopter that had been overrun by Legion's soldiers.

Korbin waved his swords in front of him as he moved toward Brock with an intensity in his eyes he had not had before. Brock threw up his sword, blocking his followthrough. He struggled with Korbin for a moment, and then the two pushed each other off. Brock backed up, putting his hands up. "Korbin, please! I know you are still in there. Try to remember who you are. Try to remember fighting hard with Katie. Fighting against the demons for years. Think about falling in love with your beautiful wife, Stephanie, who is waiting for you at home."

His sword momentarily slowed down as Korbin paused, the images conjured by those words passing through his head. Brock slowly pulled his pistol out, running his eyes over Korbin. He didn't know if he could do it. He watched as Korbin shook out the thoughts he was trying so desperately to stop and growled, coming after him again. Brock scrunched his face. "I'm so sorry, brother. I'm *so* sorry."

Brock flinched as he pulled the trigger once, shifted, and pulled it again. The bullets hit Korbin in the knees and went out the backs. The pain from the special metal hit him first, and he fell face-down on the ground, shaking violently. Quickly Brock pulled some zip ties from the side of his bag and pulled his boss's arms to his back, fastening them tightly. He went back to his bag and grabbed the rope, hanging it over his shoulder.

He glanced back, seeing Legion emerge. Brock waited for Korbin to pick himself up, wobbling, then took off at full speed and launched into him. He gripped the restraints and ran as fast as he could. As he turned the corner, the rusty old pickup squealed its tires, coming to a stop right in front of him. He threw Korbin in the bed and tied him up really fast before closing the tailgate and getting into the cab.

The British guy took off, throwing up dust and rocks behind him as he raced off. Brock, hands shaking, grabbed his phone and dialed the general, trying to keep it together.

"Brock?"

Brock twitched, glancing back at Korbin in the bed of the truck. He was still bleeding. "General, I…"

"What is it? Is everything okay?"

Brock wiped the spit off his lips. "No. Things are real fucking bad here, sir, and I'm the only one still functioning. The three we brought are part of the army or dead, and Korbin… He needs a doctor really bad."

13

With his eyes closed, he could feel the surge of his demon rolling through him, fixing whatever was wrong. Korbin was in no pain at that moment, thanks to his demon. He moved his fingers, feeling a soft cotton sheet beneath him. In the background, he could hear sounds, people, footsteps, and possibly someone in a kitchen. He wasn't sure if he should open his eyes. He wasn't ready to fight anyone off if he were in danger.

Still, he couldn't just lie there with no idea what type of danger he was in. Slowly he opened his eyes, blinking wildly to clear his vision. His vision cleared and he looked at the ceiling, which was cracked and stained. His jaw closed and he smacked his lips, feeling the dryness and smelling the stench from his mouth. Carefully he turned his head to the side and looked around. It was a stone room with dirty, dusty floors, a dresser, and an Iraqi flag on the wall. Near his bed was an old wicker chair.

The sound of footsteps brought his attention to a door to the right of the bed. A shadow fell over the floor and

Korbin tensed, gripping the sheets. The sound of the stone scraping under boots heightened his awareness, but when Brock stepped around the corner, he let out a long, deep breath.

"Hey," Brock said excitedly. "You're still alive. That's good."

A small woman, her head draped in floral fabric and wearing a dress that went to the floor, looked at him. Brock put his hand gently on her shoulder. *"Rubama bed alma' walkhubz min shanih 'an yusaeid. Shukraan lab Abyha. Allah maeik."*

The woman bowed her head slightly, her eyes shifting wearily back to Korbin. *"Bialtabe bikuli takidin. Sa'ahdar alzaytun aydana. Tushibak alsalamat."*

Brock lowered his head to her as she hurried off. He turned back to Korbin and walked into the room, pulling the wicker chair up next to him. "How are you feeling?"

Korbin took in a deep breath and slowly pulled himself up, his back resting on the wall. "Okay. I think my demon is blocking almost everything."

Brock chuckled. "Well, at least your eyes are back to their creepy, beady red selves."

Korbin shook his head. "I never did like the color purple. How did you get it out of me?"

Brock shrugged. "I got you away. I think it's only if Legion can stay in close enough proximity to you. I'm not really sure, though."

The woman walked back in carrying a tray with water, bread, and olives on it. She set it down over Korbin's lap and poured water into the cup. Korbin bowed his head. *"Shukraan lakum."*

She stared at him for a moment and then at Brock, who bowed to her as well. She hurried from the room, closing the door behind her. Korbin took a piece of bread and bit into it. "Who is she?"

Brock looked up at the door. "Someone we can trust. Someone who has ties to the general and American soldiers. She is only a few miles from where Legion was."

Korbin sipped his water. "Legion. What a damn mess."

Brock rubbed his face. He was now dressed in a long black tunic, black pants made out of a light fabric, and sandals. "That was the craziest shit I have seen out here. He seriously turned you with a look, although I thought at first he was going to kill you."

Korbin bit an olive, his eyes slightly glazed. "Everything seems so jumbled, like it happened in slow motion with my eyes closed. I remember my demon being terrified, trying to bring me back but then succumbing to the powers too. I felt no pain or no fear, but I was also very confused. It was like my life was no longer my own. I don't know. I want to think it over more before I explain. Maybe give my mind a moment to straighten out."

Brock crossed his legs and leaned back in the chair, looking at his phone. "I have to go cut wood soon for Abyha. She was the wife of an Iraqi ally who worked within the government and gave massive amounts of intel to the US during the invasion. He was killed in the line of duty about three years ago, so the US made sure Abyha got to safety. They lost their daughter to bombs about six months before her husband died. She may live all alone in the tiny stone house, but she is widely respected and hates rebels. But if she helps you, she also puts you to work."

Korbin chuckled. "That's good for you. You'll get a little exercise."

Brock snorted. "Yes, because carrying your ass while running from Legion wasn't enough exercise."

Korbin laughed and then frowned. "Carried my ass? Why were you…"

Brock grimaced as Korbin sorted out the facts in his head. After a few moments, Korbin snapped his face to Brock's. "Wait a minute. You *shot* me!"

Brock wrinkled his nose. "I know, I know. But I swear it was for a really good reason."

Korbin threw back the covers and carefully inspected the white linen pants he had been dressed in, which had gauze around them. Brock put out his hand. "The wounds are pretty much healed, but the outside is still bleeding. I am assuming your demon had to fix you from the inside out. By the time you are ready to get up, they will be fully healed."

Korbin furrowed his brow. "They?" He looked at his other pant leg, finding another thick piece of gauze. "You shot me twice? In the knees?"

Brock pointed at him. "Technically, yes, but it was for a really good reason."

"I think I get to shoot you now. It's only fair," Korbin replied.

Brock raised an eyebrow. "But I'm not assimilated."

Korbin thought about it for a moment. "Okay, you're right, so this is what we'll do. I'll fly your ass back out there, drop you into Legion, and *then* shoot you. That will make us square. Better?"

Brock blinked, shaking his head. "I still don't feel great

about it, no."

A portal shimmered open, and Katie, Pandora, and Juntto stepped through, carrying their weapons. All three of them covered their mouths, and Katie jumped back as a rat the size of a Saint Bernard strolled past her, its tail nearly knocking her over. "Jesus!"

Pandora shrugged. "What I thought was my favorite dimension doesn't have donuts. We can never go back there. It hurts so much, still. So we get giant evil rat dimensions now. I just don't care."

Katie shook her head as she opened another portal. "You need to get over it."

Stepping out onto the dusty, stony ground, Katie, Pandora, and Juntto looked around. The area was made up of rolling hills, part of it deep green and the rest brown and dusty. The only road near them was a small dirt one, evident from the tracks of tires rather than of a groomed surface. A small goat ran between them, and the sound of wood splitting turned them around.

The portal snapped shut, revealing a small stone house with Brock standing out front, a scarf over his mouth and nose, dressed in a flowing tunic and pants. He threw a piece of wood into a pile and leaned on the axe, pulling his handkerchief from over his nose and mouth. "*'Ahlaan bik.*"

Katie smiled and hurried over, hugging him tightly. A

small woman shrouded in fabric came outside, nodding at Katie and Pandora. She put her hands out to them and pulled them along. *"Sawf yaqtaluk 'iidha kunt talbis mithl hdha huna. Euqul saghirat jiddaan fi albilad."*

Pandora smirked, and Katie looked at her, confused. "What is she saying?"

"Basically, we can't go rolling around the countryside in Iraq like two-bit whores, so we need to put the jigglies away and cover our sacred crowns," Pandora replied.

The woman quickly pulled out two large scarves and wrapped Katie's head, tucking the bottom of the scarf loosely into the neck to create a billow of fabric over her heaving cleavage. She did the same for Pandora, but she had to start over with a bigger one that would stretch that far. Pandora's tits were monumental in size.

Pandora took the woman's hands and bowed slightly to her, thanking her for both herself and Katie in Arabic. They were then led into the house, where they found Brock washing his hands in a bowl of water and Korbin sitting up, looking a little worse for wear.

Katie hurried over to Korbin. "Are you all right? What happened?"

Korbin nodded, patting her hand. "I'm all right, just a bit tired. My demon healed all my wounds, even the ones I got from friendly fire." He darted his eyes at Brock.

Brock shrugged. "I had to shoot him to get him away. He went all purple-eyed and became a ninja sword master."

Pandora sat down in the chair by the bed. "What did it feel like?"

Korbin looked down at his hands. "It was terrible. Legion woos you. He uses your sympathy and compassion to get you to willingly submit to his collective. There are no commands or discourse. His words seem to pulsate through you."

Katie thought about it for a second. "Okay, then how does he make you do these things?"

Korbin shook his head. "He doesn't. He doesn't make you do anything. That is almost scarier than if he was controlling your every movement."

Katie glanced around at the others. "I don't understand."

"When you submit to his collective, it's almost like a powerful drug surging through your body. The stronger ones are able to handle it, using that drug to fuel them. The weak struggle with their bodies, trying to fight back. That is why they look like zombies, but when Legion calls, they muster the strength," Korbin explained, getting off the bed and limping to the window. "He doesn't have to make you do a thing because the reality of it is, you want to. All the loyalty and sympathy you may have had for the world now includes only those in Legion's army. That way you submit to the collective. You aren't yourself anymore. You are Legion; you are his army, you are part of him, you feel his emotions, and you never fear him."

Pandora got up and put her hand on Korbin's shoulder, sending a comforting vibe through him. He patted her hand with a thankful smile as she turned to Brock and Katie. "This is one of the most dangerous Leviathans. Not because of his strength or size. Not because of his magical powers or ability to persuade, but because as humans, we only put our all into something if we one hundred percent believe it. The enchantment or whatever you want to call the purple haze makes the human only believe in Legion and his soldiers."

Katie's heart beat a bit faster. "Have you experienced it, Pandora?"

She shook her head. "Not personally, but I have seen the handiwork of someone who has. A man allowed it inside of him, and when he could not capture his wife and two small children to take them to Legion, he killed them all with an axe and then burned the house down. His family refused to be taken, so therefore, they were no longer his family. He did not bat an eyelash, not until Legion went into hibernation again and the haze wore off. Then he couldn't live with himself. It didn't take them long to find him hanging in the tree at the site of his burned-down house."

Everyone was silent.

Pandora crossed her arms. "He could end these times."

Legion and his army marched forward, having left their dead behind and abandoned the search for the humans who had attacked them. There were far more important things on Legion's list than using his collective for small and uninteresting assaults. He led the way, wrapping his gauze tighter around him as the sun beat down. Those within the collective had stripped out of their heavy uniform jackets, cooling their bodies the best way they knew how.

Several miles into their trip, they dipped down into a valley and went over to a very small airfield. They crossed the airfield toward the main hangar bay, where the sound of clinking tools could be heard. Legion put one arm up, his voice a whisper in the ears of his collective. "Stayyyy…"

Alone, Legion glided into the hangar, stopping at the door. To the right were two mechanics, chuckling as they put their tools in the right spots. To his left was a jet, the pilot standing on the steps and speaking on the phone in Arabic. He got off the phone and waved his hand at Legion. "Who the fuck are you? Do you know whose plane this is? This belongs to the Hussain family. The great Saddam himself once rode in it. You dare bring your disease in here? Leave at once!"

The two mechanics grabbed wrenches and walked toward him. Legion put his right arm out and the wrenches flew from their hands, slamming into the walls. He kept his hand out as the two mechanics tried to charge him. As soon as they stepped close, he grabbed their necks, and their eyes went wide as they choked. The pilot tried to run, but Legion was smarter. He whipped his left hand around and flipped the pilot upside down, floating him over to the two mechanics.

Slowly he glided forward, his bright purple eyes shining in the darkness of the hangar. He leaned in and whispered to them, "We. Are. Legion."

All of their eyes changed and shimmered as their bodies convulsed, trying to fight it off. Finally, they went still, and Legion righted their stances. The mechanics grabbed their things and entered the staff part of the plane while the pilot walked up the steps and hurried to the cockpit. Legion waved to his followers as he boarded the large jet.

The army of men took their seats, their heads back on

the rests, staring at Legion. Vinders sat in the front row with two others who had strong abilities. Legion spoke to them out loud for the first time. His deep, raspy voice wavered through the air like a thick fog. "Where will we find proper armies for Legion?"

Several of the army members began to speak up, calling out from their seats in monotone voices. He got conflicting reports from them ranging from Texas to Japan to Quebec. Finally another voice, stronger than the others, spoke up. "The Damned. There is a fort in Romania filled with Damned. They are all young and barely trained, and will be easy to bring to the Legion. Their demon strength will heighten their fighting abilities."

Legion turned to Vinders, who had stood as he spoke and moved in front of him. Vinders stood at attention like a good soldier while Legion's bright purple eyes scanned him from top to bottom. The Leviathan reached slowly up with his gauze-covered arm and ran his finger down Vinders' face. "You are yourself Damned, is this not true?"

Vinders' eyes flashed from purple to red. "That I am."

Legion nodded. "Yes, I like this idea. A Legion of both Damned and non-Damned alike. We can take others in Romania." He moved back over in front of the others and Vinders sat down again, still staring straight ahead. "We need a strong army. We are not just Legion; we will be the new race upon this planet, and those that do not wish to conform will be brought in with force. But once they see the ways, *our* ways, they will happily allow themselves to be sacrificed for the cause."

Legion walked to the empty seat next to Vinders and

eyed him for a moment before taking it. "You will be my aide. My extension."

Vinders bowed his head. "I am honored."

Legion's voice turning raspy and deep again, traveling all over the plane and through the cockpit doors. "Close the plane doors, and plot a course for the fort in Romania."

One of the Legion soldiers got up and went over, closing and latching the door. The pilot had heard him and started warming up the plane; he then pulled up a map and typed in the specific coordinates that would bring them as close to the fort in Romania as they could get. The plane moved slowly out of the hangar bay and began to taxi out onto the runway.

As the plane began to take off, whimpering could be heard coming from behind a dumpster back by the hangar. A man's hand gripped the edge as he slowly peeked around it, blinking hard and watching Legion leave. Once the plane was in the air, a janitor, scared shitless, stumbled onto the tarmac. He fell to all fours and threw up, coughing and weeping.

He sat back on his feet and wiped his face, watching as the plane went higher and higher, becoming nothing more than a trail in front of him. Scrambling to his feet, he hurried inside, using the key on his chain to unlock the office. He locked it behind him and grabbed the phone, pulling it down to the floor. His hands shook as he dialed the numbers, knowing exactly who he needed to call. He hadn't always been a janitor, and he knew that the plane they were on was secretly being tracked for other reasons.

14

The general wiped his forehead as he typed quickly, trying to get the mundane portions of his job done and submitted. He had many other things to worry about, but he could not hand off the reports for several different sectors of the government when it came to the war and to the happenings around the country to his aides.

His secretary came over the comm. "General, you have a Liwa Farad on the line from the Iraqi Ground Force Operations Office."

The general raised an eyebrow. "Thank you."

He paused to gather himself before picking up the phone. "This is General Brushwood."

"General, this is Liwa Farad with the Ground Force Operations Office. We discovered through an informant that a plane has been stolen from a small but influential airfield outside Al Fatsi. This was the same field that housed, and apparently still does, the Hussain family jets, although we don't believe there is any connection with the family."

Brushwood rubbed his face. "Did the informant give you any information about who was on the plane?"

Farad cleared his throat uncomfortably. "Actually yes. Apparently, there were what looked like more than a dozen men with military-issue fatigues and boots, although none of them had anything with an insignia on it, and also several Iraqi farmers, from what it looks like. He said they all acted a bit strange, and their eyes glowed purple. We were told to contact you specifically."

The general shook his head. "You did the right thing. I will get on this immediately, and if you acquire any more information, please either give my office a call or send me a direct email."

They hung up, and he sat there for several moments, thinking about what was going on. There was still no mention of a Leviathan, but there was little else that could explain the events that were unfolding. The secretary came back on again. "I'm sorry to bother you again, General, but Katie is on line one, and it is urgent."

He picked up the phone immediately. "Katie. What do you have?"

"Korbin is on here with me as well," Katie replied. "We have unfortunate news. Legion, the Leviathan, is loose, and he's most likely on a plane that was just stolen from a small airport in Iraq."

The general's heart sank. "I just got a call about the plane. Is the rest of the collective with him on the plane?"

Korbin spoke. "Yes, General, at least most of them. We were able to take down several before I was assimilated and Brock pulled me out. Thank you, by the way, for a safe place to lay low. As of when we left them, there were dozens of men in his army, and by now there could be dozens more. They are innocent, but they have been overtaken and will stop at nothing to protect the Legion."

Brushwood glanced out the window as a plane flew high. "This is unfortunate."

"General," Korbin said, taking the phone off speaker, "I think it important that you consider the course of the plane, and although it is not what we want, don't allow that plane to land."

He gripped a pen in his fist. "I know. I know. I want to preserve life and save the innocent, but at what cost to others? I am pretty sure I can prevent that plane from landing. Send your prayers to those men. I'll contact you shortly."

The general hung up and sat in the silence of his office, staring into the distance. He had to get on top of things, but in a moment of decision like that, all he could do was let the silence comfort him. Slowly he reached over and pressed the secretary's comm button. "I will need you to call the contact for the World Council. Tell them I am calling an emergency meeting in twenty minutes. If they cannot be there in person, we will have them conference in. This is a high-level alert."

Her voice wavered slightly. "Yes, sir."

The general didn't sit down, and he didn't stand behind a podium. Instead, he planted his feet in the middle of the room, looking at the rows of council and sub-council members hurrying to their seats. One of the aides walked up and whispered into the general's ear. "Everyone is either here or conferenced in now. You may begin."

"Thank you," he said, waiting for him to take his seat before turning to the council. "Esteemed members of the World Council, I have called this emergency meeting because we are currently caught in a very unfortunate situation. Someone orchestrated the theft and implementation of technology that was restricted from council use. With this technology, they were able to locate a slumbering Leviathan named Legion. They then proceeded to send two separate unauthorized teams out to take him out."

He shifted his eyes around the room. "These strikes failed. Currently, we have a very dangerous Leviathan and dozens of soldiers assimilated from British military and US military forces on a plane heading toward Romania. This situation is dire, and decisions cannot wait. It is with grave disappointment and heartache that I bring my recommendation to the table. We cannot let the plane land. This Leviathan is stronger than any other we have faced, and has the ability to create a conscript with a single whisper. We need to keep this collective from growing."

The council all started speaking among themselves. They all seemed to be nodding their heads. The German president, once everyone had turned back around in their seats, leaned forward. "We agree with your recommendation and are putting in an order as we speak with the council's strike forces. Jets must be dispatched to take the plane down. Do we know where it currently is?"

Brushwood grabbed his tablet, flipping it over and allowing the tracking map to reload. "It looks as if they are currently over Greece and moving into Serbia."

The German president nodded. "Alert both countries of incoming military forces. We will stop this in its tracks."

Sirens blasted on an airbase in Greece. The closest forces to the plane were Greek. The US planes were just too far away at that point. The roar of jet engines echoed across the field as several of them burned down the runway and took flight.

Inside the Legion jet, the men sat unseeing or slept as they made their way to Romania. The pilot came over the speaker. "We have company; three Greek jets blasting toward us, all highly armed."

Legion turned and looked out the window at the planes coming for them. He tried to take control using his powers, but he was too far from them. For items that large, he would need to be closer and more stable. Suddenly shots rang out and the jet veered right and left, attempting to avoid the battery of bullets, but the jet wasn't made for fighting. It was a luxury vehicle.

The fighter pilots had spread out behind the jet and switched from guns to missiles. The center pilot called over on his comm to the other pilots, "Locked and loaded."

The one to his right gave him a thumbs-up. "Locked and loaded."

The pilot to his left did the same and repeated, "Locked and loaded."

The center pilot pulled down the visor on his helmet, holding the stick firm in his hands. "On my count, take this sonofabitch down. God bless our soldiers and the innocent men aboard. The angels will weep tonight. Three, two, one...*FIRE!*"

All three planes sent missiles at the jet. The first one hit the tail of the plane, knocking it off. The other two took out the wings and half the cockpit, maiming the pilot. The three fighters backed off, watching the plane immediately begin a spiral, both debris and the pilot dislodging and flying out of the plane as it went down. The pilots kept their eyes on it until the plane hit the ground below and burst into flames. "Target is down."

The crash sent a fireball shooting high into the sky. The mountainous terrain was covered with bodies and debris. Those in the front section of the plane had been incinerated on impact from the temperature of the jet-fuel-fed flames. A few people in the back corners were still alive, but very injured. They pulled off their seatbelts, climbing over pieces of bodies and stumbling away from the wall of smoke.

Vinders shook his head and opened his eyes. He was staring at Legion, who looked to be unconscious in his seat, which was no longer attached to the plane. Another guy came running up, reaching for Vinders' belt and unlatching him. He turned to leave, but Vinders grabbed his shirt, nodding at Legion. Their eyes sparkled purple as they raced through the flames, unbuckling the Leviathan and pulling him from the wreckage and out of the smoke.

Legion coughed and wheezed, floating above the ground with his back to a tree. The other survivors stood at his will, waiting for instructions. Legion's eyes opened and shimmered, and he let out a deep and profound laugh. Slowly the gauze began to unravel from his face, falling into a pile at his feet.

Vinders glanced up but immediately looked down. Legion was no longer a decayed corpse, but had the face of an emaciated little boy with deep purple eyes and a smirk on his lips. Vinders grabbed the fallen gauze and began to wrap his body again, leaving his face free. The gauze clung to his decaying skin. He led the survivors forward, marching through the valley to the base of the mountains. As they entered you could hear the men whispering,

"We. Are. Legion."

Brock, Korbin, Pandora, Katie, and Juntto sat around the bed, talking about the Leviathan, as well as a slew of other things. They were waiting for word from the general.

Juntto held up his hand and turned it front to back. "So, you see, if you use the palms, it will smash, but if you press with the backs of your hands, you will keep the juices in the dish while still creating a smoky flavor."

Korbin's phone rang and he held it up, quieting everyone and turning on the speaker. "This is Korbin and the rest of us."

Pandora snorted. "I love being grouped into 'the rest of us.'"

Katie shushed her as the general came over the speaker. "We have taken the plane down. It took just a few maneuvers and three missiles. The pilot tried to evade, but the jet was incapable of that type of maneuvering. It exploded in a ball of flames on the ground."

Brock spoke up. "Any survivors?"

"We are unsure at this time."

Katie nodded. "All right, we'll go take a look and see what we can find. We'll report back to you, sir. You did the right thing."

Brushwood cleared his throat. "Let's hope so."

They disconnected and Katie got up, joining Pandora and Juntto in the middle of the room. "We'll be back soon. Rest up, Korbin. We need you in one piece."

Pandora opened up a portal and stepped through, followed by Juntto and Katie. Before the portal could close, Brock jumped through as well, grabbing Katie by the arm. She stopped and looked at him in confusion. "You should stay with Korbin."

Brock nodded. "I am, but you can't go there. I've seen what they do. Legion might take you over. It happens in an instant. That would be a really terrible thing for you, and not just because no one wants to go through that."

Katie pursed her lips. "Then why?"

Brock's eyes shifted to Pandora and back to Katie. "Because you are one of the most powerful beings on Earth. With someone like Legion controlling you, there is a chance you could destroy entire cities and civilizations. And…" Brock looked down at the ground. "And because I love you. You have so much love and compassion inside of you, and that is exactly what Legion feeds off. He takes that and twists it, focusing it only on those within his army. You literally *cannot* feel for anyone else. Legion will use your good side against you until it is gone. What I saw with

Korbin was not only unbelievable but fucking terrifying. Let them check it out first."

Katie stared at him. She had heard everything, but was still stuck on the fact that he'd said he loved her. She wanted to say it back, but since she was standing in some random dimension up to her knees in what looked like orange juice—but from the smell, she knew it definitely wasn't—she figured it might not be the right time.

His words filtered through her brain, not just the love part, but all of it—the effect Legion had on other people and the way he used compassion and caring. She did care a lot. She did do what she did for the love of humanity. "Gabriel, the angel? He told me something one time, and until now it just sounded like one of those sweet memes you scroll past on Facebook. He said that my greatest strength would also be my greatest weakness."

Brock nodded. "And I would say that two of your greatest strengths are your compassion, and caring for other's lives." Brock put his hand on her cheek. "We all care for you so much, and you have to allow us to try to keep you safe when we can, even if it's little things like this."

A smile pulled at her lips and she leaned her face into his hand, feeling the warmth of his palm. In reality, the only thing she wanted to do at that moment—besides get out of the OJ pool—was be with him and let him protect her.

Pandora sighed, rolling her eyes, and opened a portal into Serbia. She grabbed Juntto and pulled him toward it. "Let's leave these two gross lovebirds in their own dimension."

They stepped through and let the portal close, leaving

Katie behind. Pandora's aim had become pretty good. They came out just a hundred feet from the wreckage. It was blazing and smoking, and there were small pieces all over the place. They steadied themselves and walked through, looking for any sign of life.

Pandora picked up the headrest of a chair with what seemed to be a part of a hairy scalp burned into it. "I don't know if anyone could have survived this, but if they did, they aren't here anymore."

Juntto's eyes narrowed, looking at tracks leading away from the blaze. "He made it, all right. The question is, what will his next move be?"

Back in the UK, things took on a rushed tone. Powell pulled his suitcase from his closet and threw it on his bed, shoving balled-up clothes in. He was going to escape; he wasn't going down for what had happened. He had done what they wanted him to do—for money, but still. How was he supposed to know they hadn't had the proper permission?

A knock on the door echoed through his condo. He groaned, shutting and latching his suitcase. Hurrying over, he looked through the peephole to see his dominatrix standing there with bright red lipstick on her pursed lips. For a moment, he thought about just one more time, but he wasn't sure he would have that time to spare. He unlocked the door and opened it as he walked away. "I appreciate you checking in, but I don't have time to play today."

"I don't know about that. I think you'll have plenty of time in prison," a man's voice said.

Powell froze and turned around slowly, finding his domme standing there with four military men in full uniform. He swallowed hard, staring at them, unsure of exactly what to do. However, he didn't really need to think, since the RAF was there to take him in. Two of the guys approached with their hands on their guns, but Powell didn't resist. He put his hands up and allowed them to search and then cuff him.

One of the other guys walked up and smirked. "You are under arrest, by the authority of the RAF. If you want counsel, you may ask for one. You have the right to remain silent, and anything you say can be used against you in a court of law. I don't think you'll be needing that suitcase. We have an outfit laid out for you."

His domme, her arms crossed and a smile on her face, gave him a wink. "Looks like you've been a very bad boy."

General Brushwood plopped down in his office chair, splashing bourbon on his pants. "Goddamn it! Fucking shit. I can't catch a damn break."

He swiped at the wet spots and shrugged, taking a long sip. He was drinking for two reasons: his guilt for shooting down the plane, and in celebration of catching Powell. He was a small fish, though; just some guy hired to pull off the deal. Now what they needed to do was catch the whole school of sharks and show them exactly what kind of punishment awaited those who put the entire world at risk.

15

Katie beat her wings hard, giving herself a boost high above the Serbian landscape. Pandora flew beside her, looking around for any sign of Legion and his army. Brock and Juntto were following them on land and Juntto had grown to twelve feet, putting Brock on his shoulders so they could not fall too far behind the girls. They too had their eyes peeled for any sign or evidence that Legion had come that way. Things were starting to get dreary, everyone depressed by the thought of the Leviathan building a new army of followers.

Pandora glanced at Katie, who was staring to the left, combing the tree line of a small patch of woods. "You okay?"

Katie looked at her and nodded. "I'm fine. I'm not happy that we had to kill all those people, but we figured there was no way we could let them get on the ground and mobilize quickly. We may not have stopped Legion, but we have to have slowed him down to some extent. There were a lot of bodies—and ashes of bodies—at the crash scene."

Pandora looked to her right and flipped her feet down. Katie glanced over her shoulder and swerved around, flying up next to her. "What are you doing?"

Pandora pursed her lips. "Looks like it didn't slow him down too much."

She pointed, and Katie followed her finger. In the distance, they could see a huge mass of people moving across the countryside. Katie narrowed her eyes. "They are headed straight for Romania."

Pandora nodded. "That they are, and by the looks of it, the Legion army has grown exponentially. They must be picking up Serbs as they go."

Someone whistled below them, and they glanced down to see Juntto setting Brock on the ground. As Pandora and Katie descended, Pandora clicked her tongue. "Juntto is faster than I thought he would be, especially carrying a grown man on his shoulder."

They landed, and Katie nodded in the direction of the army. "There is a huge group right over that hill, and they are heading for Romania. I think we need to figure out where Legion is and come up with a targeting plan for them."

Brock nodded. "What the hell is in Romania that Legion wants?"

Pandora shook her head. "Not wants, but needs. Legion's whole MO is to build his army as fast and large as possible, eventually bringing *everyone* into it. Once that is done, he can rule whatever he wants. But he is a scavenger, and always has been. Romania has something that not everyone has."

Katie tilted her head back. "Ohhhh—the fort. The first

one Korbin built, and the one that has the biggest group of Damned soldiers because they've been recruiting since Korbin moved on. They want the Damned for their army. They want the humans with the most strength and power, and those are the ones with a smidgen of hell inside them."

Brock groaned. "Romania was where we started. He built that fort to keep demons out, and this is the second one to attack it."

Pandora cracked her neck and her knuckles. "Legion doesn't give a shit if the town is already devastated. He cares about what he can get from it. There will be a lot of compassion and caring there at this point. The attack was very recent, and a very sensitive topic for the people. These Damned are built for this, selected carefully from those who applied."

"And Legion wants the ones that are the strongest. He doesn't want the regular humans when he can have those with superhuman powers, and that means the Damned," Katie replied.

Brock put his gun in its holster. "Look, I know all of you want to roll in and take them out before they can do more damage, but we are setting ourselves up for disaster. It is not a good idea for any of us to engage Legion's army. They are far too strong, especially with Legion in their ranks. They have nothing to fear, and nothing to lose. Legion can assimilate any of us with a few words."

Katie groaned. "There has to be some way around this. Obviously, he was awake at some other point in history, but he didn't kill off the human race or turn us all into zombies. There isn't a creature alive that doesn't have a weak spot somewhere. I will not be forced to be some mindless drone."

"Remember what Korbin said," Brock replied. "They don't force you to join. There is no pushing or bullying. Whatever Legion does to people instantly makes them want to join. They *want* to be in what they feel is their family. It's apparently a no-brainer, and you cannot turn away from them."

Pandora snickered. "Man, I wish I had that power over men. There would be dicks flying everywhere. I could give them as gifts. *You* get a dick, and *you* get a dick."

Katie turned to Pandora with a deadpan look. "Could you maybe try to contribute to the discussion?"

Pandora rolled her eyes. "Fine. I actually have an idea. It definitely has the potential to work, but it also has the potential to be a really bad idea."

"Korbin," one of the young officers said, nodding as he passed.

Korbin nodded back, continuing down the corridor in a US Army shirt and a pair of PT shorts. He didn't have any of his stuff with him, and his pack had been abandoned in the rush to get him away from Legion. When he finally had felt well enough to move, the army had sent a convoy out to pick him up and drive him over to the US Army base nearby for the time being. They had all been really nice, but he was starting to get antsy.

He made his way back to his room and closed the door, letting out a sigh. It had been a long time since he had slept on a military bed with bad springs and scratchy blankets, but it was better than cuddling up to Legion. He sat down on the bed and picked up the phone, dialing out to the US. His line was secure since he talked to the general as well as the mercenary base, so he wasn't worried about it.

"Hello?" Stephanie's voice was like music to his ears.

"Hey, beautiful," he replied.

He could hear her let out a long sigh. The general had kept her up to speed on what was going on, but it was the first time he had gotten to talk to her. "I hope I didn't wake you."

Stephanie scoffed. "Like I could sleep with everything going on. I have been dying to hear how you are doing. I'm assuming you made it to the base safely?"

Korbin ran his finger over the bubbled paint on the bedside table. "I did. Then I saw the doctor, and I just got back to my room. He said everything looked good. My demon handled the gunshot wounds, and there were no other side effects that he could see."

"Good," she said with relief. "I still don't understand what you were thinking, busting into the group like that with no idea what they were capable of."

Korbin chuckled. "You would have done the same thing —made sure the civilians were okay. Well, military and civilians."

Stephanie huffed. "Yes, well, do as I say, not as I do."

Korbin laughed. "Yes, ma'am. I actually called to tell you something."

"What's that?" she asked in a softer tone.

Korbin leaned back against the wall. "When it all happened and Legion got me, for a minute there I wasn't

Korbin anymore. My only thoughts were on the Legion. But that only lasted for a minute. When I came back to my old self again, I realized how much I love and miss you. I yearn to be near you. When I got back from the doctor and was by myself for the first time in years, I just needed to hear your voice."

Stephanie was silent for a moment. "I love you too, more than you know. When the general called and told me what had happened, I didn't know what to do with myself. He didn't want me to come out, and there needed to be someone here to protect the base anyway, but I just wanted to be with you. I laid in bed imagining myself next to you. I hope you felt me with you."

Korbin smiled. "I always feel you with me, although I do wish I could *feel* you with me, if you know what I mean."

"I love you too, sweetie. Talk to you soon. Bye," Stephanie said sometime later, holding the phone with both hands as she hung up.

She paused, keeping her hands on the receiver and her head down. Hearing Korbin's voice had been almost debilitating. There was a time where being away from each other was fine. They were both okay. But as the war progressed and every job was more dangerous, she wanted to bring him home and keep him at the base. Keep him safe. Even with all the danger, all the deaths, all the wild rides, it had never crossed her mind she might one day lose him—not until she'd gotten that call from the general.

She took her hands off the receiver, and as soon as she

stood up, the tears flowed. She had been so strong for so long, but she couldn't hold it in anymore. She stood in the middle of her office crying.

Coming from the workout room, Eddie whistled as he walked. He tossed his towel over his shoulder and pulled his phone from his pocket. Flipping through the pictures on his fake Facebook account, he laughed to himself, finding the memes even more amusing that day. He passed an open door but didn't go in. However, as he reached the other side, he heard someone sobbing. He stopped, listening for it again. Sure enough, a second later a small whimper like the squeak of a mouse hit his ears.

Backing up, he looked into Stephanie's office, finding her standing in the middle of the floor with her face in her hands and her shoulders shaking. He looked awkwardly down the hall and then stepped into the room. "Are you all right?"

Stephanie sniffed and looked at him, her eyes red and tears streaming down her face. She turned and walked straight up to him, wrapping her arms around his body and laying her face on his chest. Eddie put his hands out and kept his eyes open wide. *Oh shit, oh shit, what the hell am I supposed to do?*

Coco sighed. *Seriously? Now, I know you don't have a ton of experience with girls. Don't argue, I can hear your thoughts. But at this point, you need to not be a fucking jackass and hug her back.*

Eddie twisted his lips, looking down at the top of her head. Slowly he brought his arms in, elbows out, and patted her on the back.

Katie, Pandora, Juntto, and Brock stood inside of the gates of the US army base Korbin had been moved to. Katie and Pandora released their angel armor and folded their wings in. A corporal walked up and smiled at them. "If you will follow me, we have your bunks all made up. I'm sorry we didn't have the room for all of you to have your own space, so we had to double-bunk you in trailers. You are right down from Korbin, though."

Pandora snarked, "Oh, boy, roomies again. I bet you are very excited."

Katie yawned. "Right now, I would bunk with Juntto if it meant a bed and some sleep."

They were all showed to their bunks and then taken over to the only permanent building on the lot, which was right next to where their rooms were. The corporal talked as he walked. "This base was originally set up during the invasion, and it was a landscape of tents. Then, when no one was pulled out, they started sending builders over and placing trailers on the land for us. Then they got the word that they would be creating a permanent base. This building was the first to be finished. They are working on the barracks now."

They walked down the hall and waited for Korbin to answer the door. "Hey guys, glad you made it back. Come on in."

They piled into Korbin's room and took seats wherever they could. Korbin put his hands in his pockets. "What did you figure out?"

Katie shook her head. "Well, we found them, and they

are definitely heading to Romania. The worst of it is, we aren't sure how to stop them. Pandora thinks she has come up with something that might work, but it's dangerous."

Brock chuckled. "When is any of this stuff *not* dangerous?"

Pandora stood up and tugged her top down, trying to look professional. She put her palms together and began to pace the floor. "So, I have a plan that, much like me, is brilliant and amazing but a bit dangerous."

Brock looked at Katie and laughed quietly. Katie just smiled and shook her head.

Pandora cleared her throat loudly, staring at her. "As I was saying, brilliance is divine, which is probably why I am an angel. Anyway, not the point. I explained, and it is historically known, that Legion and his army work on compassion. Well, if you are going to send someone in there to face them, you wouldn't pick someone like Katie, a weepy sack of emotion and love."

Katie faked a cough. "Send Pandora."

Pandora shook her head. "I too have compassion. It is one of my many sparkling qualities. So, if you are going to send someone, or multiple people, you need to make sure that they are a bunch of hard-hearted motherfuckers who aren't going to give him an ounce of compassion. They need to be people Legion cannot control."

Korbin folded his arms. "Okay, who?"

Pandora smiled, pointing. "Juntto. Not him specifically, because love has made him into a sappy asshole. But frost giants from his planet—a whole bunch of them. Those angry, psycho, uncaring blue sonsabitches that don't have an ounce of compassion in their bodies. Those are the heroes of our motherfucking stories."

Korbin furrowed his brow. "And given they are like Juntto used to be, no offense, how exactly do you convince them to come over here and fight for us? They don't care about us either."

Juntto stood up, joining Pandora in the middle of the floor. "So, there are multiple layers to this, but first I would need to make it to my dimension. Apparently, Katie and Pandora have seen it before. Then, if I get there, I may be able to offer up Earth to some of my people. If I told them that Legion was the current ruler, they would go out of their way to kill the Leviathan, thinking there would be a big treasure at the end. My people were built to conquer and take what they want. They have been doing it since the first frost giant appeared."

Pandora wrinkled her nose. "Which came first, the frost giant or the egg?"

Juntto blinked at her with a blank face. "We don't have eggs."

"Yeah, I know, it was a..." Pandora waved her hands. "Never mind. Not worth it."

Brock wasn't convinced. "How do you know that they will be immune to Legion? His reputation precedes him, and very few people who get near him can withstand his need for more bodies for his army."

Juntto smiled. "I guess I don't know for sure. How would I? There has never been a Leviathan like that in my homeland. But I do know that I have all the skills of my people—the cooking, fighting, gathering, and hunting—

and his charms don't seem to work on me. He looked straight at me during the scouting trip, and I felt nothing.

"I personally think that they might have a chance at beating Legion. In fact, the frost giants might be our best chance at beating him before he makes it to Romania to recruit those Damned for his army."

Korbin glanced at Katie. "What do you think?"

Katie shrugged. "I'm not sure. It sounds like a solid plan, but only because I have seen Juntto at his work. But all in all, I don't know. Personally, I think we should do it. There is no better way of figuring shit out than trial and error."

Juntto clapped his hands. "That's right."

Korbin shrugged his shoulders. "What do you say, Brock?"

Brock smiled at Katie. "I'm down with whatever she thinks is safe and might work."

Korbin nodded, putting his hands out. "I guess we give this a shot then, but we need to take it carefully, you understand? Replacing Leviathans with rampaging frost giants is definitely not our goal."

Pandora excitedly jumped up and down. "Let's get this show on the road, then!"

Katie and Pandora stood side by side with Juntto and Brock behind them, and Pandora waved her arms and opened a portal.

16

Katie, Pandora, Juntto, and Brock stepped out of the portal onto the sidewalk in front of the building where the general worked. Several people around them froze in place, whispering to each other and jumping as the portal slammed closed behind them. Pandora picked some leaves out of her hair. "I don't know what dimension that was, but I never want to go hiking again."

Katie snorted. "Like you ever wanted to go hiking in the first place. And let me just say, usually hiking doesn't require leaping from a huge tree carrying a frost giant and a human and flying straight into a portal because giant sharp-toothed beavers with monkey arms are trying to kill you."

Juntto shivered. "That was scary."

Brock chuckled, patting him on the shoulder. "It's all right, buddy. You're safe now."

The four of them stared at each other for a moment, then went into the building. They walked through Security, who knew not to ask for weapons, and headed toward

Brushwood's office. On their way, they managed to run into every assistant that he had, each trying to keep them out of his office. They all knew just how stressed the General was. By the time they got to the waiting area, Pandora was threatening the nutsack of one of the guys, and Juntto was carrying a woman by the back of the shirt.

The general opened his door and raised an eyebrow. "I see you've met my assistants. Juntto, drop her."

Juntto sighed and obeyed, patting the aide on the top of the head. They all filed into the general's digs, Pandora sneering at the one assistant who was now fearful that all of his children would be born with dicks as fingers. She leaned into Katie. "They think I am a witch, not an angel."

Katie leaned back. "You are."

Brushwood sat down behind his desk. "To what do I owe this unexpected visit?"

Katie stepped forward. "We think we have an idea for how to defeat Legion."

Pandora and Katie launched into the plan, explaining all the details. The general kept a straight face through the whole thing and waited to speak until the end. He rubbed his chin and leaned back, taking a deep breath. "I'll be honest: I really don't like it. I was planning on outfitting the gang with all the latest gear and going in and taking that sonofabitch out. I feel like we would be inviting a whole new problem in here—no offense, Juntto."

The frost giant waved his hand. "None taken. Now, I know why you would say that, but just be aware that my people display no emotions. They will not rage out on people like I did when I was here at first. I am a special breed of frosty. They do, however, prize honor and respect, and I think if we can work mutually on something like that, they will not have any problems with the humans."

The general shifted his gaze to each of them. "And how are you going to be able to explain being gone from your dimension for so long?"

Juntto smiled nervously. "Well, that's kind of where you are going to have to trust me. I most likely will have to claim that I conquered Earth with sword, spear, and shield. Then I will tell them about the threat—Legion—and invite them back."

Pandora giggled. "What about taking your big Juntto guns?"

Juntto shook his head adamantly. "No guns. No guns. They do not understand them, and I do not want it to be a huge accident waiting to happen. No guns."

Katie wrinkled her forehead. "Umm, I don't know how I feel about you telling them you conquered Earth. Wouldn't that be a bit hard to believe? Not to mention the fact that as soon as they get here, they will know it was bullshit?"

Pandora had to agree. "You are only one frost giant, and although fearsome—"

Juntto nodded. "Thank you."

Pandora continued, "Thinking you could take down every major player in the world seems a bit unrealistic."

Juntto shook his head. "Not really, because they have no idea how Earth works. If there was a powerful enough frost giant, he would be able to single-handedly take over my world. They don't realize the massiveness of Earth. The thing is, I have to go back with a credible story, something that will really catch their attention. I am sure that

Juntto the warrior is nothing but a tale and a song by this point."

Pandora scoffed. "I want a song written for me, maybe *Ode to the Big Titties*, or *Girl, Shake that Master Rump*, or *Everybody Wants a Piece of that Pus…*"

Katie put up her hand. "So you want to tell them something that will garner their admiration and respect. I mean, I guess I can understand that. We do the same here on Earth; it just doesn't take conquering an entire planet to get it. At this point, I think we should go with it. Legion is a force to be reckoned with, and like Brock said the other day, he can turn you with just a few words."

The rest of the crew agreed, and they waited for the general's response. He sighed and waved his hand. "Fine. But if this goes wrong, you better clean it up fast."

Juntto clapped his hands. "Home, sweet home."

Brock sat down in the chair. "I'm going to hang back. Someone needs to stay behind, and I am not an angel or a frost giant. I don't want to get stuck in a world I can't survive in."

The portal sparked and shimmered open, and Katie, Pandora, and Juntto ducked through. Pandora swiped her hand to the side, closing the portal behind them, the sound of squawking monkeys fading. They all sat there, hands on knees, breathing heavily. Pandora glanced up at Juntto, who had tears in his eyes. "Sorry, buddy. I didn't mean to take us back to the weird jungle. I swear."

They all stood up and looked around, finding themselves back in the crystal tree dimension. It was absolutely gorgeous, with sparkling renditions of Earth's flora all over the place. Pandora walked forward and ran her hand down the trunk of one of the trees, watching the flickering rainbows flashing from the prism effect of the planet's sun.

She flicked the base, and it emitted a high-pitched tone just like when you tapped a crystal glass. She turned with a grin that slowly faded, realizing Katie and Juntto were staring right at her. "What? It's fucking pretty, assholes."

Juntto ran his finger over a crystal flower. "Sure, it's beautiful, and Angie would die if I took her back one, but there is no time. What are we doing here, anyway? There is not a single living creature in sight, unless they are all hard and shiny and none of them interact."

Pandora stared at the beautiful crystal rose at her feet and started giggling. "Sounds like one hell of a time to me. Hard, shiny, and doesn't want to talk. Most perfect damn date ever."

Katie turned right and left. "No. There has to be something alive, or what the heck is the point of this place?" She summoned her angel armor. Unfolding her wings, she groaned. They needed to be stretched, and she hadn't done so in a long time. Still, she focused on the task at hand. Using her angel powers, she closed her eyes and scanned the entire surface of the planet, searching for any signs of life.

When she opened her eyes again, she was perplexed. "I don't sense anything. This must be an empty planet. Weird."

Pandora shrugged. "I like it. Sparkly, and no one to bother you? It's like a dream come true. Except, no hot cabana boy—that's a letdown. Suppose I could bring my own."

Katie grabbed Pandora and brought her back over, latching onto her hand. "We have to focus and find the right dimension. We don't have time to be hopping dimensions today. There is a psychopathic practically immortal Leviathan on the loose, remember?"

Pandora frowned. "Yes. Okay. Focusing."

They stood there for a moment before both of them reached out and opened a portal.

Brock sat in the chair in front of the general's desk and they both went silent, their minds on what was about to happen. Brock had a feeling Brushwood was just as uneasy about the plan as he was. They both looked up and started to talk at the same time. Brock chuckled. "Sorry, go ahead."

The general lifted an eyebrow, opening his bottom drawer and pulling two rocks glasses out. As he poured them both some scotch, he spoke. "I have a feeling we are both going to want to talk about the same thing here: an army of old-school Junttos with no clue how to behave on Earth and the idea that Juntto is the conqueror of the whole planet. Sounds like something from a novel."

Brock took the glass with a smile. "At the same time, everything these days sounds like it comes out of a novel. But yeah, the picture in my head is probably a lot less kind and exciting than the one in Juntto's mind. From what I remember, Juntto the frost giant warrior who arose from the ice was a ruthless murderer and rapist.

Somehow, with his change, everyone seems to have forgotten that."

The general grunted. "They hear 'Juntto' and think cooking shows now."

Brock glanced up from his glass. "You watch?"

He shrugged. "On occasion. Those damn cookies are *so* good."

Brock agreed. "Here is where the plan gets a little fuzzy. We are hoping, not certain, that they can take out Legion. So, going with the best case scenario, let's say that they do. They kill the Leviathan and save the Earth from destruction by Legion's army. Then what?"

The general nodded. "Right. Then we have a dead Leviathan and a whole lot of frost giants hanging around with nothing constructive to do. Best case scenario, they deplete the Buffalo population and conquer Wisconsin. Worst case is a battle of epic proportions that leaves the world ravaged by an enemy we brought here."

Brock shook his head. "I just... I want to trust Katie's judgment. And that is ultimately what I am doing here, but history says we had a hell of a time with Juntto in the past, ultimately locking him away in a chunk of ice and somehow forgetting where we put him. The Earth is a lot different now, and a lot more crowded."

The general took a sip of his scotch and snorted. "And thanks to global warming, there is a lot less ice to bury frost giants in. I think, Brock, the moral of this story is, if it goes wrong, we are replacing one dangerous Leviathan with an entire army of invincible warriors, and no way to really do anything but fight with all our might and hope we don't end up as a society eating mutton stew again, dancing around fires and having celebrations where we battle to the death."

Brock sighed and looked out the window at the skyline. He rested his chin on the palm of his hand. "We have to remember that we brought Juntto in as a frost giant, and he has become one of us now. He is family, and we all trust him with not just our lives, but the lives of millions of people around the globe. We send him in on the hardest missions, and we eat his terrifying cooking—which is pretty damn good sometimes."

The general chuckled. "We do. He is a different giant than the one we froze so long ago; he has also become someone we trust with our most sacred and important tasks. He has never let us down, and he protects humans like they are his own people. I suppose that in a way, we *are* his people now. He has been on this planet for a very long time. Not as long as Pandora, but still long. *But...*"

"That doesn't mean we can trust his people," Brock replied. "We trust Pandora, but not a single one of us would trust other demons to not be complete and utter trash, yet we are allowing all of this to happen. The way I look at it, though, is that because he does love humans so much, especially the one he spends the bulk of his time with, Angie, that he wouldn't let the giants destroy us. I have faith that he will come through for us and he will be the frosty we love and respect. I have a hard time believing that just because his people are around, he will become a different giant. He has come too far."

The general raised his glass. "I think you may be right. We need to have faith in Juntto and trust his ability to control the situation. It's not easy integrating so many new species of beings onto one planet, especially when the bulk of them want to kill us."

They both sat there stewing in their thoughts and drinking their scotch. Brock did believe that he could trust Juntto, but he still had a ball of nerves rolling around in the pit of his stomach. "You know, even though we completely trust Juntto, I think it would be a good idea to do something for the what-ifs."

Brushwood sat forward. "I couldn't agree with you more. We would be stupid to not to cover all the minute possibilities as well. Hell, that is what the government is good at doing—spending money to cover scenarios that are completely ridiculous. Why stop now?"

Brock slapped his hands on the table and pushed back his chair. "I'll make some calls, then, and gather a Damned strike force as a precaution. They can be on call, and we'll make sure they are ready to go if any of those scenarios actually happen."

The portal opened and the three stepped through, Juntto shoving a crystal flower into his pocket that he yanked out as they opened the portal. They stumbled out into the snow, and the wind howled as it whipped wildly around them. Drifts of snow blew across them and up into the sky between the thick snow clouds, where three moons shimmered in the night. The snow came up to Katie's knees, and some gathered on her shoulder as the wind blew it in their direction.

Pandora's teeth started to chatter. "This is snow hell! It's like the opposite of hell, minus any perceived goodness. I am starting to think that scary monkeys are better than frostbite and hypothermia."

Katie reached back, breaking a piece of her hair off. They had been out there for less than a minute and were already feeling like they were being artificially frozen. However, as they began to shake and shiver in their boots, Juntto was wide-eyed, his hands out and his mouth open, catching snowflakes. He laughed like an excited child as he skipped around, throwing the snow up and watching it trickle back down.

He looked at Katie and Pandora, not noticing their blue lips and chattering teeth, or the fact that they were not supposed to be that color. "Home! I can smell it! Warm crackling fires, meat over the flames, people laughing, cheering, drinking wine, and celebrating being frost giants. It is a beautiful thing!"

He jumped up, reaching for a handful of snowflakes, his blue body growing to twelve feet tall as he did. When he landed, a tornado of snow blew up around him. He was dressed in traditional frost giant gear with a jagged leather skirt sort of piece, no shirt, leather bracelets up and down his arms, and a cape with the top part made of bone.

Ahead of them was a large igloo with smoke billowing from the chimney. He waved to the girls. "Come on, let's see where in the land we are!"

Katie and Pandora both called for him to stop, but he was already on his way. They looked at each other with chattering teeth and rolled their eyes as they ran after him, trying to keep up. When they got to his side, everyone stopped. Another frost giant stepped out of the igloo, standing just as tall as Juntto. There was where the similarity stopped; he was older and fatter, and his face was so grumpy it made Katie want to smile. He was slightly frightening to her and Pandora, but Juntto looked like he was about to cry, he was so excited.

The giant snarled at them, holding a jagged bone spear. "Who is trespassing?"

Katie and Pandora stepped behind Juntto, who waved his hand excitedly. "It is I, Juntto, returned from another dimension."

There was a moment of silence and contemplation before the frost giant yelled, *"Liar!"*

Katie just about pissed her pants as the old frost giant came charging straight at them.

17

Katie and Pandora immediately jumped to attention, pulling out their swords and taking a fighting stance. At that moment, neither of them felt the biting cold or the hell-flakes falling on their necks and melting. Neither of them noticed the enormity of the old frost giant in front of them. Neither of them cared that they were not part of that world. They were being threatened, and as far as they knew, that dimension had the same creator as theirs.

They faced off, the old man snarling at the angels as he darted his eyes between the three of them. Juntto pulled both of them back, shoving them behind him. Pandora snarled. "Bro, we've killed dickless demons bigger than this prick. Don't need your protection, blue man."

Juntto whirled and poked Pandora in the arm. "This is *my* world. This is the place I grew up and played. This is the place where my name became a legend among the people. This is not hell, and this is not Earth. Things are done differently here, whether we believe it to be the wrong way or not. I need you both to respect that and step back so that I may do what I need to."

As harsh as his words seemed, Katie understood what he was saying. She sheathed her sword and reached over, pushing down Pandora's. The other angel glanced at her with wide eyes. "What?"

Katie shook her head. "For now, in this world, we do it Juntto's way. We trust him."

Pandora sniffed and sheathed her sword, stepping back. Juntto nodded and turned back around, lunging immediately. He tackled the old frost giant and the two flew back, smashing hard into the igloo. The old giant pushed back, using his tired muscles to get to his feet, but Juntto was just too strong for him. His feet scraped backward in the ice and snow and Juntto's hand tightened around his wrist, keeping his spear from coming anywhere near him.

Katie and Pandora looked at each other with wild eyes and turned back. Pandora was impressed by their strength. "I really should have brought like popcorn or something. I didn't realize we were coming here for a battle royal. It's like some tough grandpa fighting the young guy in town. You know he's gonna get his ass beat, but you don't want to act like it, 'cause he's old."

Katie winced as Juntto picked the old man up and smashed him into the igloo, completely destroying it. "Home, sweet nope."

The old man grumbled loudly as Juntto crawled on top of him and straddled his upper body. He grabbed the bone spear and pulled, trying to pry it out of the older giant's grip. The old one fought him hard, but Juntto lifted the old man's head and smashed it down over and over, and he finally released the spear.

Juntto ripped it out of his hand and raised it over his head. The old man closed his eyes, obviously ready for death. Juntto huffed and puffed, about to kill the man, as frost giants did, but when he looked down at him, he could feel the compassion he had learned to enjoy so much seeping into his chest. He slammed the spear down, thrusting it into the snow next to the man's head before rolling off and standing up. The old man looked at him wildly for a second. "What do you want?"

Juntto removed the chunks of ice from his skin and spat in the snow. Wiping his hand across his mouth and catching his breath, he put his arms out wide and then beat his chest. "I am Juntto, King of Earth. Take me to the ruler here!"

The old giant stared at him for several moments before grabbing the handle of his bone spear. With a groan, he pulled himself to his feet. He wobbled for several moments before getting his footing.

Pandora elbowed Katie and whispered to her, "I feel like he went through all this just so we could watch the poor old frost giant stroke out like a blue Wilfred Brimley."

Katie snorted, covering her mouth. "He's got the diabeetus?"

They both snickered but Juntto ignored them, too busy with his dramatic conversation with the old giant. The old one stood, supporting himself with the spear like a cane. "I will take you to the leader. I must ask for your sincere forgiveness. You see, I assumed that Juntto was dead. I was just a young boy when you left, and I remember it oh so clearly. We all looked up to you. We all wanted to be like the great Juntto! We all wanted to hear your stories, but as the years passed, we came to believe that you were gone."

Juntto crossed his arms. "It is understandable."

The old man wobbled forward. "How are you still so young?"

Pandora and Katie both whipped their heads and waited for the answer. Pandora smacked her lips and put her hands on her hips. "Do not sit there and tell me you found the elixir of life and you've been holding out on us."

Juntto sighed. "I not only traveled through space, but through time as well, and once I reached Earth, I did not stay that long on the surface, at least not in our timeframe. Then, preserved deep under the surface in a sort of suspended animation, my body did not age. It did not wither or weather, nor did it use the life force that is in me. Basically, I kept my youth. And now I have returned a king, just as I foretold years ago on this very planet. Now, if you would, please take me to your ruler."

Legion and his army had nothing to hold them back. Although many were battered and torn, they no longer felt their wounds, because their pride and the honor of their family were much stronger in their minds. They moved even after burning and being wounded in a plane crash, hanging onto their leader and slowly mending as he grew their lost family once again. They followed blindly, not questioning what, where, or even why they were heading to Romania.

However, once in the country, they walked and walked, waiting to come upon their first town. They were heading toward the fort Korbin had built not too long before. Legion floated forward in front of them, trudging a hill. His small army joined him, lining up to stare down at the tiny Romanian town below. The soldiers all began to whisper, "We are Legion" in a chorus of light voices that spread down into the bowl that held the village.

Legion put up his fist, and the army quieted. "We move. Try to not kill, but bring them to the family."

Legion went first, gliding down the hill with his army stumbling after. When they reached the edge of town, Legion paused, staring down the central street. In the distance was what looked like a castle perched on the edge of a cliff. The crew moved through the town, most of the people immediately hiding in their homes, watching through the cracks in their doors and shutters.

Legion floated into the castle and looked around, finding many different glass cases filled with weaponry from the medieval period. Vinders walked up next to him. "It is a museum. A place with things preserved from the old times."

This highly interested Legion, and he took so much time browsing through the museum that the people of the town began to come forward, curious as to who this visitor was, with his army of purple-eyed soldiers. The curiosity in this case might not have killed the cats, but it definitely made things easier for Legion to assimilate pretty much the entire town in one fell swoop. Those who didn't come out were quickly apprehended by those who had, and they were turned in the town's square right in front of the medieval museum.

Once that was completed, the women went immediately to work, pushing all the children out of the way and, like it was actually the 17th century, they began making preparations to take care of the men. To them, there was nothing more important than their new family. Legion opened the gates to the museum, taking all of the relics and weapons and passing them out to arm his new troops. There were no guns, but there were many swords, and bows and arrows were also prevalent. By the time they were done, they looked and felt like a true medieval military, some even going so far as to carry shields and wear chainmail to protect themselves.

Legion took a walk through the city, many of the people in his army following a few feet back, waiting to bestow anything they could on him. He stared into the open doorways of the homes, curious about the time and place he'd ended up in. The last time he had walked the Earth, there wasn't such a thing as electricity, but now there were gadgets and gizmos that he didn't understand and didn't want to.

Legion passed a sports clothing shop and paused, seeing his reflection. He turned toward the glass and held up his arm, finding that the gauze was unraveling from his body. Leviathan or not, he wanted to look good and not walk around like a complete heathen. He snapped his fingers and Vinders came up next to him, completely calm.

The Leviathan moved forward, Vinders hurrying to open the door for him. Legion floated through the store, trying on different hats and various items of clothing. He then searched the racks to find something he would be comfortable in. When he reached the soccer section, he glanced at Vinders, unsure what soccer was.

Vinders looked around and grabbed one of the balls off the shelf. "You kick this ball down a field to your teammates and try to set it up for a goal. You go back and forth, them defending their goal and your team attempting to protect your own."

Legion twirled a piece of his loose gauze as he flipped through the rack. Finally, after three racks, he stopped on a red and gold shirt, holding it up in front of him. Vinders pointed to the logo on the front. "This is Manchester United in England, a very popular team. That is indeed a good one."

He walked over to the changing room. Entering, he began to work on his gauze, winding it around, tucking in pieces here and there and smoothing it as best he could. When he was done with that part, he took the shirt from the hanger and pulled it over his head. Outside, but still in the store, Vinders waited, whistling to himself and looking around. Suddenly the changing room door opened and Legion walked out, putting his hands up.

Vinders looked at him for a moment, appraising his handiwork. Using the loose gauze from the rest of him, he had put together a pair of gauze shorts that slightly resembled a diaper. Pulled down halfway over it was his new Manchester United jersey, and boy, was he proud. "Looks great. Anything else you need?"

Legion shook his head, looking at himself in the mirror again. Vinders glanced out the front windows and back at Legion, who was hovering a few inches above the floor. "I will take you and the army somewhere if I am permitted. It has what you have been seeking."

Vinders waited for him to agree and then followed him out, watching as he began to send small whispers throughout the town, drawing people from their houses to gather in the square. When it was time, he handed the reins over to Vinders, who lead them up a steep hill. When they reached the top and looked out, they could see a lava-covered town with Korbin's first fort.

The old frost giant's long beard blew wildly behind him, slapping his bare blue skin. He kept one arm up, allowing the snow to pummel his body as he pushed through the drifts. Behind him, Juntto walked tall, enjoying his frozen homeland. Before leaving the old giant's igloo, he had made sure that Katie and Pandora were wrapped in thick Heflin fur and covered with deep and warm hoods. The girls had no idea what kind of animal the fur came from, but it felt like it had magic in each strand.

As soon as Katie pulled it around her next to the disheveled and broken-down igloo, all of the cold disappeared. Pandora had the same experience and was more than happy to accept the clothing from the old giant.

Katie pulled on Juntto's arm as they walked. "Do frost giants always try to kill each other and then help each other reach the place they want to go? I mean, it wouldn't surprise me. Boys are the same way. They can choke the other person to inches from death and the next day be best friends again."

Juntto watched the old giant as he walked. "He is not a friend. He lost in his battle, and therefore he is technically my slave now."

Katie was taken aback by this, and Pandora shook her head. "I'm sorry, but isn't that one of your jobs? To save the innocent?"

Juntto stopped and looked sadly at them. "Not all innocents are worth saving."

Katie's lip twitched. "That is nuts, Juntto; I won't lie. That's almost... Not almost, that's wrong on so many levels. We humans figured out that slavery was wrong a long time ago, although we haven't worked on passing the laws to the full extent...but that's beyond the point."

Pandora shrugged. "I have to admit, after being on Earth for so long, I am inclined to agree with Katie. I mean, don't get me wrong, I've had a few slaves in my day, but it has always been consensual." Pandora elbowed Katie and snorted. "You know what I mean?"

Katie shook her head at Pandora. "Not the time."

Juntto sighed. "Look, this is the world I lived in. If you want their help, you are going to have to play along with me. I'm not saying it's right, but for here, it's normal. If I were to tell him he was free of his duty without earning his honor back, he would not only be shunned by everyone else in our world, he would relieve his soul out of embarrassment."

Pandora blinked. "Relieve his soul? Do souls do that? I mean, if they do, do we think that shit is all over the apartment? Like black-light city?"

Katie rolled her eyes and let out a deep breath. "He

means kill himself. Good God, you are hopeless sometimes. I don't know how you remember to breathe."

The old giant led them down a narrow pass between the peaks and into a clearing. When the drifts of snow disappeared, a huge castle lay in front of them. Katie's mouth dropped open, and Pandora pushed her hood back and gawked. "Whoa. So uh, is this leader single? Because I've seen worse."

Posted on either side of the fortress' gates were two frost giants in leather armor with spears that shimmered like diamonds. As soon as the group got close, they shifted, crossing their spears over the entrance to the palace. The old giant bowed his head and stepped to the side, allowing Juntto to pass.

He walked up to the guards, his chest puffed, standing easily two feet taller than them. "I am Juntto, King and Conqueror of Earth. I have come to speak to whoever rules here. It is of dire importance."

One of the guards stood at attention, but the other kept his stare on the angels, his spear still in the way. "That would be Lord Kraggen, our leader and warrior king. Lord Kraggen does not see anyone without a direct invite."

Juntto held his posture. "I am not here for his mercy or grace. I am here to request his assistance in a matter that affects us all. I have been gone for nearly a millennium, but now I come as a warrior king, just like he is. I will not be turned down out of childish whim. You are to tell him at once that I have arrived. We have much to discuss, and time is of the essence."

The guard who was standing at attention glanced at him and then at the other soldier, who was starting to look a bit nervous. "I am sorry, Your Highness, but we cannot allow anyone through without proper clearance. Perhaps if you come in the morning and summon the duke, he will be able to find time in the calendar for the king to give you counsel."

Juntto growled, and although the guards kept their stance, they were nearly quaking in the snow that reached their knees. Katie looked at Pandora, and they both nodded. Untying the fronts of their fur cloaks, they shrugged them off and spread their wings wide. Both of the guards jumped, immediately pulling their spears back and unlatching the gate.

The girls picked up their cloaks and smirked as the first guard put out his arm. "I will escort you inside."

18

Juntto, laden with furs from his new slave's shelves, walked through the massive halls, which were obviously built for giants his size and larger. Katie and Pandora had folded their wings and walked close, staring in awe at the beautiful white marble castle. Very few items hung on the ornately carved walls besides massively tall paintings of the giant kings of the past and the tattered banners of the rulers' foes, past and present.

The guard led them into the throne room, stopping halfway. "I will summon the lord. Please wait here, and do not touch anything."

Pandora sneered. "Rude. I don't want to touch your shit anyway."

As soon as the guard had left, Juntto turned to Katie and Pandora and whispered, "Lord Kraggen was around when I was a young boy. He is a fierce warrior, or was, at least. He fought with my father in many battles and was there when he was honorably killed. Still, he can be a tyrant, and tyrants are not what we were hoping for."

Katie scratched the top of her head. "If you are at least a millennium old, then how is he still alive?"

Juntto stood back up, straightening his furs and his armor. "When you look at a lifespan of a millennium, does fifteen years older than me really sound that ancient? Our people do not live forever; we are not immortal. However, we do live a very long time here. We have hibernation chambers where we spend hundreds of years of our lives, and they rejuvenate us. That is why you will often see young-looking lords. The poorer you are, the older you look."

Katie shook her head. "Why is that not surprising? No matter what dimension we end up in, they all have the same bullshit rules: push down the lower classes and raise the ones with money. It is sickening. And slaves, too? Look at all of these...female giants standing by to serve. They should be the ones on the throne instead!"

Juntto turned back to her, patting his hands on the air. "Please lower your voice. This is not the way you want it to be; I get it. If we ever stop this war, you can come back here and start an uprising."

Pandora just stood there looking over their heads at the torn and bloody banners of Kraggen's conquered foes. They had lined the halls and now also billowed above their heads in the throne room. Footsteps and a loud voice could be heard approaching.

Kraggen walked to the doorway and narrowed his eyes. "How can we know this is him? It would almost be impossible."

The king was more than a bit suspicious. Juntto had left eons ago, rushing out to conquer other worlds. Still, he didn't want to offend the giant if he was truly Juntto. So, he took in a deep breath and tugged down his armor as he walked from the shadows, putting his arms out. "By Crtagul's frozen tits, can this be Juntto, the Great Warrior of the Frost Giant Lands? The missing king?"

Pandora gave Katie a side glance at that last comment. Juntto walked forward with a jubilant smile. "Lord Kraggen, I am very much alive, and still have the heartbeat of a king. I have finally returned, with glory beneath my belt."

Lord Kraggen put his arms back as his servant girls pulled off his armor and put on his formal robes. His eyes moved feverishly over Juntto. "I see that you have. Conquered Earth, huh? And if you conquered Earth, then what dire issue would bring you to my doorstep?"

Juntto chuckled. "To make peace with the other frost giants and claim the army that is mine by right of conquest. I have traveled through many dimensions, the exhaustion of battles clinging to the twisted metal of my sword. I have come to be seen and heard again, and request my people's help in a time of grave sorrow and struggle. What giant likes to be swindled of their rightful property? None."

Kraggen slowly circled Juntto. He looked at his furs and his women, having not seen such fair skin on a female in many years. Instead of excitement, though, suspicion was what filtered through his blood at that moment. He needed a way to determine if this indeed was the Juntto from many years ago.

Kraggen stopped in front of him, reaching out in greeting. Juntto smiled and reached out as well, laying his hand over Kraggen's and gripping his forearm tightly. Kraggen threw his hands up. "If you are indeed the brave warrior Juntto, then you know very well that true honor demands there be a battle so that the famed Juntto can prove that he is here in the flesh."

While Katie and Pandora were shocked, Juntto had known before they came that he would not get away without a fight. However, this was not his moment to display his skills. It was time for a different type of battle, one that brought leaders to the edge of their seats. It was the crucible of the giant world.

Kraggen lifted his arms to face level and turned, clapping for his servants. Two young warriors stepped forward, donning frost giant armor with angry looks on their faces. Kraggen whirled around, bowing to Juntto. "I will offer you my two strongest warriors. If you are truly the king of Earth, then you should offer me two of your warriors."

Juntto smiled. "As you wish. I will offer up my two slaves."

Pandora furrowed her brow. "What slaves?"

Katie growled. "That big fuckin' blue asshole means us."

Turner tripped, calling out to Eddie as he laughed, whizzing past him. Sean chuckled, pumping his arms to the rhythm of the wheels crunching over the sand, gravel, and grass. He wasn't too far behind, and he definitely wasn't giving up this "guns run." He got too much shit from them on a regular basis to even think about quitting before one of them.

When Eddie came back around, Sean acted nonchalant until he was right next to him. Suddenly he jerked his wheelchair and knocked Eddie to the ground. Sean looked back, laughing loudly as Eddie rolled head over heels, coming to a sliding stop at Turner's feet.

Turner pointed at him. "That's what you get, cheater." He pumped his fist. "And the cripple wins again!"

Sean wheeled over to them and put on the brakes, then clasped his hands together and shook them to each side of himself. Eddie sat up and leaned on his hands. He nudged Sean's wheel with his foot. "So, how's admin?"

Sean rolled his eyes. "I can't really do anything in there. I mean, what can anyone do on this base with practically no security clearance? Just knowing this place exists requires a higher security clearance then I have. It's fucking pathetic."

Turner shrugged. "You could be the head chef. Unless we have potatoes spying on us, I think we can trust you."

Eddie shook his finger. "Or you could be the chief latrine cleaner. Put mop heads on those wheels and just ride around all day. It would be a piss-free establishment."

Turner nodded. "I think it's a great idea. And if you get good at that and you are rocking it with your wang definitely not out, you might get a promotion. You could become one of the janitorial staff here. Those guys are always quiet, and they know everything that's going on anywhere they work. You would have all the secrets and no security badge, which in my opinion is way cooler."

Sean slapped his hands on his legs. "As much as I appreciate your attempt to find me a career, I think I'd rather leave here and go be normal somewhere. I saved people's fucking lives and I killed fucking demons, and I didn't do that so I could clean toilets. I mean, I love the janitorial support people, since they make everything nice and sparkling, but that is not me, dudes."

Eddie scrunched his nose and tilted his head. "Well, aren't we pretentious!"

Sean smiled. "No, I just want to be treated right. That's all. Right now, I'm like a fucking Roomba. I fucked up, but they forgave me. Still, I'm stuck."

Eddie slapped Sean's leg. "I have one! You could be a guard. We would get you one of those Jeeps with the gas and brake levers on the steering wheel, and you could patrol the base."

Sean nodded. "Actually, that sounds like something I would be totally down with."

"Hey, numbnuts!" Calvin was over by the barracks waving his arms at them. "Meet me downstairs in Conference Room 3 in ten minutes!"

The three of them looked at each other for a moment, then Turner grabbed the handles of the wheelchair and pushed Sean down to the barracks building. When they walked in, Sean peeled off, letting them go to their meeting.

As he was about to turn, Calvin yelled for him. "Where you going? This meeting is for you too."

Sean smirked and rolled down the hall fast. As he approached the door, he stopped one wheel and turned hard on the other, making a squealing turn into the room. Calvin closed the door behind them and dropped a file on the table. Eddie, Turner, and Sean stared at it and back up at him. "I just got off the phone with the general. Now, that's a routine thing for me. Normally we would discuss past events and shoot the shit, and he would give me a directive for Katie. This time was a little weird."

Turner narrowed his eyes. "How weird?"

Calvin let out a deep breath and flipped the folder open, showing them Juntto's face inside. "Juntto, Katie, and Pandora are trying to bring an army of frost giants to Earth, so he wants everyone prepared."

Sean shook his hand. "They are doin' *what*? Did I miss the part where Katie lost her mind?"

Calvin shook his head. "This is happening because they realized the frost giants may be the only ones who can defeat the Leviathan. Katie and Pandora, or anyone else, could easily be swayed to join the Legion, and that would be a really bad thing for everyone. So for now, everyone is on standby."

Eddie snarled. "I feel like we've been over this before, but aren't we guarding the base? We weren't mobilized for the Rio fight. Why is it that when they need bait for these things, we automatically end up toasted? Besides, we have our guns and ammo."

Calvin stretched his arms over his head and yawned loudly. "The reason, Eddie, is because special metal doesn't work on Juntto the way it worked on me and several others. You three are some of the best Damned mercs that we have, well, except for Sean, who isn't anymore, and the keyword in this scenario is Damned. We need the extra strength when going after that sonofabitch. So, yesterday you defended the base, and that's awesome. But your duty station has changed and broadened. Today, the three of you get to realize that this base is on Earth. And that means, without a shadow of doubt in my mind, that you are protecting the planet and every living creature on it. Consider this right here the most important protection detail ever to be assigned, and we won't see it even when it finishes unless you royally fuck up."

"I remember the days of the angels and the demons," one of the frost giants said to his friend. "It was an interesting time. I know those guys think this is going to be easy, but I'll tell you right now, they are in for a surprise."

The other frost giant grunted. "Just a couple of women with wings. I personally think it's offensive to those guys."

Another of them chimed in, "Think about it this way: they are Juntto's slaves. That means he went to Earth, conquered it, and then conquered the angels too. That takes balls."

The other two had wide eyes, whipping their heads to the right and watching Juntto. "He bested the damn angels! I never thought about it that way. He might as well be royalty. I would give my blue left nut to have a couple of angels as my slaves. You think he…" The frost giant nudged his friend, winked, and clicked his tongue. "You know. Takes care of business with one of them. Probably the one with the huge tits."

They all laughed, but their voices couldn't be heard through the freezing wind and blowing snow. Juntto's planet was definitely not the friendliest place to visit, especially for a human. Even for an angel, it was fucking cold. Katie kept her hands to her lips, trying to warm her fingers. Pandora turned toward her, sticking out her chest. "My nipples are so hard! Fuck glass. These bitches could cut motherfucking diamonds."

Katie chuckled, shivering. "Great, so why don't you take down a couple of frost giants with those things? You would become a legend."

Pandora looked down at her chest. "Maybe they would erect a statue of me and my girls."

Kraggen, wearing a blue and gray fur-lined robe, stood in the middle of the field. "Today we find out the authenticity of the so-called warrior king Juntto. He has offered his two slave angels, names unknown, to battle my fierce and strong warriors Skaal and Pivvo!"

The frost giants cheered as the two soldiers stomped out, shaking their fists. Their scales shimmered blue and gray in the light from their moons. Pandora snarled. "Talk about toxic masculinity. Earth seems like a dreamland, compared to this place."

Katie pulled the sword from her back and spread her wings. "It's time to take them down a ballsack or two."

Pandora howled, pulling her sword out. "That's what I'm talking about, bitch!"

Kraggen backed up when he saw their wings and walked over to his side. Juntto nodded at them, standing still with his arms crossed. Skaal and Pivvo stepped forward, whirling their spears to try to intimidate. Katie maintained a stern look, while Pandora had a smirk plastered on her lips.

One of the frost giants blew his horn, and the battle

began. Pandora and Katie didn't hesitate, running straight toward the giants. They clashed in the middle, where Katie grabbed Skaal and spun him in a circle using the momentum of her wings. She smashed the hilt of her sword into his face, knocking out two teeth.

Pandora ran too, but just inches before clashing, she slammed to a stop, spread her wings, and flipped over him. As she soared over his head, she put both arms out, her sword extended. The blade cut right through the leather armor and gashed his shoulder. Pandora landed and smiled widely. After a moment's pause, all four slammed into each other, blocking and slicing with their weapons. You could hear the clanging for miles, even in the cold and bitter winds.

Katie ducked a thrust of Skaal's spear and cut across his belly right below the armor. He wailed, hissing loudly as blue blood dripped down his legs. It was just a flesh wound, but it distracted him enough for her to leap into the air and come down hard on him. At the same time, Pandora, just having taken a straight punch to the chin, got really angry. She dropped her sword and gripped Pivvo's face, slamming her knee into it over and over.

Skaal and Pivvo went down, both dropping hard and shaking the ground. Pandora picked up her sword and sheathed it, looking at Katie. Skaal and Pivvo were still on the ground, and Katie nodded her head at their feet. A huge smile came to Pandora's face, and they leaned down and grabbed them by the ankles.

Katie's and Pandora's wings beat hard as they lifted Kraggen's warriors. The frost giants scrambled for control, but before they could do a thing about it, they were dangling from the angels' hands, their spears on the ground below. Up and up the two angels went until the air was so turbulent, they had to stop to keep control. Still, they were in a good place, everyone below looking really tiny.

Pandora grunted. "Here's the deal, assholes. Either you submit, or Katie and I will let you slip right out of our hands. You are big dudes, and if you don't die from the fall, I promise you will never walk again. It's your decision."

Pivvo looked at Skaal, nodding as fast as he could. Skaal grumbled and the two frost giants pumped their fists, making hand gestures that signified their submission. Skaal growled loudly, "Now, take us to the ground carefully."

Pandora pursed her lips and lowered her eyebrows. "As you wish."

She drew her wings in, and the two rocketed toward the ground. Pivvo screamed, as did Skaal when Katie followed suit. Both angels waited until the last second before deploying their wings and coming to a stop with the frost giants' heads just inches from the snow-covered ground. Smirking, the girls released the giants, letting them fall the last few inches to the ground.

Kraggen looked put out but he walked to the center, gesturing toward Juntto. "The Warrior King, the Conqueror of Earth and the Tamer of Angels, has won the competition. Welcome back, Juntto! In light of these events, I will keep my word. We will send an army to Earth with you to take care of whatever is forcing these extreme measures."

19

Screams could be heard from the small town in Romania. It was reminiscent of the fiery hell and demon massacre of a few months ago. Legion and his army were raiding the fort and everything within the lava-covered Romanian town. Last time, almost everyone fighting or caught in the lava had been killed, but this time around, only a few lives were lost. A few precious lives, but they did their best to save the precious souls for Legion's army. These attackers might have been under his spell, but they were much more intelligent than the demons.

Everyone the army could get their hands on was assimilated by Legion, including the military members and Damned at the fort. With every assimilation, a whisper blew across the hardened lava and debris. "We. Are. Legion."

Legion stood back in his Manchester United shirt and gauze shorts, watching the army begin to fall into place. As soon as they had calmed after the assimilation, the Damned began training with the other Legion soldiers, showcasing their strengths to the group. Legion watched with excitement on his emaciated young face. He loved his new, strong Damned soldiers. They were just what he needed. He could tell they would be the ones who fought in the front lines. The ones that became legends. With an army of Damned, Legion would be virtually unstoppable. The angels would struggle to keep up.

But that was not where it was going to end. Legion had gotten a taste of the Damned's abilities. He had seen them bleed but continue to fight. He had seen them battle, fall, and get back up to fight some more. Vinders walked up next to him, his eyes fading from purple to red and back again. "What do you think, Master?"

Legion stared at his soldiers. "They are perfect for this, but I want more. I must have a full army of Damned. I must have my champions on display when we battle the large cities for their souls."

Vinders crossed his arms, thinking. "I might know of a place. There are more in Paris."

Legion stared at Vinders and smirked before telling them all through their minds to prepare for another march. As they moved away from the pathetic attempt of the Romanians to stay in hiding, Vinders put his fist in the air, stopping the troops. Standing on the dip down of the land, Vinders and Legion stared at the Romanian army forces.

"Move back!" screamed the commanders. "Move back!"

Although the troops had been ordered back, a few brave souls attempted to break ranks and race toward Legion. When they got within a few steps, he flipped his wrist and the three soldiers floated off the ground, their weapons dropping. Legion walked up to them and assimilated them, not touched in the least by their brave actions. He was not going to be weak. He was going to show them that he was a very powerful creature.

The ground shook as the frost giants moved around, some of them attempting to speak to Juntto while the others filed in, but he was too busy trying to keep track of everything going on without revealing his concern. The army of frost giants was suiting up, grabbing weapons, and preparing themselves for a battle in a land they had never been to.

Juntto stopped next to the doorway, watching them go through the lines. They began by stepping up to a platform and allowing the armorers to measure their bodies. There were racks and racks of armor hanging behind the platform. When they had taken the measurements, the armorer would jog to the correct spot and grab the closest size. The frost giant would put his arms out and they would dress him, strapping his leather armor on and making sure his leather crotch guard was good and steady.

Pandora could see them from outside, getting their junk rattled. "I think I have the wrong job. Dead serious. I could do some work on these blue guys."

Katie watched the end of the line. After they were armored up, they were handed shields, spears, and other unsightly weapons that were like something from a Greek war movie. "Where are all the women?"

Pandora glanced at the line of male giants. "Well, I am

assuming there aren't any women soldiers. Think about how they treated them earlier, and how our world tries to treat human women. There is no respect when it comes to honor and valor. They are just females to them."

Katie turned to her left, spotting a line of female frost giants carrying everything from dishes to linens toward the training facility. It was obvious just from their appearance that the giant women were fierce.

She stepped up next to one of the guards. "Can you tell me why your women don't fight?"

The guard snorted. "Our women are strong, but only men fight wars on our lands. There is no place on the battlefield for a woman. They take care of things here. Their motto is, 'The men wage war over there, while we wage war here to protect our country.'"

Katie nodded and glanced at Pandora, and at Juntto as he walked back over toward them. They met in a space in the center of the courtyard, observing the chaos around them. Katie looked at Juntto and expelled the air from her lungs. "Are you sure you can control them? They are much wilder than I assumed. I knew they would be somewhat the same way you were when you first met me, but I also hoped that they would be calmer. It has been many, many years since I worked with anyone like them."

Juntto watched the soldiers roar, facing one another and slamming their fists on their armor. He scoffed, waving his hand. "Of course I have this. I mean, why wouldn't I?"

As Juntto said that, a crowd began to gather in a separate part of the training compound. Katie walked over with Pandora and Juntto and crossed her arms. Kraggen came down the steps, stopping at the bottom and throwing his robes off his shoulders. Katie flinched, turning her head as he stood there completely naked and flexed for the other frost giants.

Pandora, on the other hand, tilted her head to the side, bit her bottom lip, and grunted. "Now, I know I have seen your blue ass naked, Juntto, but that right there is the definition of perfect. Those chiseled abs, the muscles rippling along his back. This is what makes my job so worthwhile."

Kraggen faced the crowds as several woman slaves belted on his leather and metal armor. "I will come to Earth with my men!"

The crowd cheered.

"I will lead you to the victories that Juntto the King wishes to see. I will not back down, and I will not leave any giant behind. I will swing my sword with the same desperate anger that each of you feels on the battlefield. There is a whole new world out there, one we didn't know existed. A millennium ago, a much younger Juntto decided to pack his things and head out into the unknown. He looked for the stars no one could see. His unslakable thirst for more is the entire reason we are standing here, ready to go to a new world. We will watch one of our own defeat a ruthless creature, and we will attempt to reach out and touch him in every way possible."

Pandora made a gagging sound. "So, what? You get hand jobs while you're out there fighting demons? I feel like I got screwed in this fucking deal."

Katie chuckled, still watching Kraggen. "I think we would have a lot fewer men on the fence about joining the service."

Pandora laughed. "And a lot more women staying as far away from their machismo as they can, because no one wants splash in their eyes and a sword in the back. That's just fucking rude."

They looked at Kraggen when the crowd erupted. He had grabbed one of the slaves and planted one on her, his tongue and mouth basically swallowing her face. Pandora held her stomach and shook her head. "For real, this time, I am pretty sure I am about to blow chunks. He is so bad at being a king. Just want to put that out there. He is terrible at this. Do any of these women actually find him attractive?"

Katie shrugged. "His bankroll, awesome castle, nice body. The rest you can just ignore."

Pandora looked at her wildly, and Katie shook her head. "I didn't mean for me. I meant more like those three sisters that are all over everything. The K-Hos is what the media calls them, but they are worth a lot of money."

Pandora nodded in understanding. "Oh yeah, those chicks with the yachts and clothing and makeup and everything. Their dad became a woman. Super brave, too, former Olympian and she said, nope. No more dick on me, only in me. Fuck you. I'm proud."

Katie nodded. "That was their only redeeming grace, in my opinion."

Pandora whipped around to Katie. "So let's get on the same page here. Are you as worried about Kraggen the idiot being a problem on this trip as I am?"

Katie laughed loudly, then stopped short. "Fuck yes, I am worried about that. Are you kidding me? He might be the one who brings us to our knees."

Making a dimensional shift was the only way to get the frost giants to Earth. Both Pandora and Katie decided the best choice was to go through the crystal world. That way, considering the giants were a bit rowdier than they had initially thought, they wouldn't destroy anything vital.

Pandora stayed on one side, holding open the portal to the frost giants' world. One of the frost giants came through, grabbing Pandora's ass cheek with gusto. Slowly she turned her head and looked at his hand, then up at him. "You mind getting your hand off my ass, bro?"

The frost giant laughed. "Little woman telling *me* what to do? Yeah, right. You do what I tell you to."

Pandora smacked her lips and reached for her dagger. Before he knew what she was doing, she had spun around and lopped his entire hand off. He wailed, grabbing the arm and running off. Pandora lifted her eyebrows and turned back to Katie, who burst into laughter as she held the portal leading to Earth open.

The army steadily poured through one portal and out the other. They were stoked to get going and see what Earth was really like. The frost giants only thought they were ready. No one was ever fully ready for the lifestyle of Earth. Even the demons struggled, and they had visited for a long time. It was only to be expected.

Pandora let go of her portal and walked over to Katie's, holding it open so Katie could go to Earth. Pandora, as she climbed out of the realm, grabbed a relatively long and pointed piece of crystal and shoved it between her breasts. When she turned around, she put her arms up and cheered. Several of the frost giants cheered with her, while the rest glanced at her but paid little notice.

Katie shook her head and stood back while Juntto and Kraggen stepped forward, ready to command the troops. The army was already forming up around them, getting into ranks and beating a warlike tune on their chests. Kraggen and Juntto stared at each other awkwardly for a moment, then Kraggen cleared his throat. "I think this will need a bit of finesse from a still-active leader."

Juntto stepped forward. "And you will get just that opportunity, but I am going to lead on my land. I am the King of Earth, but I will appreciate your leadership on the battle line. You chose to fight, and that is where we are all going, noble birth or not. We will stand hand in hand as we walk toward the vicious killers who plan to rage war on our kind and the entire human race. It will be only a short time until he reaches our planet as well. So, learn from this, take it back with you, and strive for greatness, King Kraggen."

The king didn't seem too happy about that, but he relinquished his position, turning and walking back to one of the lines of soldiers. It took over an hour to get everyone in their spots, but once they were, they were silent.

Juntto paced as the military commander talked about the inches, times, and moments that could save your life. His speech was uplifting and motivational, something Juntto had forgotten about since he no longer got to be around his family or parents. All had died when he was young, leaving him in the care of a teacher. He hadn't minded, though; he had learned to be the warrior he was, and nothing could take that away from him.

Pandora and Katie had taken flight and were doing circles in the sky, looking for any sign of Legion and his collective. After several hours of marching, they finally spotted a large group of people walking. They both swooped down and told Juntto about the men. It was without a doubt Legion's army.

Juntto stopped the troops and put up his hands. "They are right over this ridge. We meet face to screen first, then we can talk about what to do next. I want to remind you that he is the most dangerous being on this planet right now. What he can do with a mind is almost perverted. Keep your body loose, move around, and line up in ranks. It's time we sent this Leviathan where he is supposed to be, and that is not the fuck here!"

The troops grunted and stomped their feet, making a massive amount of noise. They began to move down the hill and circle the Legion. The Leviathan and his army stopped, looking around. The frost giants continued, doing the war dance of their people. They roared and hissed, slapping their huge hands on their thighs and then doing it all over again.

Juntto's slave stepped up in front of him. "I want to be at the vanguard, so I can restore my honor. I want to do it for you, and I wish you fruitfulness for years to come."

Juntto smiled and reached out, shaking his hand. "Kill the sonofabitch."

The man roared as he rushed the crowd surrounding Legion. "I will kill this *gifr* for you!"

The armies of Legion shuffled around, none of them willing to fight a giant. Instead, they moved apart, allowing the old man to run straight at the leader. He stopped just feet away, shocked to see the face of a skinny boy. Legion had been hibernating longer than any of the others, and it had taken a toll on his health.

Legion moved forward, his eyes glowing brighter and brighter. The old giant could almost see the movement of the energy inside of him. He whispered "We are Legion" over and over, moving closer until he was just inches away. He said it one last time, swiping his finger across the giant's chest and moving back. His eyes dropped when he realized that the frost giant had not succumbed to what he was trying to do.

Juntto touched Katie on the shoulder. "It's fucking working. They are immune to that shit."

They were all excited, watching the old giant stand triumphantly in the center. He reached onto his back and tugged out his sword, holding it in two hands. As he lifted it, he stared at Legion, ready to redeem himself. Juntto put his arms up in celebration, but suddenly the Legion's Damned army jumped out of the crowd of soldiers and piled on top of the old man. They used their weapons, their hands, and their will to rip him apart.

His screams echoed across the valley and Juntto turned his back, feeling the pain of the old giant's death. Katie put her hand on his arm. "It was an honorable death. He earned his honor back."

Juntto nodded. "I guess you are right, but I'll tell you this right now: Legion will not make it past this field.

These giants and I will get him, and we will show him what an eternity of pain feels like."

Juntto gritted his teeth and stared angrily at Legion, whose eyes shifted to him. Slowly a smile moved over the Leviathan's lips. Juntto tilted his head back and screamed, beating his chest. One by one the others followed along until the air began to vibrate around them.

20

General Brushwood walked Brock out of the building to the car waiting for the two of them. The former rock star looked at the tinted windows and private driver, which raised his suspicion. "Should I be worried that you're going to off me instead of taking me to the airport?"

The general stood in front of the car door and to the side, waving Brock in and wiggling his eyebrows. "You will only know once you've gotten into the car."

Brock shrugged. "Can't be that much more dangerous than fighting Leviathans or walking into hell. Besides, being killed by the famous General Brushwood? It could be worse."

They climbed in and shut the door, and the car headed down the street. They weren't very far from the airport, but the general wasn't feeling the walk. "I've walked more than a whole city of people in my life, from the jungles of Vietnam to the hallways of Congress. I think I might just take a car everywhere from now on. Hell, I might just get myself one of those old people scooters and run into my assistants in the hallways."

Brock laughed. "You've earned it, sir. You can run over anyone you want, except me, of course."

The general furrowed his brow and pointed at him. "You're first, kid. But in all seriousness, this whole thing makes me incredibly nervous. At the same time, though, I am hoping that we don't need you guys. Juntto, Katie, and Pandora are more than capable of handling the situation, unless of course something unforeseen happens. But that's why you'll be there. And between you and me, if something happens to change Juntto, I don't want you to think twice about him or innocent civilians. That is nothing against the big blue ox. I would say it to him about you if the roles were reversed."

Brock looked down at his clenched fists. "I know, sir, and I appreciate your unbiased view on things. I know you keep it fair."

The general groaned, putting his arm over the back of the seat. "Yeah, you know what they say. Old Brushwood, the guy who will take you out no matter who the hell you are."

The car pulled up next to the hangar and came to a stop. The driver got out and came around to open the passenger door. The general dipped his head, looking at the plane. "Have a good flight, and call me when you have any intel. And try not to let the world know we brought the frost giants here."

Brock smirked. "If I do, I'll make sure to let them know it was your idea."

He hopped out of the car and grabbed his bag, slinging

it over his shoulder. He hurried toward the plane and the flight attendant waiting at the top of the steps. Brock was shocked to see it was a personal jet and not a military plane, but then again, their mission wasn't on the books. Smiling at the flight attendant, he turned the corner and stopped. Eddie, Turner, and Calvin were already on board and chilling in their seats.

Calvin put his fist up. "The fearless have arrived. It's about damn time. What were you doing, schmoozing with the bigwigs?"

Eddie glanced up and smirked. "How do you think he started getting all the good jobs? Apparently, his aim is nothing compared to his suction."

Brock rolled his eyes and put his bag up in the overhead. "I'm sorry you guys suck so much that you can't believe I could actually just be good at my job."

"Right, and I have working legs," a voice said behind him.

Brock turned around to find Sean moving from his wheelchair into one of the seats. Brock shook his head. "But you're not Damned."

Sean raised an eyebrow. "I can't walk either, but I'll still punch you in the dick, dick."

The Fasten Seatbelts sign came on, and Brock sat down, laughing. The plane taxied onto the runway and they were on their way, soaring into the sky. Turner took the earbuds out of his ears, rotating his jaw to get his ears to pop. "I swear, Brock, you go to Europe more than anyone I know."

Brock turned in his seat, his hand running over his scruffy chin. "Yeah, but under the circumstances, I would say it really doesn't count."

Everyone got serious for a moment. "Do you think Juntto is going to be able to control himself with a bunch of his kind there, all bloodthirsty and ready to kill everyone?"

Brock shrugged. "I can't say I'm one hundred percent on it, but at the same time, we have no reason not to trust him. After the change, he became a solid member of this group, not to mention that he is as tough as nails. It was worth the shot."

Turner stood up and pointed hard at Brock. "Damn right. I've seen that motherfucker take a missile in the back and go to his knees, only get back up and throw the fucking thing back at them. He's tough as shit."

Sean agreed. "Not to mention that he loves Angie, and has more than once expressed how much he loves his life now. I really don't think he would throw it all away. Of course, people have done crazier things. But, no—I think he's gonna play a tough fucker like he was before to get the help we need, and then he'll drop it."

Turner shrugged. "I think we all give way more credit to an alien species we know very little about regardless of how close we seem to be to them."

Sean laughed. "He's a person. A giant, as close to human as you can be while being a different species. You talk about him like people talk about adopted wild animals. He *is* wild, no matter how much he seems to love you. Come on, man."

Eddie leaned forward, rubbing his tired face. "I don't understand why the Army just doesn't take care of this.

Drop a fucking nuke and take them out. Why is this being dragged out?"

Brock unbuckled his belt and stood up, holding onto the back of the seat when there was a small bit of turbulence. "I don't think you guys fully appreciate the full magnitude of the power this Leviathan has. I've stood before two of them. I've watched them attack. Within two seconds, Korbin went from talking to me about strategy to pulling his dual swords and trying to decapitate me. His eyes glowed, and he just seemed to not be in there anymore. It was incredible."

Calvin turned around, hearing the story. "He's all right now, isn't he?"

Brock nodded. "Yeah, of course. He's at a base in Iraq, and probably getting ready to head back home. After I shot him…"

Calvin's mouth dropped wide open. "Hold up. Did you just say you shot the man?"

Brock gave Calvin a small grin. "I did. Technically I shot him twice, once in each knee."

"And you're still alive?" Calvin was baffled.

Brock put out his arms, chuckling. "So far."

Calvin whistled, shaking his head. "Lucky son of a…"

The fucking insane battle raged wildly in the curving and twisting hill-covered Romanian landscape. The sounds of the fight could be heard for miles: battles cries, screams, and shouts of pure terror from both sides. The frost giants started on one side, looming several feet above the Legion soldiers. But although their size was a factor, the Legion army's only thoughts were about what they had to do to protect their family. What they had to do to protect their leader, Legion.

It was the frost giants versus the Legion's Damned soldiers, the strongest of the troops and the alphas among them. Their desire to win matched the frost giants', but they weren't quite as strong. Even with demons inside them, entranced by the idea of Legion, the giants' sheer size made it hard for them to begin to understand how to handle them.

The battle was bloody on more than one level. Limbs flew overhead in arcs, spraying blood over Legion's Damned. With every leg, arm, or torso, the murderous screams could be heard for miles. The blue giants raced across the field, grabbing the Damned by the heads and ripping their purple eyes straight out of their skulls.

Legion watched from a distance, standing behind a guard of Damned soldiers. Vinders stayed with him, never leaving his side for more than a moment. Legion peeked through the cracks between the Damned, narrowing his eyes at a large blue giant tearing his men limb from limb. He stretched his arms out and pushed his men apart, stepping out into the open. Immediately Vinders came up next to him, ready to protect him from anything and everything.

"We. Are. Legion," the Leviathan whispered, focusing his attention on the giant in front of him.

The giant continued to rage, grabbing a Damned around the waist and slamming him into the ground until there was nothing left but a bloody pulp. Legion tried again, pushing the giant to assimilate, but he got nothing more than a small twitch of a muscle, and even that was questionable. He slammed his hands to his sides and went behind his Damned guards again.

On top of a hill on the other side of the field looking down over the battle, Katie, Pandora, and Juntto reluctantly stayed put on the frost giants' side. It was the safest place they could be and still watch the battle rage. None of them could chance being taken over. The results would be terrifying for everyone involved. Not just for the people in the field, but if Juntto and the two angels were under Legion's control, the world would have no one to protect them. At that point, the fight or flight response would be the only factor deciding whether anyone survived or perished—a decision the three of them didn't want people to have to make.

Lucifer sat back in his chair and shook his head, glancing at Baal. They were watching the shit show from the comfort of Lucifer's throne room. Lucifer threw out his hands. "Jesus Christ."

Baal recoiled, and Lucifer rolled his eyes. "I can say it. Don't be a pussy."

Baal covered his mouth as he watched body parts soar through the air. "I just don't get it. Up until now, besides the whole bombing hell thing, the humans have played it relatively safe. This just doesn't make any sense to me."

Lucifer shook his head. "Me either, little slave, me either. The humans must have fucking lost it. Thrown their hands up and said, 'Hey, if we're going down, we might as make it a fucking blowout.' That's the only reason I can think of to bring the frost giants in. Total insanity."

The frost giants were really getting pumped up. The ground was already covered in blood and body parts, but they seemed to be just getting started. Their rage grew with every strike and every blast of the Damned Legion's weapons. They weren't really hurting them, but their amusement had run its course, and now the giants were just done. They didn't want to keep letting them play. It was time to get down to business and make sure that anything left of the Damned Legion was unable to be reattached.

Katie bounced her foot up and down and wrung her hands as she watched what was going on. With every human death, Damned or not, Legion or not, she couldn't help but think about the plane full of soldiers who would never have the chance to break the spell. The ones they'd sacrificed. She wasn't sure now if it had been the right thing to do.

After a few minutes, Pandora looked at her, just as anxious. Katie shook her head and marched over to where Juntto and Kraggen stood. "Excuse me."

Kraggen glanced at her. "Your little muse is speaking."

Katie narrowed her eyes. "I'll say it again, but this time, I am warning you that I fucking mean it. You need to tell your giants to not kill everyone."

Kraggen put his head back and began to laugh. "That is

adorable. You are still trying to act as if being an angel means you have the ability to save these people. They are obviously weak if they have been taken over by that pathetic Leviathan."

Juntto glanced down at her, his eyes wide, watching her jaw clench and unclench. Her fists were so tight that they were almost paper-white. She reached up and poked Kraggen hard on the shoulder. "Look, I know you think you are tough because you are bigger and stronger—and who knows, maybe it's true—but those humans out there are not bad. They were once very good and very important soldiers. They have just been taken over, that's all."

Kraggen eyed her for a moment. "They were soldiers? You mean, human warriors?"

Katie nodded, and Pandora walked up next to her. "They were held in high regard, having saved sometimes upward of a thousand or more lives with one single action. They are Damned, yes, but they are good, and they were working to clear the Earth of demons."

Kraggen thought about it for a moment but still shrugged her off. "They are going to get what they are going to get. It is that simple."

Juntto put up his hand. "Now, hold on. These are people from my world. Humans who have worked, not just for my cause, but for everyone's. Do you think you are immune to hell's demons? I think not. One of the reasons it took me so long to get back was because they attempted to brainwash me and use me to kill others."

Kraggen smirked. "So, you are *not* as strong as you seem. Too bad for you. I will not order them to stop killing."

Juntto gritted his teeth, tired of being told no. He grabbed Kraggen by the shoulder and leaned in close. "I think you have forgotten your place, Lord. You are no longer in our dimension. You are on Earth, and on Earth, *I* am the king, the ruler, the almighty. Now, pull your guys back, or you and I are going to have some very serious problems. I don't believe you truly want to be stuck on this planet, now, do you?"

Kraggen snarled and crossed his arms, trying to figure out whether he had been had or if he would get a choice in the matter. The problem was, Kraggen was used to being the big shit. He was used to always having his way with no one questioning him. But now there was Juntto, who had rolled in on his noble steed of bravery and nobility, and Kraggen had to bow down.

After a few moments, though, he realized that fighting Juntto was probably incredibly stupid. He was not in his dimension, he did not have his weapons, and he needed the girl to get them back.

Finally, after far too much contemplation, Kraggen threw his arms up. "Fine, you get your way this time, but only because I am on your territory."

Kraggen shook his head as he walked forward, putting his hands to his mouth and shouting out in a language that neither Katie nor Pandora had ever heard before. They didn't know what he was telling them exactly, but moments later the carnage began to slow. Instead of ripping them apart, the giants were ripping the Damned away, pulling them as far back as they could go in order to free them from Legion's influence.

It was almost too simple. As soon as they crossed the

threshold of power, their eyes cleared and they found themselves blinking up at the giants. It was a little hard for some of them to take, since they didn't know what had happened to them, not to mention seeing giant blue men standing over them. Katie and Pandora were able to help that part, though. They used their angel magic to send a wave of comfort and understanding across the Damned, helping their bodies and their minds relax and clear from the assimilation.

Pandora and Katie had bodies all around them again, but this time they were alive and well. Even the demons were sending vibes of thanks instead of fear to Pandora. But still, the fight was not over. It would never be over until Legion was as far away from Earth as he could get. Or dead, which was preferable for most of them.

Katie stepped to the edge of the hill and watched as the frost giants cleared the last of the Damned Legion from the grounds. They began to circle, chanting, slapping their hands loudly on their thighs. Their bodies moved sinuously, dancing to their ancestors, to their victories. Dancing to the capture of a creature that didn't belong on Earth. He didn't belong anywhere that they knew of.

Vinders stepped in front of Legion to ensure that no one harmed him. Facing out, all he could see and hear were the eyes of the frost giants and their bellowing calls. The ground shook with each stomp and the circle closed in, trapping the two with nowhere to go.

21

"Aye yay a ya yaaaa!" one of the frost giants bellowed in a high-pitched tone, piercing the deep voices of the others and causing all the sound to cease instantly.

Vinders looked around frantically as the giants stomped again, then the front row took a knee. Through the ranks of the frosts, one of the higher-ranking warriors stepped through. He had black tattoos up his neck and across his face. His long silvery hair was shaved on one side and his clothes were thick, small bones hanging from every seam.

Shaking his head, Vinders put his hands up in front of himself. The warrior roared and lunged, grabbing Vinders by the throat and the legs and ripping his jugular from his body. He slashed the remaining limbs apart, tossing them in all directions. When he was done, the entire group grunted, jumping back to their feet.

Every other giant took a leap forward, and they repeated this until they were close enough to reach him with their spears. Legion just stood there with no fear in his eyes, unconcerned about their proximity. One of the giants in back clapped his hands hard over his head and rubbed his palms together quickly.

Then he stopped and grunted, which was followed by the others aiming their spears. Every giant close to him slammed their spears into Legion, thinking that would be the end. They speared him again and again until every last tip of their bone spears had broken off. They all stopped and slowly backed up, holding the spears in their hands and looking at them wildly. They had never imagined something like that could happen. The beast could not be killed.

Pandora narrowed her eyes. "Even if we can't kill him, he still needs to get the fuck out of here."

Katie cracked her knuckles. "I have to agree with you on that one."

They had to think fast. Legion was beginning to regain his strength, and a hell of a lot of people had been released from his control. She wasn't willing to even think about giving them up again. They had survived it, and they deserved her protection.

Pandora's eyes grew wide and she reached out, grabbing Katie and pulling her close to her. She whispered in her ear, and Katie smiled broadly. They nodded to each other and took off down the hill, waving at Juntto. He was on the sidelines, watching in dismay as Legion endured attack after attack. He saw them running, and Pandora pointed two fingers at her eyes.

He started toward the group as Pandora and Katie stopped about ten feet back. Katie licked her lips and pulled the energy in, concentrating hard on one specific place. She pulled her hands apart and flung the portal to the Crystal dimension open wide behind them.

Juntto waved his arms. "Throw him in! Throw him in the portal now!"

One of the giants glanced back at the portal and dove over the others, grabbing Legion by the neck. He tossed him under his arm to another giant, who flipped him back over his head to the line closest to the portal. The closest frost giant held him tightly in his hand, and with one smooth swipe, he punted Legion straight into the portal. The Leviathan sailed through, hitting branches and leaves of crystals as he tumbled head over heels and then hit the ground, skidding through the sharp stones and leaving blood behind him.

The frost giants all took a knee, waiting for the perfect moment to celebrate. Pandora gave the Leviathan the finger before slamming the portal shut. The frost giants jumped to their feet, throwing their hands straight up. Deep wild cheers echoed around the Romanian landscape.

Katie dusted off her hands and Pandora hip-checked her, both of them grinning. It was the first cheerful moment they'd had since they'd brought the frost giants back with them, and although they still didn't know if they would become a new problem, at that moment neither Katie or Pandora cared. They had been successful in the first part, which was vital.

Pandora shook Katie's arm and pointed at the other hill. What looked like hundreds of people came over the top, dazed and confused about where they were. Their eyes were no longer purple, and they had been given their lives back. They were the ones who weren't Damned and had been kept in the shadows for safety. All the Damned who had been spared no longer had purple eyes, returning to the deep crimson they were used to.

Juntto lumbered up to them and nodded. "That was quick thinking. Fucking Leviathan deserved to be ripped apart starting with his mummy dick, but I guess some time in the crystal dimension will do him good. Besides, I doubt he will live long there. There is nothing to sustain him."

Pandora patted him on the back. "Sorry about your slave, dude. I mean, I'm pretty sure it would have been an issue here anyway. The humans don't take too kindly to the word 'slave.'"

The frost giants had gotten even rowdier in the background, and Juntto looked over his shoulder with a glint of excitement in his eyes. Katie shook her head and waved him off. "Go be with your people. I know it has been a very long time. Just try not to break the planet or start any wars."

Juntto smirked. "We will do our very best."

It was a celebration of giant proportions. The rest of the valley, starting half a mile from the bloody battle site, was transformed from a rocky and barren landscape to one reminiscent of Viking times on Earth. Kraggen's army made camp where they stopped. Tents that seemed massive to humans but were just tall enough for the giants sprang up, bonfires were stoked, and the smell of meat and ash filled the stagnant air around them.

Katie called in a favor from a friend close by, having

crate after crate of tequila dropped at the campsite. The boxes of liquor outnumbered the boxes of ammo, but ammo wasn't what they needed to celebrate with. The tequila, on the other hand, was a hit. The giants couldn't get enough of it, and were trying to figure out how they could make it back in their dimension.

There were giants all over, singing, dancing, telling stories of battles past, and generally having a good time with their fellow beings. Juntto wasn't missing out on the fun either, standing atop a pile of trees they had gathered for the bonfire from the forest a mile away. He toasted his relatives, his ancestors, and the giants' blood that ran through them all. He made speeches honoring his old slave and all those who'd died.

Juntto was hailed as the King of Earth and celebrated for his valor and ability to know when he needed his fellow giants to help him through the difficult times. Kraggen's men even made him a throne of wood and steel. He sat perched at the head of the party, enjoying the sights and sounds and feeling the energy of the others pulsing through him.

The general smiled when he got the short text from Katie letting him know that the Leviathan was gone. At least one thing was off of his shoulders. The phone on his desk rang, and it was too late for the secretary to still be there. "This is General Brushwood."

"Please hold for the President of Romania," the pleasant voice said.

The general tapped his fingers on the desk as he waited. "Brushwood. You're still in the office."

"Yes, sir, I am always in the office," he replied. "How can I help you?"

"Well, I was just kind of wondering where the blue monsters are going to go? You know, the ones currently staging a melee in the valley."

The general rubbed his face. "I'll have to get back to you on that one."

Calvin, Brock, and the rest of the team pulled their bags from the overhead bin and loaded up. They walked down the steps of the plane and into the hangar, where two HMMWVs sat waiting for them. Calvin carried Sean down the steps of the plane, and Turner unfolded his chair at the bottom. Seeing the waiting vehicles, Calvin laughed. "What, we have one cripple, and they send us the nice cars?"

Sean smirked, holding onto the arms of the chair as Calvin set him down. "If it *was* on my account, you're welcome. Let my legs be the bribe."

All the guys laughed, heading over and loading in their luggage, and, of course, Sean. The drive over was calm and quiet, and they didn't get to see the scene of the battle. Then again, they had seen so many in the past that it would be kind of a waste of time. They pulled up at the Damned encampment, looking out at the many soldiers and civilians who were obviously resting from their assimilation into the Legion.

Eddie shook his head. "These dudes and dudettes got the shit end of the duty stick. Yes, I would like to join the military, be taken over by a maniacal overlord, and almost get killed by frost giants. What's that? Would I like to add in being saved by two angels? Sure, why not?"

Brock chuckled, opening the door. "The things we do for our country."

The guys hopped out, Calvin taking a moment to get Sean situated. Pandora and Katie came over to greet them, having spied the caravan pulling in. It wasn't hard to spot since they were in a pretty secluded area, one road in and out.

Eddie and Turner pushed Sean while Calvin gave Katie a hug and stepped back so Brock could do the same. Their hug was slightly different. Calvin furrowed his brow as he stood there, hearing music of sorts and deep laughter off in the distance. "I feel like there is a giant frat party going on."

Katie giggled. "It's something like that. Those giants really know how to throw down. They are very glad they were able to get rid of the Leviathan."

Brock nodded. "Yeah, tell us all about that, please. Sounds like there was a battle from hell minus the demons."

Katie rolled her eyes. "It was definitely intense."

Pandora scoffed. "Intense? Try, 'the most stressful freaking battle ever.' Try, 'I've never actually seen someone's eyeballs plucked from their heads.' Try, 'there were fucking slaves, and the giants think that Juntto is the king of Earth and he conquered the angels.' Talk about letting a lie get away from you! This one is rolling downhill with no plateau in sight."

Sean looked around. "So, are most of these Damned the ones who got caught up in the Legion?"

Katie nodded. "Yep, although there were so many more of them than this. I had a hard time getting the other frost king to start pulling them back instead of killing them. Finally, Juntto jumped in and fixed it, but there are more than enough body parts in the valley if anyone needs them. We are going to have to send a cleanup crew to collect them so we can return them to their families. I'll make sure that the general knows. Right now, they dealt with Legion, and everybody is partying down."

Pandora put her hands up. "All right, enough talking about it. Let's get over there and show them how humans get down."

She looked around, finally spotting one of the soldiers who could help. "Ah. *Garçon!*"

He raised an eyebrow. "My name is Rick."

She patted his chest. "Mmhmm. Good. Okay. I need you to take these guys' belongings to their tents. Can you do that?"

Rick nodded. "Sure."

Pandora smiled. "Chuck, you are the best."

He blinked at her. "Rick. My name is Rick."

Pandora sighed. "I'm sorry. I'm the worst with people's names when I just meet them."

Rick threw his hands up as she walked away. "You just pulled me into the shower thirty-five minutes ago!"

The crew headed out to the party, arriving just in time to see one of the giants doing a headstand while guzzling a bottle of tequila. Turner and Eddie grabbed Sean and rolled into the party, ready to get wasted on whatever alcohol they could confiscate from the frost giants.

Pandora pushed up her tits and slapped Katie hard on the ass, making her squeal. "Time for me to wine and dine the king, and I don't mean of Earth. That castle was fabulous."

Calvin, Brock, and Katie laughed as she strutted off, garnering a few whistles from nearby giants. Calvin turned to Katie and Brock. "While I'm here, I might as well have a sip and hang out a bit. Maybe go pay homage to King Juntto."

Katie groaned, rolling her eyes. "Kick him in the balls for me, and tell him it comes with love from his slave Katie."

Calvin hurried off and Brock turned to Katie, pulling her into him. "I say we tour one of these huge tents and see what we can discover."

Katie wrinkled her nose. "I don't want to discover the giants."

Brock laughed. "Not the giants I was talking about."

The next morning, the smell of cooked meats and bread wafted through the tent city. Kraggen had hosted a feast for the leaders of the armies, giving thanks for all that was done. For the humans invited, the hangovers were stark, but the giants seemed happier and livelier than ever.

Calvin, Brock, Katie, Pandora, and Juntto were there, while the other three stayed in their tents, half-dead, with hangovers that would last them until the war was over. The only one out of the five who had any issues was Pandora, but that was mostly because she had gone to bed alone after beating on a few rude giants and being turned away from talking to Kraggen. Not that she had really wanted to, but she figured he would be fun to play with.

They all sat around a makeshift table Kraggen's troops had put together. He stood up at the end of it and raised his chalice, which had been hand-carved overnight. "Thank you all for coming to this breakfast. I know a lot of you had more fun than you could handle last night, and that is the way it's supposed to be. Of course, none of it would have been possible without Juntto and me and my men."

Pandora leaned into Katie. "He's a real modest one. Douchebag."

Katie snickered, hiding her smirk and clearing her throat. Kraggen took a sip of his drink, which Katie for some reason figured was tequila. He swished his hand in front of him. "I also have an announcement to make. A very important one, and it is personal, so no one need feel obliged to join me. Either way, I have decided that I will not be leaving Earth. I want to stay here."

Katie dropped her fork, and Pandora giggled. That really wasn't the way Katie had hoped things would go, but it looked like she might just be screwed. Her eyes shifted to Juntto, who was able to keep his composure. She had to give it to him; when it came to matters involving his people, he had become a professional at keeping calm.

Kraggen smiled at the giants who were nodding their heads. He shrugged and looked at Juntto for a reaction. When he didn't get one, he continued, "I want the Earthly nobles under Juntto's control to pay me homage, as is my right. They need to know how deep his roots really go. What do you think, Juntto? I'm sorry...*King* Juntto."

Juntto gave him a mocking smile. "I think that may be unnecessary. Our people will be chomping at the bit to give you gifts and rewards back on our home planet, and it might be too much to carry. Besides, humans don't worship us, they fear us. They don't give deep-rooted love; they give you attention so they can survive. You'll be much better off at home."

Kraggen's smile slowly faded, and he set his cup down. He began to chuckle angrily, shaking his head. "You know, Juntto, you almost had me fooled. I don't think you conquered Earth. I don't think you rule this planet. And do you know how I came to that conclusion? Your little angels over here. They are too comfortable, and you are too happy to look to them for answers. A true king would never need that. A true king would always have the answers."

Juntto smirked, his eyes shifting downward. "And you believe you are a king of that sort?"

Kraggen smiled, picking up his cup again. "I *know* I am that kind of king. Therefore, since there is no leader, I am declaring myself the new King of Earth!"

All of Kraggen's men stood and cheered, raising their glasses to him. He waved his arms and looked at Juntto and the rest in warning.

22

Lucifer took a gulp of his drink and glanced at the screen just as Kraggen declared himself King of Earth. Lucifer choked, spraying his drink all over the floor in front of him. He gasped for air, wine running down his chin. He leaned over and slapped his paws on his thighs, his laughter reverberating through the throne room. It became almost manic and high-pitched, and he let go of the chalice he was holding, spilling the wine all over the floor.

Mania and Baal quickly stood up, glancing at each other. They had never seen him act that way, and usually when laughter was involved, it wasn't a good sign. It most often was followed by the extreme torture or death of one of the demons. Neither of them wanted to be next, so they simultaneously began to back away from him. Lucifer hadn't noticed that he was scaring the hell out of them, and they kept looking at each other, unsure of what to do.

But the reality of it was that Lucifer wasn't upset. He was actually thrilled at the way everything was going. He looked around for Baal and Mania, who stopped moving and grinned. "Oh, that is the perfect thing. Absolutely the perfect thing. Can you believe it? I can't. I mean, I love all of this. The way it is blowing up in their faces by bringing the frost giants to Earth! Oh, the glory of it all. If the other idiots had just waited, they would see that humans will just kill themselves off with stupid decisions."

Baal and Mania looked at each other again, and Mania let out a deep sigh. She sauntered back over to the chairs and took a seat. Baal wasn't as sure about his chances, so he took his time making his way back. The last thing he wanted to do was end up lashed to a pole with only one testicle and no limbs.

Lucifer stood up and let out a deep sigh. "Oh, man. That's just so great. I'm really hoping that somebody finally murders that asswipe Juntto. He's a fucking lunatic; that's why we used him in the first place."

Baal smirked. "The Leviathan who grew a conscience. Disgusting."

Lucifer quickly pointed at Baal, making him jump. "Exactly right. Exactly fucking right. I'll be honest, though, I'm more interested in how Lilith is going to deal with this. She has a tendency to think without touching. Not to mention that if you give her one victory, she will be headstrong and stupid about other situations of the same magnitude. That's how she ends up getting her dumb ass into cracks."

Baal looked at the footage. "Do you think she can take this frost giant down? He's pretty cocky."

Lucifer shrugged. "She brought Juntto to heel, but man, I don't know. I don't know if this bitch can bring Kraggen under her control. He isn't the same as Juntto was. He cares about fame and the other fucking stupid shit humans cling to. I'm not mocking it; it's what fills my quota of beautifully disgusting demons. But it's still different than Juntto. He was ruthless, just like her. He was...beautifully disturbed. A being after my own heart...if I had one."

"I want everyone to understand," Brock explained, pacing in front of the Damned. "The frost giants were the ones who made it possible to get rid of Legion. They are also incredibly hard to kill. If we don't have to fight them, we won't. This is more an intimidation tactic than anything. Nobody here moves until me or Katie gives the word. No need to accidentally start an incident."

The Damned had gathered together at Brock's request. They had a problem on their hands, one that Katie wanted to deal with as quickly as possible. The Damned were humanity's best hope, but at the same time, they wanted to avoid a massive outburst. A fight with the frost giant army would most likely not end well for the Damned or the world. When the call was sounded, though, everyone came. Every Damned who had been put down by the Legion showed in support of their promise to protect the world, not just themselves. Sure, the frosts had saved them, but that didn't give them the right to attempt global domination. They weren't going to allow it.

Korbin had arrived and was finding the newest development more than a bit disturbing. He walked into the comm tent and looked at all the Damned gathered there.

He noticed their solemn faces. The idea that they needed to protect the country from those who had saved their lives was hard for them to swallow, especially after such a short amount of time. Still, it was a dire situation, which was why he'd come as soon as he heard the news.

The tent flap was pulled back, and Sean rolled himself inside. Calvin nodded at him, knowing full well it was his choice to be there. Sean hadn't come all that way to sit it out. He had come there to help. He knew he would get pushback for it, but it was what it was. He was not going to spend any more time being pushed because his legs were wheels and his stature not as high. He had spent a huge portion of his adult life as a Damned, and just from that, he was tougher than most.

Eddie was worried about him, though. He saw him roll in and to the side, listening to Brock. When they had been sent to the airstrip for the trip over, Eddie had jogged ahead to catch up with Sean. "Hey, man. I really think maybe you should sit this one out."

Sean just shook his head and kept wheeling. Eddie sighed and jumped in front of him. Sean stopped and lifted his eyes to Eddie's face. "Move, Eddie."

Eddie put his hands up. "Just hear me out. Not only are you dealing with bad motherfucking beasts, but they are massively larger and much more highly trained. I think it's fucking amazing that you want to stand behind this, but I don't want to see anything happen to you."

Sean released some of his anger. "I really appreciate you caring about me. I do. It means a hell of a lot. But this is my choice, and I know the risks. If you want to be my friend, you'll support that."

Eddie narrowed his eyes as the crew headed out. Finally, he nodded. "All right, man. I got your back."

Sean held out his hand and Eddie fist-bumped it. "Come on, let's catch up."

The entire Damned group walked together toward the frost encampment, with Katie and Pandora leading the way. When they arrived, the frosts stopped, staring from each side. Juntto was there, and Kraggen had begun to walk toward them. "What is this?"

Katie walked up to Kraggen. "I am here representing the people of Earth. This planet has gone through more egregious and terrifying scenarios in the last three years than most civilizations go through in a lifetime. We are not willing to allow you to continue that with your presence. You need to go home."

Kraggen glanced at Juntto and began to laugh. "Juntto, is this another one of your jokes? A welcome from your people?"

Katie gritted her teeth. "I assure you, Juntto had no knowledge of this. I can also promise you that if you and your army of frost giants do not peacefully go back to your world, there will be consequences."

Kraggen smirked. "Like what, little angel?"

"Like motherfucking paperwork. That's what, you rude-ass blue blob," Pandora spouted.

Juntto gasped, putting his big blue hand to his chest. "Come on, now. I think that's too harsh a punishment even for the frost giants. And are you forgetting that these are also people that assisted you in getting rid of the Leviathan and saved the entire world in the process? Regardless of your feelings about them being here on this planet, we will not torture them. That is disgusting, even from you."

Kraggen nodded. "Thank you, Juntto, although I don't know what this paperwork torture is."

Juntto hadn't finished. "At the same time, Kraggen, you *must* return to your own planet. Although your presence and comradery have been amazing in our darkest of moments, you do not belong here, nor will you understand the customs and lifestyle. Do you agree to leave peacefully and without confrontation?"

Kraggen's mouth was hanging slightly open. He shook his head, trying to wrap his mind around the treachery he felt had just been brought to a head. "I will not. I have a right to be here like anyone else, and you will not make the decision for me. Not you, and not that whore claiming to be an angel. This is not your choice."

Katie laughed. "I think you are wrong. Seeing as how this is my planet, rather than yours or even Juntto's, I have the right to kick hate out of this world. And you, sir, are looking for nothing more than adoration and slaves. We are free here, mostly. We don't need you to bring that perversion here. Trust us when we say we've seen the worst of a frost giant, and we are prepared to protect our lands."

Juntto put up his hand and shook his head. "This is not going to go down like that. Is it, Kraggen? No, see, I'm going to help you on your way to becoming a more intelligent frost giant, who knows the best way forward is through a portal back to the snow. What do you say to that?"

Kraggen licked his big blue lips, looking around at the

others with a laugh. "You, sir, are in no position to be barking orders at me or anyone else in this army. We will do as we please, and when we have had our fun with these humans, we will decide when to return home."

Juntto chuckled, shaking his head. "You are incredibly stubborn." He breathed deeply through his nose and unlatched the fur robe from his back. "I guess we will just have to settle this the old way. I, Juntto, warrior king, rightful heir to the throne, descendant of the Great Allam of Frost, challenge you, Kraggen, to a fight. Whoever wins will have the right to rule the Earth."

The Damned moved into a semi-circle to the right and behind Juntto. The frost giants did the same behind Kraggen. All parties, once settled, dropped to one knee and waited for the fight to begin. Sitting in the center of the line of Damned, Sean rolled forward and put the brakes on his chair. He looked at Juntto and nodded his head, the blue giant nodding back. Eddie walked up on one side of Sean and Turner stood on the other in solidarity with him. With Juntto. With the freedom for all beings on Earth.

Juntto rolled his shoulders, facing Kraggen. "How would you like to conduct this fight?"

Kraggen sucked a whole lot of air into his lungs and blew out, the stench of liquor hitting almost everyone. "I think this should be brute force. Let us solve this age-old question: who is stronger, the warrior king or the king of all? So, no weapons. We should only need our strength anyway. That is what we are known for."

Juntto nodded, reaching down and pulling off the three knives strapped to his legs. He dropped them near Sean and grew to his full size. "I agree. This should be me showing you what it means to be a warrior."

The two giants nodded and turned to their lines, preparing themselves. Juntto walked over to Pandora and Katie, who looked at him reverently. "We will be above you at all times. If there is anything shady going on, we will know about it."

Juntto reached out and put his hands on both of their shoulders. "It is vital, no matter what happens in there, that you allow me to fight on my own. No picking up the pieces."

Pandora snorted. "You are saying that if he bests you, to let you die. Sorry, you big blue fuck, that is not how we roll here."

Juntto squeezed her shoulder lightly. "I appreciate your friendship, but this is the way it must be done. You should expect the same from his side."

Pandora looked at the ground and back up at him. "Be careful in there."

Juntto shook his head, looking around at all of the kneeling Damned waiting for the battle to begin. "I will not. I live on Earth now. I am one of you now. I will *not* be careful. I will be fearless in my love for this planet and fearless in my compassion for its humans. Angie taught me a saying, and I think this applies here. 'Fortune favors the bold.'"

Katie smiled. "Be careful with that. Many of those who have pushed forward under Fortune's protection have died."

Juntto cracked a smile. "That is not on my list today. Today I will be a hero. Kraggen, if he were to rule the Earth, would rule with an iron fist. It's time for me to send him home."

As Juntto walked into the battle ring, Katie and Pandora took flight, soaring high into the sky. They began to circle like vultures, watching the crowd from all angles. Neither Katie nor the rest of them trusted the frost giants or Kraggen for a moment. Korbin led several of the Damned outside the battle area to watch the frost giants for any signs of a coup. Brock did the same, and Sean stayed put on the front lines.

Kraggen stepped out, his armor and furs gone, cracking his big knuckles. He had an amused smirk on his face as he glanced at the angels above them. "Look, Juntto, they are waiting for your dead body so they can pick you clean."

Juntto smirked. "I believe that they would much rather have a chance to go at you themselves, but for the same reason they would not pick me dry: they don't like scraps."

Kraggen's lip twitched as he frowned. Both giants lunged, slamming into each other. Juntto pushed Kraggen back, his feet creating huge divots in the ground beneath him. Juntto shifted to the right, spinning on his foot and then dropping low, knocking Kraggen's legs out from under him. The Damned began to chant quietly, repeating Juntto's name over and over.

Kraggen leapt back to his feet and jumped forward, grabbing Juntto by the back of his neck. With a whip-like motion of his arm, he threw Juntto down and punched him hard in the chest. The air left Juntto's lungs and he grunted, grabbing his chest. Kraggen laughed loudly and turned, putting his arms out to the Damned.

Juntto climbed to all fours and Kraggen turned, rearing back and kicking him as hard as he could in the head. Juntto's body spun, and he landed on his back with blue blood covering his face. The frost giants all stayed quiet as Kraggen gloated, pumping his fists. "A true king is able to keep the riffraff down. You made a mistake, Juntto the Warrior: you should have never come back. I took that home from you, and now I will take this one as well."

Juntto heard him but sat still, collecting his strength. Up above Pandora hissed, clenching her fists and preparing to go down to help him. Katie grabbed her arm, shaking her head. "He made us promise. Give him a chance. Do not believe for a moment that Juntto is done yet. He is smart, and even more so when it comes to his own kind. I know it's hard to watch."

Pandora screeched in frustration. "I want to fly down there, reach through Kraggen's asshole, and pull his balls out the back."

Katie wrinkled her nose. "All right. Yeah. But right now, let's keep our hands out of his butthole at the request of our big blue warrior."

Pandora flipped her legs down and hovered. "Man, if I ever tell you some bullshit like that and you see me getting my ass beat, you better fucking help a bitch out. If you don't, we will not be friends anymore."

Katie flipped forward like Pandora and put her arm over her shoulder. "I'd stick my arm in a butthole for you any day."

They both chuckled, their faces going straight as they

watched the battle rage on. They would never admit it, but a very small part of them feared Juntto wouldn't survive the fight.

Angie pushed the vacuum, listening to her music with the television on just for the news headlines. She danced a little, swaying her hips to the soft beat in her ears. As she turned, her eyes caught the screen as Juntto's bloody face flashed across it.

She stopped moving, flipping off the vacuum and taking off her headphones, then curled up in the large chair in the room and turned up the television as the live footage rolled. It was her Juntto, and someone she assumed was the king of Juntto's dimension. He lay there on the screen with blood on his face and Angie covered her mouth, staring at him as the moments passed.

She leaned forward and gripped the chair's arms. "Get up, baby. Get up."

Suddenly Juntto's eyes opened wide. He flipped to his feet and took off, lunging for Kraggen.

"YES!" Angie screamed, throwing her hands up.

23

The two frost giants broke from the circle, wrestling and rolling across the ground. Their bodies bounced wildly, knocking huge chunks of dirt from the hills. The Damned and the giants turned to watch, staying far enough back to not get beat to hell themselves. At the edge of the valley was a forest with tall, thick trees.

Juntto slammed his foot into Kraggen's chest and ran over, yanking a huge tree out of the ground. He lunged forward as Kraggen got up and pulled back, sling-shotting the trunk around and hitting Kraggen in the ribs. The blow threw him several hundred feet, and he smashed into a group of fat old trees. He growled, grabbing one of them as he pulled himself to his feet.

Before Juntto could get another shot in, Kraggen raised the tree over his head and slammed it down on Juntto's, splitting it straight down the middle. They went back and forth, beating the fuck out of each other. Juntto kept swinging, even after Kraggen looked as if he were slowing.

He ripped a thinner tree from the ground and used it

like a baseball bat, knocking Kraggen around like a rag doll. As the frost king wavered on his big blue feet, Juntto patted the ground with the end and wound around, bringing it down and under like he was driving a golf ball down the course. The tree trunk hit Kraggen under the chin and lifted him off his feet. He landed with a thud, not moving for a moment.

Juntto stumbled, blood dripping down his chin and bruises growing darker all over his arms and legs. They had beaten each other to a stand-still, both almost too tired and bruised to continue. He limped over to where Kraggen was, kicking him in the leg. Kraggen groaned and rolled over, heaving himself up. He teetered and thrust out his arm, catching himself on a tree.

Kraggen coughed and spat a mouthful of blood on the ground. One of his eyes was already swollen shut, and there was a huge bruise forming over his entire abdomen. He stepped forward to continue, but dropped to all fours, hacking. Blood and spittle dripped from his lips to the ground. It looked as if Kraggen was on his last legs.

Juntto knew he could end it right there, but he hoped beyond hope that Kraggen would fold and surrender. He was not a warrior, so he saw no shame in saving his own life. Juntto felt that as the king of his world, no matter how much he was hated, he deserved that respect. Finally, Kraggen got to his knees and wiped his mouth with his arm.

His eyes shifted to Juntto, and anger surged through them. He flipped his arm out and pointed at his army. "Fools! I order you to attack this frost giant! He threatens our freedom, and he has soiled your king!"

The frost giants looked at each other. Kraggen snorted and clenched his fists, shaking them at his warriors. "What are you waiting for, you good-for-nothing sacks of shit? Attack him!"

Juntto turned and looked at the frost giants. They all climbed to their feet but did not move. They watched Kraggen struggling on the ground for several moments, then their eyes turned to Juntto, a legend they had only heard tales of. A legend who in their minds represented their land much better than Kraggen did. Slowly one of them took a knee again.

"Why are you not attacking?" Kraggen screamed.

Juntto looked at him. "Because they are something you will never be."

Kraggen spat again, a tooth landing on the ground this time. "Oh, yeah? Please, by all means, Juntto, enlighten your king about what that might be."

"Honorable," Juntto said as he bowed slightly to them.

Kraggen watched with a dropped jaw as every single one of the frost giants bowed their heads in return before slamming their arms across their chests, their fists striking their shoulders. They cried out in a simultaneous battle salute reserved for kings. Juntto was truly touched, and if it weren't for his swollen tear ducts, he would have shed a couple in return for their kindness.

The giant soldiers dropped their arms, and one by one looked down at the ground. This was their way of giving Juntto permission to finish Kraggen. They were not permitted to watch their king die; it would be a shame to their honor, and when they died, they would find themselves in the grasp of their own version of Lucifer.

Juntto turned to Kraggen, who had fallen again, barely able to hold his head up. He reached down with a groan and picked up one of his daggers. He stared at the blade for several moments. Visions of his former life on his planet flashed before him, but the violence he had formerly practiced was not enough to ignite the flame of killing in his chest. He looked at Kraggen again, imagining the travesties he had subjected his people to, but as he stepped forward to finish him, Angie's face floated through his mind.

The compassion in her eyes and the innocence of her soul sent shivers down his spine. He dropped the dagger to the ground point-down and marched over, grabbing Kraggen by the shoulder. The beaten and battered king opened his one good eye and blinked at him.

"Finish it," he whispered. "You have been given that right."

Juntto stared down at him and shook his head. "That would be an honor for you."

Rearing back, he screamed as he slammed his fist into Kraggen's face, knocking him out. Kraggen's body fell to the ground, unmoving. Juntto shook his hand out, wincing. The Damned stood up and looked at him, confused. Juntto waved at them, nodding at Kraggen. "Put him in chains. Make them tight, and wipe the blood from his wounds. He belongs to the people of the frost planet. They will decide his fate. I have only set foot in my land once this millennium. It wouldn't be right."

The Damned nodded and hurried off in different directions to retrieve materials to chain him with, cloth, and his cloak. They went to work chaining him tightly at the ankles and wrists. A couple of the giants came to help, making sure the bonds were tight enough to hold him if he came back to a conscious state.

Juntto stumbled forward and took a knee in front of the giants. They all rose and began to surround him, humming in a deep, low tone. They circled him, each of them running their left hand across his shoulders and over his head.

Above them, Katie and Pandora watched uncertainly as Juntto rose and the giant army began to cheer. Katie shook her head, very confused. "What is this? What are they doing? He just beat the hell out of their leader."

Pandora's face was contemplative and slightly uncomfortable. "He is no longer their leader. They don't allow losers to be leaders, unlike humans, who seem to flock to the most ridiculous people out there. It looks to me as if Juntto has an army now. A real one."

Katie and Pandora slowly flew back to the ground and moved to the side, staying out of the way. Juntto had not acknowledged them or the Damned, with the exception of ordering the soldiers to chain Kraggen up. Instead, he stayed surrounded by his new army, a huge grin on his face.

This all made Katie a bit uneasy. Pandora, too. She watched as the giant army continued to congratulate him, bringing his cloak, cleaning his daggers, and tending to his wounds. They were honoring him, and his eyes sparkled as he pointed out the different things he wanted, being waited on hand and foot.

Pandora turned back to Katie and crossed her arms. Katie looked almost sad. "He has forgotten his life here. He is consumed by his giants."

Pandora nodded. "And he's starting to look like the old Juntto, the one who really likes to fuck shit up. The one who meticulously plans every move."

Katie looked at Kraggen, who was still unconscious. "Like not killing Kraggen."

Pandora nodded. "Like not killing Kraggen."

Lucifer pursed his lips and waved his hand, getting rid of the screen. He sat silently for several moments, staring off into space. "I really thought this would be the end for Juntto. I really, really did. I also thought that by the end of it, Lilith would have been returned to the land of the dead."

Baal felt the sense of being let down that Lucifer was emitting. He had been waiting for Lilith for far too long, and he wished there was a way to bring her back to him. But from the way it looked, not even an army of frost giants could fix that problem. Plus, she was still an angel and wouldn't end up in hell if she died, but Baal was not about to remind him of that.

Baal let him wallow in his grief for several minutes before speaking. "Would you like me to plan an attack after the frost giants are gone? They will be looking forward to getting back to their lives. It would be a surprise attack. We would catch them out of nowhere. I have observed in the past that when they are caught off guard, they tend to be a lot less effective in their fights."

Baal went quiet, knowing he had said enough. Lucifer would reply when he chose to. He sat with his head in his hand, leaning his elbow on the arm of the chair. He waved his other hand. "No, I suppose not."

To Baal's surprise, he was actually relatively thoughtful about the subject. He leaned back, pressing his horned head against the headrest and glaring at the picture on the wall with the burned spot where Lilith had once stood. "In all honesty, I could not do that to her. I have always admired one thing about her; one thing that never wavered. I always madly respected just how batshit-crazy that broad could be. In my opinion, she flourished as Queen of the Damned. She was on point with everything."

Baal smiled. "Well, she *did* bring frost giants to Earth. To me, that means she was either confident in their abilities or she was absolutely insane. Not judging either way, but it did cross my mind."

Lucifer smiled. "It is most likely that she is insane. I won't say she isn't intelligent since she has bested me a couple of times, but crazy is the first word I would use to describe her. To be honest, I can't stop laughing at the thought of her convincing the humans that having those big frozen bastards on Earth was a good idea. If she could do that, I am pretty sure she could do anything."

They sat there for a couple of minutes, chuckling at the thought. Baal worked with Lucifer for quite a while during Lilith's time in hell, and he knew that everything Lucifer was saying was the absolute truth. "My Lord, may I ask you a question?"

Lucifer lifted his eyebrows. "Sure. No one really ever does."

Baal nodded. "What will you do with Lilith when you

have her here? At this moment, she seems to be the complete opposite of who she was before."

Lucifer shrugged. "That is a complicated question, my dear slave Baal. Love is a complex thing. Infatuation and lust can be even more so, especially with someone as blatantly stubborn as her. There are two sides to this fence. Maybe I want to torture her for a thousand years, showing her that no one leaves this kingdom. Or maybe I want to bed her and show her the same thing, just with different tools. I know she would prefer the second option."

A smirk came to Baal's face, and he looked away. Lucifer noticed, though and he laughed. "Why, Baal, you find me amusing?"

Baal shook his head. "No, my Lord. I find the idea of love amusing. Love is apparently so powerful that even our king is not immune to it."

Lucifer grinned. "I suppose you are right, Baal. Not even I am immune to it. Whatever I end up doing with her, I know for sure that I just want Lilith back…preferably in one piece, but I can work with several if it's necessary."

Pandora and Katie walked next to each other, finding the giants even more brazen than before. They whistled and commented as Katie and Pandora passed them. Pandora took Katie's hand, squeezing it tightly. "Take a deep breath. We could handle these idiot pricks, but I think talking to Juntto is more important."

Katie nodded, trying to let their blatant disrespect go.

"Right. We need to make sure he isn't reverting back to his old self. That is what is most important right now."

Pandora nodded. "Exactly. Eyes on the prize, and those jerks can just be extra treats."

Katie chuckled. "I can't believe I am thinking like you these days. Usually I am the one who calms you down."

Pandora shrugged. "Sometimes you have to swallow your own crazy and help your main bitch out. What good would it be if both of us were completely whacked out of our minds?"

They could see Juntto lounging beneath a tent, eating fruit. They hurried forward but stopped short when two frost giant guards stepped in front of them. "If you are going to speak to him, you will have to kneel."

Pandora smiled and walked up close to his face. "If I kneel, I'm going to put your nuts in a meat grinder. So fuck off."

The giant laughed for a moment before he looked her in the eyes, seeing that she was dead serious. He slowly stepped out of the way. Pandora smirked and patted him on the chest. "Good choice."

They approached Juntto, who looked up and smiled at them. "Fruit?"

Katie shook her head, crossing her arms over her chest. "No, thanks."

Pandora nodded at the chair. "So you're a king?"

"I am," Juntto replied.

Katie lifted her eyebrows. "With an army."

Juntto bit into an apple. "The most powerful army in the world."

Katie pursed her lips and tilted her head to the side.

"And, king, what exactly are you planning on doing with the most powerful army in the world?"

Juntto tossed the core over his shoulder and slumped to the side, staring out at the giants. He looked extremely bored, which surprised Katie. She figured he would be reveling in his newfound fame.

Juntto closed one eye and pretended to squish the giants with his fingers. "Ask them to subscribe to my YouTube channel, then send them home."

Katie and Pandora looked at each other, surprised. Juntto sat up. "This planet is not big enough for all these assholes, and I am pretty sure that if I let them stay, Pandora would go through their toxic masculinity like the plague."

Pandora snapped her fingers. "Damn fucking straight I would."

Juntto groaned and stood up, stretching his arms over his head. "So, let's get this show on the road. You guys got the portals?"

Katie nodded. "Of course. We got this."

Katie and Pandora went to work building a large enough portal for the frost giants to easily get through. Luckily for them, they got the dimension right the first time around. Juntto made an announcement, thanking them for their help and giving them instructions on what to do when they got back. They would need a leader, but they were to choose wisely. "Make the decision from not only honor and valor, but from your hearts as well. Lead with your hearts, and your kingdom…our kingdom…will flourish. Thank you for the honors bestowed, and please take that asshole with you. Earth doesn't want him."

Kraggen yelled as they tossed him through the portal, still chained. Juntto put both of his hands up, making peace signs. "And smash that Follow button for my show!"

The giants lined up, not wanting to go back but knowing they didn't have a choice. Korbin and the guys lined up at the portal, making sure to shake each of their hands as they stepped through. They wanted them to know they were truly thankful for what they had done for Earth, even if they were only doing it for Juntto.

Standing back, they watched the last of them go through, each carrying a box of tequila with them. There was no way they were going to go back to frost hell without that amazing liquor to keep their huge bodies warm—and their wives happy all night long. The humans couldn't help but laugh.

24

To think that Pandora, Katie, or the guys would actually allow all of the tequila to be taken was seriously a laugh. When the giants began taking it, Katie had motioned to Pandora, who had motioned to Sean, who used his lap and chair as a wheelbarrow to hide as much as they could. It was a team effort, which was good, since it would also be a team effort to drink it all. Not a single person was complaining.

Pandora came out of a tent carrying several bottles and began passing them around. "Take a shot, pass it around, ninety-nine bottles of tequila going down!"

Everyone was going to do a shot. Well, more like shots, plural. Once they got going, the excitement of the success of their mission was almost overwhelming. Katie stood next to Pandora as she passed out bottles. "Do you think everyone is so excited because they all thought, somewhere in their minds, that we would fail?"

Pandora shook her head. "No. I think it's because

everyone was afraid that we would fail. Fear can definitely sober you up."

Pandora handed Katie a full bottle and took one for herself. She hopped up on top of the boxes and raised the bottle. "Holy shit, people, we succeeded! For one more day, we kept the Earth safe."

Everyone cheered. Pandora whistled for a moment, swaying with her bottle. "First and foremost, and in every sarcastic way we can imagine, take a shot in honor of KING JUNTTO!"

The whole group lifted their shot or bottle and cheered in unison. Juntto laughed and jumped up and down in excitement. Pandora took a shot and wiped her mouth with the back of her hand. "Next, to the FROST GIANTS! You big blue assholes were more than a bit useful."

Again, everyone cheered and took a shot. Pandora hopped down, and Turner climbed up. "We didn't get to see this, but we have to say, a shot to the empty crystal dimension that's now a prison!"

Cheers, screaming, and guzzling of tequila.

Eddie jumped up with Turner. "And last, but definitely most important. Without Sean, and his lame legs, we would not be enjoying this delicious tequila. It would all be freezing in the snow hell that is Juntto's home. So, everyone down a shot to Sean's sweet-ass wheelchair!!"

Sean got the biggest cheer of all, everyone breaking out into conversation, laughter, and even song after that. Katie and Pandora high-fived Sean and shook their heads at Eddie and Turner as they attempted to race the tequila bottle. They lasted all about three seconds on that one.

The phone in Katie's pocket began to buzz, and she

pulled it out. Looking at the number, she nudged Pandora and flipped her head to get them over to where it wouldn't be as noisy. They made their way over and Katie answered, putting it on speakerphone. "This is Katie and Pandora."

"Whoop!" Pandora yelled out, taking a swig of the tequila.

The general laughed. "Sounds like a real party out there. Good thing you hid some of that tequila."

Katie narrowed her eyes. "Are you spying on us?"

"What good are satellites if you can't use them to see what your favorite mercs are up to?" He chuckled.

Pandora giggled. "I'll make sure to leave my curtains open...farther."

"I do draw the line at some things," he replied.

Pandora wrinkled her nose. "Ah, too bad. At least all this nightmare is over, and now we can move on to the next stupid crisis."

"Wellll..." the general replied.

Katie's face dropped. "Oh, man."

He tried to calm her anxiety. "Not to worry. It is not anything as insane as what you just pulled off. And congrats for that, by the way."

Katie and Pandora high-fived. "Thanks. So, what is this new situation?"

"There's still a dangling thread in this whole thing," the general replied. "I hate that we didn't address this earlier, since it would have been a lot simpler. But Powell, the one using Timothy's program, had a partner, and that partner, Xian, was actually the one to fully figure out the system. The problem is, he is still out there. He stormed off when Powell refused to take things seriously."

Timothy typed quickly on a keyboard, moving from one to another. He had a vendetta against this Xian guy, and he was determined to track him down. The dungeon seemed almost too quiet that day, and he was glad that some more intel had come up on the case. He wanted every last bit of it taken care of and gone—not only for him, but for Sean too. He knew that until it was all resolved, Sean wasn't going to be able to move past it. Not on that base, at least.

"What are you doing?" Stephanie asked, leaning over his shoulder.

He glanced at her and then at the computer. "Right now, I am running as many searches as I possibly can, everything from his name to his handles on his social media accounts. Anything that will tell us where we can specifically find him."

"Does it come up with different people?"

Timothy scooted forward a bit. "Sometimes, of course, especially with how much the internet has grown over the years. People put weird words on all kinds of stuff. But the info I just got will make it a bit easier."

Stephanie followed him, her body touching the back of his chair. He cleared his throat and shifted himself in his chair, but she wasn't catching on. "Honey, do you need to stand over my shoulder like that? I mean, I love you and all that jazz, but I can seriously feel the rumbling of your stomach right now. Have you eaten lately? I am telling you, 'Ethiopian child' is not coming back into style. It is all about loving your body."

Timothy got up and walked fast around the room,

pulling papers from the printer, flipping through one of the binders he had made, and coming back over to type something else into the computer. Stephanie stepped back and crossed her arms over her chest. She watched him run back and forth, back and forth.

"First of all, yes, I am eating," she replied. "Secondly, honey, you are running around like a chicken with its head cut off. I think this is the second time I have ever seen you sweat."

Timothy gasped, touching his forehead and sliding into his chair. He pulled out a compact and began patting his forehead, chin, and around his nose. "I cannot handle a shiny face. That is just off-limits."

Stephanie put her hand on his shoulder. "Then slow down."

Timothy dropped his hands in his lap. "I am trying, dammit. I spend all my time in this dungeon alone. I have to get things done, and there are really no distractions, so I just speed around doing things."

Stephanie pursed her lips and gave him a look. Timothy sighed and turned toward the screen, watching the system do its job. "Fine. I was used to having Sean wheeling around and getting in the way. He was always here making me scuff my leather shoes and forcing me to stub my toes. It really was a huge pain, but now that it's gone...I don't know. I just try to pass the time to get out of the silence of the place. Not to mention, I redecorated for him, and now I just have all this handicap space. It's like being forced to use the handicapped stall in the store. You feel awkward, and there is far too much room."

Timothy put both hands on the keyboard and added a

few more search parameters to the information that was coming back, then swiveled his chair back around. "So anyways, it's just fucking weird being here all alone like this. I tried talking to myself, but I am not the greatest conversationalist. I agree with myself far too often to satisfy my argumentative side."

Stephanie tried to hide her smile, but she couldn't. She hurried over and put her arms out, bending down and hugging him tightly. "Aww. You miss him."

Timothy tapped her shoulder, grimacing. "No. I miss… cripples. So easy to feel superior."

Stephanie pulled back. "You can admit it to me. I understand."

Timothy rolled his eyes. "No. I don't even miss…"

The computer alarm sounded, and Timothy spun back around. He hit a few keys, and then one more to bring the information up on the screen. "We found something."

Katie and Pandora stepped out of the portal into an alternate dimension. They kept low as they moved in, trying to be sneaky. The last thing they wanted was to accidentally open a portal into the crystal dimension and end up releasing Legion all over again.

Pandora stood up and pouted at her former favorite universe, where everything was gorgeous and hot people were walking all around naked. One guy with perfect abs jogged by them, winking at Pandora. Her lip started to quiver. "No donuts. They don't like…"

Katie quickly opened another portal and pulled Pandora through.

The portal opened fast and Katie stumbled through, pulling Pandora along behind her. She released her hold on the portal and let it slam shut behind them. Katie turned to Pandora and grabbed her by the shoulders. "I know you're struggling, but I need you to hold it together, at least for right now. I'm sorry we ended up there, but Xian needs to be found. Okay?"

Pandora took a deep breath through her nose and nodded, trying to keep her lip from sticking out. Katie pulled up the address the general had sent them. "All right, this is where we need to go. It's in the city, so I think the best thing would be to catch a cab so we aren't seen walking around. I don't want to fly until we get to the complex. Hopefully, this city has transportation like that."

Pandora snorted. "It's Singapore. You can pretty much just pluck people off the street and ask them to carry you, and for the right price, they will!"

Katie and Pandora moved out of the alley and out into the busy street. Pandora put her hand up, and several cars and a bike-pulled carriage stopped. They looked at each other and then climbed into the carriage, figuring it might help people ignore them pulling up in front of the complex.

Once they were situated, Katie glanced at Pandora. "I really think you are too hung up on that place to not be part of it. I was always told, no matter how scary it was, no matter how many times I had to move things around to make something happen, I should never let a good thing get away from me. It's a really good way to have regrets."

Pandora nodded, looking sad. "But that's a really big thing. I mean, no donuts? How can they believe they have lived a full life without the amazing wonder of the hole-punched dough of God?"

"I know what you are talking about." Katie sighed. "You want that perfect place, but you've been here longer than I have. Is anything perfect? Or as humans, will we always find something wrong with everything? I just think it's unhealthy to expect that we will find something we love and it will not have any imperfections."

Pandora groaned. "But, *donuts*! Donuts. How can I find a place like that and consider spending my free time there, and not be able to go down the street and grab a donut? How can I look myself in the mirror without finding crumbs between my tits?"

Katie wrinkled her nose. "That's kind of gross, I won't lie. Nonetheless, we both have lived in times where we don't know if there will be a tomorrow. We still live that life. We still wake up each morning wondering in the backs of our minds whether we will die by the next morning. At first, it was traumatic, and I just wanted to be normal, to not feel scared or sad. But then I came to my own conclusion, pushing my emotions back. Do you know what that is?"

Pandora slowly looked at her. "That you should never be a therapist?"

Katie rolled her eyes. "No. I learned that if I want something, I need to just go after it. And that is what you should do, too."

Katie turned her head away and put her hand to her mouth, emotions surging through her. Pandora felt bad for bringing all of that up, seeing at that point that the things she was talking about didn't just go for her. They went for Katie, too. Pandora wondered if those emotions were attached to Brock. If they were, then she was in love with him, something Pandora knew would be extremely scary for her. But at that moment, in a bicycle carriage bouncing all over, it was not the time or the place for it. So instead, she reached over and squeezed Katie's hand.

The carriage came to a stop in front of an older apartment building on the outskirts of the city. It wasn't dingy or dirty since it was Singapore, but it should have been. There were bars on the front windows, even ten floors up. Katie pulled some money out of her pocket and gave the driver a generous tip, and she waved and smiled as he left. As soon as he was around the corner, though, she dropped both the wave and the smile and turned toward the building.

Pandora sniffed. "It smells like a cross between body odor, trash cans, and Chinese food. I don't like this at all."

Katie nodded, walking around the corner and finding the fire escapes. She looked up and then back down at her phone, counting up to the seventh-floor window. Pandora walked up next to her. "Is this the right side of the building?"

Katie sighed and looked at her and then around. "Of course. I think I've done this long enough to…"

She pursed her lips and walked down the alley to the

other end of the complex and counted up. "All right, fine. I had the wrong side. Sorry. Anyway, he is right up there. There are lights on in the place. We should fly up and just go for it."

Pandora nodded. "Right, then. Let's go."

They stood there awkwardly for a moment and then spread their wings, shooting straight up the side of the building. As they came over the fire escape, Katie grabbed the metal rail above her head and punched with her legs, breaking through the glass window. She landed on one knee and looked back as Pandora stared at her, opening the window frame easily and stepping through. Katie shrugged, standing up and brushing the glass off her sleeves.

They heard laughter coming from the other room and carefully made their way to the door. Apparently, whatever was going on in there had masked the sounds of their arrival. Pandora pressed her ear against it, listening closely. Katie waved a hand at her. "Watch out. No reason to wait."

Pandora stood up and put her finger up. "I really might wait if I were…"

Katie kicked the door off the hinges. Pandora finished, "You."

Storming into the room, Katie stopped and turned, covering her eyes. Xian was standing up on the bed, a long silvery wig on and two prostitutes lying on their backs with their mouths open. Pandora walked in and turned her head to the side. "I never understood asses if they weren't taken care of. They are like wide and flat, and there's just so much wrong with it."

The girls gasped and grabbed the blankets, scooting

back to the head of the bed. Xian furrowed his brow and turned around quickly, holding a Fruit by the Foot and letting it unroll as he stared at them. "Who…what…who *are* you?"

Katie swallowed hard, trying not to look. "First, you two girls get the hell out of here. Secondly, uh, put on your boxers or something."

Pandora just stood there laughing wildly. The girls got up and grabbed their things, holding them to their chests and running out of the apartment. Xian stepped down to the floor, dropping the fruit snack and covering his junk. Pandora laughed even harder. "Oh, don't flatter yourself— you only need one hand. And your wig? It's…kind of…"

Pandora was making the motions with her hands to help him move it a couple of inches around. Katie threw out her hands. "Enough of this." She grabbed a pair of shorts off the dresser and threw them at him. "Just put these on."

He looked at them for a moment and then at Katie. "But these are—"

Katie had her back to him. "Just put them on, goddamn it!"

She could hear him struggling. When he stopped, she turned around, staring at him in a pair of very small jean shorts that didn't button and only zipped half of the way up. Pandora was wheezing, she was laughing so hard. Katie groaned and pulled her sword from its sheath, walking forward and pressing the tip to the side of his neck.

He gasped. "What do you want?"

Katie narrowed her eyes. "Give us the last copy of the program you used to track the Leviathan. And if you fuck me over, we will come back and make sure you never have the ability to fuck a prostitute again."

Pandora giggled and leaned forward. "She'll cut your dick off."

Xian's eyes grew wide, and he hurried over to the dresser and pulled it away from the wall. Reaching behind it, he ripped the flash drive off the back and tossed it to Katie. She held it up and then looked up at him. "Good. And put some fucking clothes on."

25

Angie paced in her apartment, chewing on her fingernails. Her eyes darted around, and she could hear her heart beating in her head. A knock on the door made her jump, and she ran over, flinging it open. Juntto stood on the other side, currently the size of a normal human. He was holding a bunch of hand-picked flowers, with a single crystal one in the center.

Grinning from ear to ear, Angie ran forward and wrapped her arms around him, hugging him tightly. Juntto pulled back and kissed her forehead. "I am an Earthman."

Angie giggled and raised an eyebrow. "From what I heard, you're the King of Earth."

Juntto nodded, puffing out his chest. "Yes, I suppose I am. But see, the thing is, it just wasn't right. So I gave it all up for you."

Timothy and Stephanie left the barracks and walked into the courtyard of the base. The wind was low, the sun was shining, and it didn't seem very cold with the sun shining. Timothy gave Stephanie his arm, and she smiled as they walked toward the airstrip.

Stephanie leaned her head on his shoulder for a moment. "I really hope that one day we get to have a summer vacation. Last year I hoped it would be this one, and most likely this year I will hope it will come next year."

Timothy smiled. "I'll tell you what. If we can't jet off into the sunset this year, we'll pick a room in the barracks and create a vacation spot. Then we can go from room to room taking pictures and having drinks. I think we could probably hit up every major city in the world in an afternoon."

Stephanie laughed. "Man, that sounds freaking spectacular, but at least one of the rooms needs to be a beach. It will probably stay a beach all year, too, because who wants to vacuum the sand up?"

Timothy scowled. "Fine, but it's off-limits to the Triplets of Terror. I don't want to find their grossness buried in the sand a year later."

Stephanie nodded. "It's a deal." They walked up to the airstrip and watched as the jet made its way toward them. "I'm really glad they were able to recover the last copy of the program. It will be nice to be done with this. And the guys get to come home safely. That is really the biggest thing."

Timothy nodded. "Yes, girl. It was nice and quiet the first day, and after that, I was starting to think I would go nuts. Where were the idiots making fart jokes and blowing fruit up?"

They stood back as the plane touched down and came to a stop at the end of the strip. Several soldiers pushed the stairs up to the side door, and they waited for it to open. When it finally did, Eddie jumped out, stretching his arms wide. "Ah, back to our wonderful, fantastic home. Oh look, you came to wish me a happy arrival!"

Timothy's nostrils flared, and he whispered to Stephanie, "I take it back. Can we put them back on the plane?"

Stephanie giggled. Calvin came out the door, carrying Sean in his arms. Sean waved at them from above, and Turner grunted as he carried the wheelchair out behind them. They made their way down, then Brock carried his luggage and Sean's to the bottom. Stephanie and Timothy hurried up, giving the guys hugs and welcoming them back.

From above, someone loudly cleared his throat. Stephanie glanced up, then put her hands to her mouth. Korbin was standing there with a smirk. "Surprise.!"

He hurried down the steps and Stephanie jumped into his arms, wrapping her legs around his waist and cupping his face in her hands. "You are such a jerk."

He chuckled. "That wasn't quite the hello I was expecting, but I love you too."

They kissed, and she hugged him tightly before jumping down. He patted his jacket and reached inside, pulling out a brown sack and gently opening it. "I brought someone with me. Her name is Jasmine Sambac."

Stephanie raised an eyebrow. "If you pull a small person out of that bag, we are going to have a talk."

He smiled as he pulled the plant out, beautiful and vibrant. "This is the Grand Duke Supreme, a very rare but amazing plant for our garden area. I have wanted to get you one since I first saw you. Radiant and mysterious, but once rooted, it is strong and loyal."

Stephanie was surprised and held it gently in her hands with tears in her eyes. "It's beautiful. And that was beautiful. For such a hard-ass, you can sometimes be the sweetest man ever. *My* sweetest man ever."

She leaned forward and kissed him, making sure to protect the tree. Looking at it, she laughed through her tears. "I haven't the faintest clue how to plant or take care of this tree. Will it grow out here in the desert?"

Korbin shrugged. "I'm sure it will, with the right additions. But I'm here with you, so I promise that I will help you with it."

Behind them, the guys walked toward the barracks, trying to give them some privacy. Brock walked alone in the front, pulling out his phone and texting Katie to let her know he had arrived back at the barracks safely. Eddie and Turner raced toward the door like a couple of children, and Timothy brought up the rear, pushing Sean inside.

Sean pointed at the elevators. "You can drop me in there, and I'll go back to my hole."

Timothy smiled and pushed him down to the dungeon door, stopping and pulling a keycard from his pocket. Handing it down to Sean, he smiled widely. Sean carefully took the card and looked at Timothy in confusion. "What is this? I'm not allowed in there."

Timothy waved his hands. "Girl, that is so last week. Get in the present, I am tired of living in the past. You've got your clearance back, so come on. You have a lot of annoying to make up for."

Sean slid the card down, and Timothy pushed open the door. He started to wheel inside, then stopped and looked up at Timothy. "Thanks, buddy."

Katie and Pandora were shown into the general's office. Pandora glanced over her shoulder at the assistant from before, giving him a death glare. He put his hands in front of him and crossed them over his junk, turning his head in the other direction. The secretary closed the door behind them and the general stood up, clapping his hands.

Katie chuckled, and Pandora took a bow. They sat down in the chairs in front of his desk, and he joined them, smiling. "Thank you, ladies. Thank you for always coming through. I don't know why I fear anything when you are on the case."

Katie shook her head. "Because, angel blood or not, we are still part-human, and all humans fail and make mistakes from time to time."

Brushwood nodded. "Nonetheless, thank you for dealing with Legion and the army of frost giants. They would have been a very scary threat to this world. I thought nothing would be worse than the demons, but life continues to show us that nothing is absolute."

Katie took a deep breath, her shoulders moving up and then back down again. "Really, we couldn't have done it without Juntto. He was a different frost giant when he was dealing with everything. He never lost his temper, and made all the right choices."

The general seemed pleased. "I'll have to make sure to give Juntto a medal or something like that. A big thank you."

Pandora put her arm up enthusiastically. "You could give him a medal shaped like a giant blue d…"

"Pandora, don't," Katie interrupted.

Pandora furrowed her brow. "What? I was just going to say…" She giggled. "Okay, I was going to say 'dick.'"

The general laughed and shook his head. "Now, of course, I would never ask you here without having your next mission ready for you to consider."

Katie smirked. "I know. Okay, what it is?"

Brushwood leaned forward, tapping his fingers on the desk. "It's a special mission this time. The appearance of Legion, though terrible, made me realize just how much of a threat having these Leviathans out there can be, especially when discovered by the wrong hands. Now, although they went about it badly, those people had a good thought in mind: to destroy it. But the next time, we might not have a positive outcome. Ultimately, I would like the two of you to find the last Leviathan."

Katie looked at Pandora, whose face had gone serious. "The Unnamed Leviathan. He is the only one left—a terror so great that everything in the universe could be destroyed in the blink of an eye. It is the ticking time bomb of Earth. Left here long ago, buried or trapped, but we have no idea where to look."

The general listened to her, fear bubbling in his stomach. "I know it is dangerous, as is everything else I ask of you. But if this Leviathan is as fearsome as you say it is, I would rather have the two of you find it than anyone else on Earth. I know I can trust you to do the right thing."

Katie and Pandora paused, looking at each other. They didn't need to say a word to know what the other was thinking. This mission could mean their deaths, but at the same time, it could be the one that saved the world—or ended it, depending on the outcome.

Katie nodded at the general. "For whatever reason, I was given these gifts, and my life has become something that means more than just one life. So, yes, I accept."

Pandora clicked her tongue, as she always did when she got nervous. "I've done enough bad things in my life that saying no would put me in a hole deeper than the one I am already in. For the first time in my life, I have a purpose. I accept too."

The general sighed in relief. "Thank you. I know I ask more of you than anyone should."

Katie shrugged. "The Leviathans are a pain in the ass. They have been for a very long time. They have been used as weapons by the demons, and when they aren't being used in that capacity, humans have accidentally woken them and set us on a course of possible death and destruction. I suppose it's better to find the last one, the Unnamed, before he pops up and surprises us. That is not the kind of surprise I would like to get."

Pandora shook her head. "Yeah, me either—especially now that I am half a person and half not, only the person side does me no good. I would like people to remember me, for fuck's sake."

The general started. "Oh yeah, that reminds me. I have something for you, Pandora."

He pulled out an envelope and handed it to her. She narrowed her eyes and opened it, pulling out a driver's license and a Social Security card. She blinked at them for a moment and looked at Katie. "We are apparently related."

The general nodded. "I didn't know your last name, so I gave you Katie's. Figured you were like sisters anyway. I used her address as well. Made more sense that way."

Pandora sniffed. Katie appropriated the documents and looked at them. "Pan, this is awesome. You're a real person now. You can even open a bank account if you would like to. You can do anything you want now."

Pandora nodded, fighting back tears as she looked at Brushwood. "Thank you, General. In all my years on this planet, I have never been considered to be a real person. Now, as an angel and one tough bitch, I can finally say that I am someone. That I am a person too. This is the best gift you could give a girl."

The general smiled and reached out, patting her hand. "You deserve it more than anyone. I am proud of you. Both of you."

The cab pulled up in front of the downtown bank. It was pouring rain outside, and the streets were a lot emptier than usual. The cab driver was paid, and the passenger door opened. A black and white round-toed heel appeared, splashing in the standing water. A black umbrella popped up out of the top and opened. Standing up straight,

Pandora smoothed her tight black dress. It fell down to her calves and had a gold zipper straight up the back.

She closed the door behind her and walked toward the bank, closing the umbrella after she walked through the doors. The vice president of the bank gave her a small wave and hurried over. "You're ready to open that account?"

Pandora nodded, pressing her bright red lips together. "I've been ready for thousands of years."

He looked at her strangely for a moment and then took her back to his office. She used a check from Katie for all the back wages they'd agreed to pay her up to the moment they threw Legion into the crystal dimension to open the accounts. But she didn't deposit the entire thing. Instead, she withdrew a pretty large sum and stuffed it into her clutch.

The VP took her to the door and made sure she was covered all the way out to the cab. She was, in fact, a very big account for him now. She went from there to Krispy Kreme, where everyone asked where Katie was. "She had her own things to take care of. We don't do everything together all of the time. I called in an order this morning?"

The girl went back into the back, and when she walked out, she was carrying several bags. Five, to be exact. Inside each one was two dozen donuts, ten dozen in total. Pandora smiled as she paid the woman, gathering her bags and heading out of the shop. She turned the corner and glanced around before opening a portal. She really didn't want to cause a scene.

Smiling, she stepped through the portal and breathed a lungful of fresh air. The portal closed behind her, and she stared up at the beautiful tall buildings, the flying cars soaring overhead, and the animated holographic advertisements spiraling around the different buildings. It was her favorite place to be, although not because of the flying or shining buildings.

She clutched the handles of her bags in both hands, turning in a circle and looking at all the beautiful people walking down the streets completely naked. Their skin was perfect, their bodies toned, and everyone had pleasant smiles on their faces—tits and dicks bouncing all around her like her best dream ever.

A guy walked past her, turning his head and smiling at her. There was a gleam in his eye, and she could feel the heat in her belly. She bit her lip and nodded at him, stopping him in his tracks. As he turned back, her eyes flitted down, and she giggled in excitement. He gave her a gleaming white smile. "What is all that there? You've been shopping."

Pandora puckered her lips and gave him a sexy smirk. "How would you like a long, hot cream-filled donut?"

He tilted his head to the side. "A what? I've never heard of a donut. What do you do with it?"

Pandora tilted her head back and began to laugh. "Well, there are many things you can do with a donut, but using your imagination and your mouth is probably the best way to go about it."

He tapped his finger on his chin, looking as confused as an airheaded puppy. It sent chills up her spine, and she stepped closer. "Would you happen to be free this afternoon?"

The handsome guy seemed to be hooked on her

already. "Actually, I am. Of course, I am pretty sure I could never tell you no."

Pandora moaned, rolling her eyes. "Perfect answer. Come with me, kind sir, and I will give you delights you have only dreamt of. But first, let's have a little taste of what is to come."

He began to reach up. "Shall I get your zipper for you? You seem so uncomfortable in those fabrics."

Pandora giggled loudly. "There is time for that, but first..." She opened one of the boxes of donuts and held it in front of him. "A little taste of heaven from a goddess you will learn to pray to every time I leave."

AUTHOR NOTES - MICHAEL ANDERLE

APRIL 3, 2019

THANK YOU for not only reading this story but these *Author Notes* as well.

(I think I've been good with always opening with "thank you." If not, I need to edit the other *Author Notes*!)

RANDOM (*sometimes*) THOUGHTS?

So, I play a lot with different stories and different thoughts, and sometimes I want to be involved in something that is fun. Other times I am annoyed with something I sense is wrong.

Mind you, this is *my* opinion of wrong, not a general consensus, and I want to write about the subject.

A few months ago I was agitated over the injustice (as I see it—once again my personal perspective) of the education system. Not only as a homeowner (Yes, if I pay taxes I want them to go to the local school that is educating my child) but also from a higher vantage point, looking at what is good for humanity.

And I found it a bit lacking.

AUTHOR NOTES - MICHAEL ANDERLE

I tend to think about the future. No big surprise. Since I cut my teeth writing science fiction, you might expect that from me.

Witch of the Federation is one of the latest projects I have created, and it tells the story of the Federation's first witch.

And how she came about.

I pull from Earth's myths the tiniest bit and stretch a concept into the future, where the Earth has had some hard weather patterns that messed up society, but we've also been visited by aliens.

Aliens with magic.

Add in another race of aliens, and we have a Federation.

Our (eventual) hero is a genius, but she doesn't know it. The school system that is supposed to support someone of her caliber without financial means to go to a university is corrupt.

She ends up tested by the AI that runs the Virtual World (the area most advanced students use for post-secondary education.) When she isn't chosen to go to a university under a scholarship system the government has in place, things start to change.

And now, an AI is involved outside of his Virtual World programming.

It was only slightly shocking to me that the huge scandals rocking the university admissions process across the United States exploded two days (I think) before this book was released.

Dammit, I missed a perfect marketing opportunity! Hope you pick it up anyway.

NOTE: This book is about 3 times the size of a normal WOTA (or PBTD) book.

http://books2read.com/WitchoftheFederation

AROUND THE WORLD IN 80 DAYS

One of the interesting (at least to me) aspects of my life is the ability to work from anywhere and at any time. In the future, I hope to re-read my own *Author Notes* and remember my life as a diary entry.

Maestro's underneath The Cave in the Sky (™), Las Vegas, NV

So, I'm hanging having dinner at the back table in the bar area at Maestro's. (Should you ever come here to eat, just tell them it's the table by itself off in the corner.) I'm not allowing myself to have the dinner order go to the kitchen until I'm done with these *Author Notes* and the blurb for this book.

It's a bit of an incentive. Not too much, since I've just had warm sourdough bread and fresh butter.

'Cause, priorities. (And cheating...I was famished.)

It's Wednesday night, and the bar has a few people hanging out chatting (they look like a business group) and one small group dining in the bar area already.

I'm supposed to be on a diet campaign that Craig Martelle (whom I'm going to nickname HE WHO HATES ME) is pushing.

So far, I've only been able to cut out most of my Coca-Cola consumption. It's a start, but I'm not dropping the weight like I thought I would after cutting out all the extra calories.

So, either the Splenda is adding calories to my tea...

Or the idea that Coke is causing weight gain is a damned lie.

I'm so very tempted to believe it's a lie.

FAN PRICING

$0.99 Saturdays (new LMBPN stuff) and $0.99 Wednesday (both LMBPN books and friends of LMBPN books.) Get great stuff from us and others at tantalizing prices.

Go ahead. I bet you can't read just one.

Sign up here: http://lmbpn.com/email/.

HOW TO MARKET FOR BOOKS YOU LOVE

Review them so others have your thoughts, and tell friends and the dogs of your enemies (because who wants to talk to enemies?)... Enough said ;-)

Ad Aeternitatem,

Michael Anderle

CONNECT WITH MICHAEL TODD

Want more?

Find us On Facebook

https://www.facebook.com/Protected-by-the-Damned-193345908061855/

BOOKS BY MICHAEL TODD

PROTECTED BY THE DAMNED

Torn Asunder (1)

Killing Is My Business (2)

And Business Is Good (3)

Sit Down, Shut Up, And Pull The Trigger (4)

Welcome To The Jungle (5)

Metal Up Your Ass (6)

Dirty Deeds Done Dirt Cheap (7)

For Whom The Bell Tolls (8)

WAR OF THE DAMNED

Resurrection Of The Damned (1)

No Quarter (2)

Dark Is The Night (3)

Dim Glows The Horizon (4)

Waking The Leviathan (5)

Subversive Giants (6)

Juntto (7)

Redemption (8)

WAR OF THE ANGELS

A Sacred Pact (1)

Katie's War (2)

Baylahn (3)

Personal Demons (4)

There Will Be Blood (5)

Can't Touch This (6)

His Name Is Legion (07)

DAMIAN'S CHRONICLES

Crucifix (1)

Renegade (2)

Apostle (3)

Upgrade (4)

BOOKS WRITTEN AS MICHAEL ANDERLE

For a complete list of books by Michael Anderle, please visit:

www.lmbpn.com/ma-books/

All LMBPN Audiobooks are Available at Audible.com and iTunes

To see all LMBPN audiobooks, including those written by Michael Anderle please visit:

www.lmbpn.com/audible

www.ingramcontent.com/pod-product-compliance
Lightning Source LLC
LaVergne TN
LVHW091713070526
838199LV00050B/2374